COURTING THE TIGER KING

JADE CHURCH

ALSO BY JADE CHURCH

Standalones:

Temper the Flame

This Never Happened/Snowed In With You

Three Kisses More

One Last Touch

Frost

Desired by the Dragon

Sun City (College romance):

Get Even

Fall Hard

Strip Bare

Still Yours

Living in Cincy (Romantic suspense):

In Too Deep

Tempt My Heart

Kingdom of Stars (Sapphic romantasy):

The Lingering Dark

The Clarity of Light

Ashvale (Paranormal vampire romance):

The Vampire's Thrall

The Vampire's Kiss

The Vampire's Touch

AUTHOR NOTE

This book is written in UK English - meaning colour is spelt with an 'ou' and realise with an 's', as well as other common subtleties.

Courting the Tiger King contains themes and content that some readers may find triggering, this includes but is not limited to: *blood, gore, death, violence, death of a parent (off-page), alcohol, murder and threat.* Please note, this book also contains on-page sex, swearing, and nudity.

To all the women who ever wished for sharp claws and teeth...
This one's for you.

COURTING THE TIGER KING

JADE CHURCH

CHAPTER ONE

WREN

"Fucking fuck!" He shook out his hand to ease the sting, squinting against the dusty darkness in the tunnels that had them all stumbling around like blind idiots. If the witch would hold still for just two seconds, then maybe she'd know that they weren't there to harm her.

It was difficult to communicate that while being struck with her sparks of silver lightning though.

They'd hunted her down over the course of weeks until his men had received word that the witch had been spotted in the forest that precluded the shore. If she left his kingdom now there was no telling when they'd be able to find her again, and he didn't have time to waste. Not with the curse breathing down his neck.

"I don't have time for this," he muttered, following the sound of the witch up ahead around the curve in the tunnel. How she'd known the tunnels were here, he wasn't sure. There were not many secrets that his kingdom held that he did not know about and yet she'd managed to evade them for an impressive amount of time. Louder, he called, "For the last time, Sonnet. We're here to—*Ouch!*" The pain sparked his anger, the beast within snapping at the reins and Wren decided he had no reason to hold it back.

The change was a warm cascade over his skin. Heavy paws hit the dirt floor as his senses sharpened, the tunnel no longer appearing pitch black. A metallic scent tickled his nose and he chuffed, suddenly understanding why the witch hadn't utilised anything more than sparks to dissuade them from following. She was injured, which meant she likely didn't have much more magic in her reserves since it depended on the life energy of the user.

He moved quickly, his stride long between his paws, and he caught up to the witch easily. She spun, silver eyes widening as she lifted her hands between them and only the faintest flicker of magic answered her call. Blood coated her side and the pallor of her face was chalky, panic overtaking any logic she may have had until Wren knocked her to the ground with the press of one large paw.

Perhaps it was the pain that jolted her out of the panic, or maybe being face-to-face with a tiger knocked the sense back into her, because she stopped trying to fight and instead breathed a sigh of relief. "Your Majesty."

Sensing it was safe and that the witch was at last in her right mind, Wren let his beast fade away in favour of the man. With barely a thought, the magic of the change reproduced his clothes and he offered the witch a hand, frowning when she grasped it weakly. She couldn't die.

Not when he needed her. She was the only known lunar witch left of her line and, consequently, the only one who could perform the spell he needed.

"Sonnet," he acknowledged. "What trouble have you got yourself into now?"

The infirmary was largely empty, affording the witch privacy as his team of healers worked to cleanse and erase the wound that stretched from her hip to her ribcage. Sonnet had fallen unconscious on the journey back to the palace and Wren could only pray to the Goddess that the witch pulled through.

"Thank Selene you found her when you did. The worst is over now." Gabe clapped a hand on Wren's shoulder, making him grunt. He wished he could believe that his friend was right, but the ceremony he needed Sonnet to perform was only the first step in thwarting his curse. Gabe sighed, like he could see the doubt churning in Wren's mind behind his eyes. "Come, let her rest. There's nothing you can do here while the healers work."

That much was true at least.

Wren accepted Gabe's hand up as he stood from the uncomfortable wooden bench that lined the outside wall of the infirmary. He'd been out on the hunt for weeks and was desperate for a bath, whiskey, and bed. Not necessarily in that order. He didn't like to spend so much time away from court, but needs-must and this wasn't a task he could let fall to anyone else. Only his most trusted soldiers had accompanied him in an effort to keep their task under wraps. If he hadn't needed Gabe and Skye to be his eyes and ears at court, he'd have brought them too.

He followed Gabe out of the room and into the stone corridor, their footsteps muffled by the green runner that wound through the halls. Wren must have looked worse than he'd thought if the unusual tightness of Gabe's jaw was anything to go by.

"Tell me," he said quietly and Gabe nodded, scrubbing a hand over the blond stubble on his jaw before heaving a sigh. His amber eyes were weary when they met Wren's.

"More of the same. Whispers mostly, that the king would rather be out fucking and hunting than looking after his court."

Wren snorted. If only that were true.

The hour was early, most of the palace hadn't yet stirred as the sun began to stream weakly in through the windows that lined the corridor. But still, he was careful to guard his words lest someone be lurking unseen. In a kingdom full of shifters, you couldn't trust anything you saw—sometimes the fly on the wall was a grown man in disguise.

"Someone is going to a lot of trouble to sow discord," Gabe continued, the early morning light washing over him and dyeing his white skin momentarily gold. "But whoever it is, they're being careful."

"Well, hopefully this should be the last hunt I'll have to go on for a while." Then they would have no reason to complain or spread rumours.

The entrance to his chambers was a welcome sight and he nodded in greeting to the two guards who stood sentry before he turned to clasp Gabe's shoulder.

"I need to rest, will you and Skye—"

"We'll keep an eye on your witch," Gabe confirmed, voice pitched low enough that the human guards wouldn't have picked up the words. "Rest, brother."

Wren smiled, the look fleeting as Gabe nodded and walked back the way they'd come. Gabe wasn't a brother by blood, but he had grown up with him and Skye and the three of them were close. The doors opened quietly beneath Wren's palm and the familiar scent of his rooms tickled his nose and relaxed his body automatically.

The hearth was cold but Wren couldn't be bothered to heat it, instead he wandered to the small golden cart in one corner of the room and poured a healthy measure of the amber liquid into a crystal glass. He sat down heavily into one of the plush armchairs arranged around the low, large oak table as he sipped.

He had his witch and had collected all but one of the ingredients Sonnet would need for her spellwork. This curse had been in his family for generations, so he was well versed in what it would entail. Lunar witches like Sonnet were beyond rare, they specialised in matters of the soul— a magic that many felt was too powerful to be allowed to exist. As a result, they had been hunted. His family had done what they could to protect the witches, but they were a stubborn lot and Wren was forced into secrecy; any hint of his curse could be perceived as a weakness that the court and their adversaries may pounce upon.

Worse, Wren wasn't sure that he could blame them for questioning his fitness for the throne if they discovered the truth. He'd only learned of the curse himself that same year. The ceremony Sonnet would perform could only be done during the cursed's twenty-fifth year. Now he had less than a year to find and bond with his mate, or the curse would take effect.

The only comfort was that Wren wouldn't know that he'd failed if that happened. Trapped in his animal form, Wren wouldn't know much of anything. He couldn't say the same for the kingdom and the throne. The chaos would leave them weak, scrambling for his replacement, perfectly poised for their enemies to close in.

He swallowed back the last of the drink, frowning in the darkness at the morbid turn his thoughts had taken. The glass thunked as he set it on the table, the sound loud in the quiet of the room as he stood and walked to the drapes and tugged them open until a small slither of light cut through the gloom.

His parlour space was where he did his best thinking, aside from when he was in the bath, it was also where he spent the most time with Gabe and Skye. Normally accompanied by drink and cards as they worked to clean out his coffers.

Dust motes swirled in the small beam of light, returning some warmth and brightness to the room as he turned and walked into his adjoining bedroom. A balcony waited to his left, the drapes shut to keep the sun out while he slept, but despite the security risk he often liked to sleep with the doors open, enjoying the smell of fresh air that carried the scents of the forest below up to his room. He pulled open one drape, leaving the one closest to the bed closed to keep it in shadow, and opened the door, breathing deeply and enjoying the hint of earth on the air.

The bed took up most of the room, carved wooden

posts forming the vague shape of trees and birds guarding the bed below like a woodland canopy. A copper tub sat in front of the empty hearth, steam curling up from the water within and he hesitated, gaze flitting between the promise of the bed and the heat of the bath calling to him.

His simple tunic and trousers hit the ground, discarded next to his boots and the small horde of weapons he'd had hidden on his person. The need to be clean was too strong to be ignored and he slipped into the water with a groan. After the rough sleeping of the hunt, endless days spent in the underbrush of the forest and the odd tavern, the opportunity to soak in the bath was heavenly. One of his attendants had even added his favourite jasmine oil to the water and the scent had his eyes falling closed.

Water slipped over his nose and he spluttered, jerking upright and blinking the moisture out of his eyes. Fuck. He'd spent all this time trying to break the curse, only to nearly drown in his bath.

Wren dunked his head and reached for a bar of soap, lathering his hair and body and rinsing quickly in the rapidly cooling water. How long had he been asleep? He wasn't too pruney yet so he had to assume it hadn't been a long time.

A large towel had been placed onto the fabric seat of the wooden chair beside the hearth and he reached for it as he stood, toweling off roughly and pushing the dark fabric over his hair so the semi-long strands wouldn't drip down his back. There was also a small pot of cream on the chair, scented similarly to his favoured jasmine, and he scooped up a portion with two fingers before working it across his face and hands. Spending so much time outside would leave him with weathered skin as thick as a bore's hide if he wasn't careful.

Mostly dry, he stumbled over to the bed and promptly collapsed atop the sheets face first. He was asleep before the sun finished rising.

CHAPTER TWO

WREN

Wren slept all the way through the afternoon and right into the evening, waking only when the grumble of his stomach refused to be ignored any longer.

Gabe waited for him in the parlour, a plate of food on the table in front of him that he pushed toward Wren when he stumbled into the room and blinked blearily. "As much as I love our naked dinners, maybe you'd be more comfortable with some clothes on?"

Wren glanced down and cursed before walking back into his bedroom and tugging on a loose pair of trousers that cinched with stays at the front. His hair had dried in strange, kinky waves, and he ran a hand through the mess as he sat down heavily into the chair opposite Gabe.

"Thank you," he murmured, digging into the still-warm bread roll on his plate. "All quiet last night?"

Gabe nodded. "The witch didn't stir and nobody

disturbed us. She's awake now, looks about as good as you feel I'd wager."

Wren scowled. "I feel fine, prick."

Gabe smirked and let Wren finish his meal in silence. "You going to the temple?"

Selene's temple was where Wren would get the final ingredient for Sonnet's spell—a blessing from the Goddess. Not easy to come by and typically only granted in dire circumstances, or in traditional ceremonies like weddings and mate bonds.

"Yes." He would remain in worship until Selene saw fit to bless him. He couldn't proceed with the ceremony until he received a token of the Goddess' favour. It was one of the things that made soul magic so difficult to perform, the lunar witches had a stronger connection to the Goddess than most. It hadn't been enough to protect them from the fear of the masses, however. "Is Skye still with Sonnet?"

Gabe nodded. "We didn't want to leave her alone. Though she's likely recovered enough that she can defend herself if needed."

"I'd rather it not come to that," he murmured and Gabe agreed with a grunt. It would only take a glance for someone to know what Sonnet is—the silver irises of all moon touched were a dead giveaway as to their heritage. "You'll watch her while I'm at temple?"

"Of course."

Wren pushed up and away from the table, retrieving a tunic top for his room and slipping it on, buttoning the front deftly. A decent night's sleep and a solid breakfast-dinner had him feeling reinvigorated. He was so close to what he'd worked so tirelessly for all this time. Now he could only pray that Selene would grant him this boon.

———

The Goddess' temple was outside of the palace, in a secluded part of the grounds half-shrouded by the forest. It was only fitting for the temple to be out in nature, for Selene was the Goddess of the moon and wild things. To entrap her place of worship among the court would be an affront. As it was, the only material permitted for use to build the temples was moonstone that made the structures hold a glow all of their own.

Wren had always found the Goddess' temples to be a place of peace. The first step through the arched entry-way made his shoulders relax, cool air embracing him as he walked further inside. No lights would be found inside the temple, the glow of the stonework enough to guide the pious to their destination.

His tension slipped away the further he walked through the temple's tunnels. If he followed the path all the way around, he knew he would end up in the main chamber of prayer where a moonstone statue of the Goddess watched over those who sought her guidance. But amid the main tunnel were several offshoots that led to hollowed out nooks with just enough room for one person to stand inside. It was one of these prayer holes that Wren sought out. For what he'd come to ask, he wanted privacy. Plus, only the Goddess should see the king kneel.

The path widened and Wren took the first offshoot he

passed, the walls of the cave-like hollow closing around him in a soothing cocoon of luminous stone that made him feel as if the Goddess had wrapped him in an embrace.

Wren tended to pray at the temple several times per year. Selene was the Goddess of wild things and, as such, didn't demand tithes or strict examples of devout dedication. Though, they did tend to celebrate the Goddess when the moon was full, or in ritual ceremonies like that of a mate blessing or wedding, as well as death rites. More often than not for him, communing with the Goddess had been for a joyous occasion and revelries, but for his task now a more formal tone seemed necessary.

His knees hit the cold ground and Wren didn't flinch at the impact as his eyes slid closed and his chin tilted upwards. A pressure settled between his shoulder blades, the feeling not entirely comfortable, and he knew the Goddess' attention was placed squarely on him.

"Selene, I have come to ask for your blessing as I attempt to locate the mate who will break my curse." The words were spoken quietly, muffled as they sank into the stone surrounding him. The pressure at his back didn't lessen, but nor did anything else happen. Wren frowned. He needed this blessing from the Goddess in order for Sonnet's spell to work.

A nudge at his back made him sway, as if a palm had rested on his spine and pushed him to continue. Perhaps the more formal route wasn't what the Goddess needed from him.

Instead, Wren cleared his mind and focused on what he imagined for his mate, for their bond. He'd been so focused on the need to break the curse and secure his Kingdom that he hadn't considered much about the mating itself, beyond it being a necessity for his survival.

The beast within him awoke and Wren shivered, images flashing in his mind's eye. Running beneath the moon, the heavy thud of paws echoed in the presence of another, warmth and bite and power... An equal. That was what he wanted in a mate. Someone who would fight for him and the kingdom with a passion that rivalled his own sense of duty, but could also look past the crown to the man beneath.

A tingling swept through his body and when Wren opened his eyes, his lips parted at the glowing markings that encased his hands in sweeps and flourishes of silver swirls that reminded him of tiger stripes. His mate would be like him, then, a shifter. And shifter forms always matched that of their mate. Soon, if everything went to plan, there would be more than one tiger roaming the halls of the castle.

"Thank you," he murmured and pushed up to standing as the glow in his hands faded but the silver marks remained, looking a little like a long-healed scar. The presence around him slipped away and Wren breathed in deeply before letting the breath out in a slow exhalation. It was time to see a witch.

Wren returned back to his quarters where he'd been told Gabe and Skye were waiting, no doubt with Sonnet in tow, and his jaw unclenched as he saw the three of them in his parlour.

The colour had returned to Sonnet's face, her silver eyes gleaming as she stood and curtsied. "It's good to see you again, my king."

"Are you well?"

She nodded and brushed a strand of dark hair out of her face. "Much better, thank you."

They'd only met once before, last year after his father's death when his mother had finally confessed the truth about the curse on their bloodline. Nobody knew where the curse had originated, some said one of their ancestors had displeased a god, others that their kin had spurned a witch. Wren didn't care about the particulars, just about breaking it—though, even if he thwarted its hold on him it would still be passed on to his children unless he found a permanent solution.

It had been a short passing of time, and yet Sonnet looked as if she'd been wearied by the world in the year that had elapsed. Her eyes were not as wide and bright, and a perpetual tension sat in her shoulders as she assessed the room.

She looks like prey, he realised.

Her eyes dropped to his clasped hands and she nodded to herself. "Selene was amenable."

Gabe and Skye peered at Wren's hands, a furrow in each of their brows as Wren lifted his palms up to let the markings catch the faint light that came in through the window that overlooked the low oak table.

Selene's blessing was the last component needed for

Sonnet to perform the ritual and, somehow, being so close to completion felt much more precarious now than it had months ago when he'd gone searching for the other ingredients the witch would need. It felt like a sword, swinging over his head and ready to drop at any moment, snatching his victory away before it could be claimed.

"When?" he asked, and the question hung in the air as a tension fell over the four of them. Skye and Gabe shared a look, amber eyes meeting blue, and Wren ignored their obvious concern. Yes, finding his mate was a big step, but he had no choice in the matter. It was either perform this unquiet magic or lose his mind to his animal form.

"Tomorrow night," Sonnet replied, the words firm despite his huff of impatience. "We need the full moon and I need time to replenish my energies. Gather your witnesses, cleanse yourself for what is to come."

She made it sound… Frightening. "Will it hurt?" The words slipped out before he could help himself and he grimaced.

Sonnet stood and walked to him, her hand touching his forearm briefly as those disconcerting silver eyes stared into his soul. "No, there will be no pain. But that does not mean you won't have to give something of yourself." As if that explained everything, Sonnet inclined her head. "I must prepare. Do you have a room for my use?"

Wren jerked himself out of his swirling thoughts and nodded. "Gabriel will escort you."

Gabe nodded, knowing without asking that Wren meant for him to stay and guard the witch.

The door closed behind them and Wren sat down in

one of the abandoned chairs and closed his eyes. He'd nearly forgotten Skye was there until he spoke.

"Who are your witnesses?"

Wren jumped and scrubbed a hand over his eyes tiredly before looking up at his friend where he leaned against the wall by the window, peering outside.

"My mother, my uncle, you, Gabe, cousin Rela, Jamison and his second." Jamison was the captain of the guard, and Rela was next in line for the throne until Wren had children of his own—though not everyone was keen on a female reigning monarch.

Skye nodded, expression indecipherable. Unlike Wren and Gabe, Skye wasn't a shifter, but he was one of the most incredible fighters Wren had ever known. Part of it was sheer skill, but it helped that Skye had witch ancestry that had manifested into a subtle gift for precognition. He often knew exactly what move you were going to make before you made it, rendering him a formidable opponent even before his powerful ancestry came into play—his line was much akin to royalty amongst the witches and the consequences would be costly if it were discovered he was aiding a lunar witch.

More than any of that, Skye's friendship was one of the few constants in Wren's life. Between court machinations and now the curse, Wren was sure he wouldn't have survived if not for Gabe and Skye keeping his head on straight and his back protected.

He was taller than Wren and when Skye turned, his piercing blue eyes left no room for escape. Skye often reminded Wren of the Valeneos trees that were his kingdom's namesake. Shockingly tall and solid, with a sombre dignity that spoke of a wiseness beyond Skye's years, and dusky brown skin that matched the bark of the Valeneos trees almost perfectly. He'd known Skye his whole life and he hoped he would know him for many more.

"I take it that there's no dissuading you from this course of action?"

Wren smiled slightly. Skye may not have killed Sonnet on sight, but that didn't mean he trusted her magic. "I've come this far."

"The magic of the soul is dangerous—"

"And so is my curse." Wren raised a brow and Skye sighed as he rounded the table to fold himself into the chair at Wren's right.

"For all you know, her line is responsible for the curse in the first place."

Wren lifted a shoulder and let it drop. "That may be. But right now she's the only chance I've got. Unless you've had any luck in finding a cure?"

The words hadn't been a taunt, nor a reproach, but Skye frowned as if it had been meant as such. "Not yet. But—"

"I'm running out of time, Skye." The words were quiet, featherlight, and the pain on his friend's face tightened the skin around his eyes and darkened his irises to cerulean.

"I know," he said gruffly. "I just don't like this. I don't like that I can't *see* the outcome. Too many pieces are shifting, and altering the soul…"

They'd had this discussion before. Wren understood Skye's beliefs, but he didn't agree with them. "If the lunar witches weren't supposed to exist, the Goddess wouldn't have gifted them magic."

Skye frowned, the expression darkening his face until he looked almost unrecognisable. Usually, his friend was one of the most easy-going people Wren knew—but maybe that had more to do with his ability to know what futures were in motion, the strands of fate visible to him in a way they weren't for the rest of them. This loss of control had them all on edge. "You know my thoughts about that."

He did. Skye, and the majority of all witches, believed the lunar witches were accidental magic, a perversion of the natural order. Wren couldn't say either way for sure, but it seemed unlikely that Selene would bless this course of action if she disapproved.

"Will you be there?" It was the question Wren had been most anxious to ask his friend. Skye's presence would be a balm, knowing there was someone there who would unfalteringly watch out for him, but tolerating the presence of Sonnet was a different matter to being present while she performed her magic.

Skye glanced at him, surprise flashing across his face. "Of course. I don't like this path you have set us on, but I do understand it. And I wouldn't leave you alone in the hands of that witch either."

Wren refrained from reminding Skye that he wouldn't be alone, his family would be there, but he knew that didn't count as far as Skye was concerned. None of them were witches. If something went wrong, Skye would undoubtedly consider it his responsibility to right it.

"Thank you," he said instead and Skye nodded.

"I just hope you know what you're doing."

His hands squeezed the wooden arms of the chair and made the structure creak. "So do I."

The moon was full and bright the following evening, a beacon against the sky that spilled silver light onto the rounded balcony of the palace's highest tower. A crisp chill made their breath fog, though nobody complained as adrenaline and anticipation kept their hearts pumping fast and their blood hot.

Sonnet had arranged them all into a circle with Wren standing in the centre as she walked the inside with burning incense. She spoke quietly under her breath and Wren didn't try to listen for the words, instead keeping his eyes closed and his mind as clear as possible even when Sonnet approached and wafted the sweet smelling smoke over his form and made his skin tingle.

Her hands clapped together and Wren jumped, eyes flashing open as all of the candles set out at the edges of the circle flashed into life. The flames didn't flicker despite the breeze and the fire beneath the bowl on the podium he stood in front of seemed to have a silver glow, like it was reflecting the moon itself.

Steam wafted from the silver bow atop the podium and curled into the night sky and the stars seemed to sway in response, like a reflection rippling in a lake and Wren could have sworn he heard the Goddess laugh.

Warm hands gripped his and Wren blinked, coming back to himself as he looked into the solid medallion gaze of Sonnet's eyes.

She nodded and Wren breathed in the incense in three deep breaths, just like she'd told him, before flipping his hands to be palm up inside of the witch's.

Chanting began, the words unfamiliar, but Sonnet had talked him through each step of the ritual before and so he knew that she was calling to Selene, asking for the Goddess' attention, to grant them magic so that he might find his mate. In some ways, this ceremony was similar to that of the marriage and bonding rites, but when magic rose up in the air around them Wren knew it was an entirely more powerful ritual.

The energy raised the hair on his arms and he heard his mother gasp when his skin began to glow silver-white. Sonnet's hair lifted, drifting in a wind that nobody else could feel, and for a second Wren felt an overwhelming swell of peace fill his body.

Then the burning began.

His head fell back, a hoarse cry ripping from his throat as the magic plunged into him, coiling around his essence as it searched every inch of his mind, his soul. It wasn't quite pain, but it wasn't pleasurable either. The magic delving inside every crevice of his being to find the small thread that would tie him to another.

Warm words brushed against his mind, the voice unfamiliar, unintelligible, a slow sweetness pushing through his veins like liquid caramel and in it he could feel *her*.

He had no name, no images, just the warmth at his centre that pulsed harder and harder until his eyes re-opened and a lance of silver light shot out from him, lighting up the clouds from within, as he slumped, falling to his knees.

"Don't." The words were harsh but Wren barely heard them, his body wrung out, sweat coating his skin, and an intense longing filling him in a way he'd never felt before. Like he'd been missing a part of himself and hadn't realised it until that moment.

He blinked, sweat dripping into his eyes and making them burn, and he made out Skye's blurry form stepping back into the place Sonnet had assigned. "I'm okay," he rasped and Skye nodded, eyes burning brightly as he watched Sonnet the way a predator sized up prey.

Sonnet reached for him, unflinching when Skye hissed out a warning, and took Wren's hands, helping him to his feet and guiding him on stumbling steps to the silver bowl.

Her dagger gleamed brightly, the hilt plain silver and the blade reflecting his own feverish gaze back at him. She cradled his palm in one hand and pressed the tip of the dagger to his life line, tracing the thin line so delicately he nearly didn't feel the sting of the cut.

The droplets of blood fell into the bowl and his stomach dropped as the magic took what it needed from him, energy or magic or both, Wren couldn't tell.

A map of the kingdom was laid out on a small table in front of the bowl and his blood sank into the depths of the mixture. Sonnet's hands glowed as she placed them on either side of the altar, her head falling back as light erupted from her form until it faded. She murmured her thanks to the Goddess and when the bowl spilled onto the parchment, it moved languidly like it had thickened.

His muscles shook, the energy the magic had taken

from him leaving him weak, but he couldn't move, couldn't take his eyes off of the place where the mixture met the map and began to fade as if it had been absorbed, leaving only a ring marking the parchment.

As quickly as it had come, the energy in the air dissipated and Sonnet murmured under her breath, the candles extinguishing with only a motion.

"Did it work?"

Exhaustion pushed at every inch of his body and remaining upright was taking more effort than he had. Sonnet looked nearly as wrecked as he felt.

Her fingers traced the ring on the map. "It worked."

Relief made him dizzy and Wren leaned gratefully on Skye when he approached before accepting a skein of water from Gabriel and gulping it back. It helped some, but sleep was the thing he needed most right then. He'd known to expect the energy drain though, so his men were readying themselves to travel out and retrieve what was his.

"Where?" The words were half-gasped as hope squeezed the breath from him.

"Midmyr Forest." Sonnet smiled and Wren reached for her, squeezing her hand in thanks and then wincing at the lingering soreness in his palm. It would heal, but not until his body rested. He had too little energy right then for his magic to tend to the wound. "Your mate can be found there."

"Half a day's ride," Gabe murmured and Wren nodded shakily. His mate had been so close this whole time. "I'll instruct the guard."

"Thank you." He sagged and then his mother was there,

clasping his face in her cool palms as she smiled at him, green eyes twinkling.

"I know this was a necessary evil, but I'm so proud of you, cub."

Wren pressed a kiss to her cheek and knew he needed to leave before he fell down. "Skye," he murmured quickly, sensing the encroaching bliss of sleep as his body demanded rest and recovery. "Look… after Sonnet."

The words were all he was able to sigh out before his eyes closed and his body fell limp.

CHAPTER THREE

NEAH

The manor house amid the trees was dark when Neah approached. It had taken her three days to reach Midmyr Forest and she'd opted to eat and replenish her energy in a tavern in the nearby town before proceeding to Zennon's estate.

Her thighs were sore from the ride and she smelled more like horse than she typically liked, but the information she'd stumbled upon was more important than her discomfort. So she'd ridden hard and fast, desperate to reach the part of her kingdom that she'd once called home, before anyone could realise what she'd discovered and stop her from warning the king.

She'd arrived in Midmyr yesterday evening and had made camp in the trees, waiting to see if she'd been followed. No such pursuer appeared, but Neah still couldn't relax. Instead, she'd walked the cobbled streets of the town and did what a spy did best: listened.

The chatter was minimal, mostly local gossip about

whose wife was cheating and how the price of grain had increased thanks to the ongoing tensions with nobles in the further northern reaches of the kingdom.

When Neah was satisfied that she wouldn't be bringing chaos to Zennon's doorstep, she'd set off for the house and had found it unnervingly quiet.

The trees rustled in the breeze and awareness skittered across Neah's spine. She couldn't place what it was, but something wasn't right here.

Her footfalls were quiet against the compact earth, her dark cloak barely stirring the leaves that littered the ground as she leapt over the high hedge that surrounded the estate and flanked the heavy gates that protected the property.

She may not have been able to shift, but her senses were still sharper than that of a human and her strength and speed were heightened too. Maybe one day her animal form would come out of hiding, but admittedly she'd begun to doubt the excuses her parents offered of her being a 'late bloomer'.

The thud of her feet hitting the ground was minimal, but she froze in place all the same, waiting for a sound to indicate she'd been caught. When nothing moved, she continued toward the house looming up and over her in a dark silhouette.

Where were all the guards? Zennon was a noble and typically had a small retinue to look after her and the grounds, yet nobody had noticed Neah's presence. While she was good at what she did, she wasn't sure she could claim this as a result of her own, sheer talent.

A trellis clung to the side of the manor, leading from

the ground to the middle of the wall, just a small amount of space away from the window she knew led to Zennon's bedroom.

The wood creaked slightly under foot as Neah climbed, the small vines beneath her palms saving her from the worst of the splinters, and when she reached the top she eyed the distance between the trellis and the window ledge.

She could make that. She hoped.

Not giving herself time to chicken out or worry, Neah launched herself from the trellis and gripped the edges of the stone sill with her bare hands as she painstakingly lifted herself up until she could swing a leg onto the ledge. It was just big enough for her to crouch and she frowned when she tried the window and found it unlocked. Making a mental note to yell at Zennon later, Neah assessed the room's interior. She shouldn't have been able to break in so easily.

The window had opened soundlessly and Neah slipped inside the room, the familiar scent of sage, lavender, and honey filling her senses and relaxing her somewhat.

It was dark inside, and the house was quiet, only the gentle breathing of the figure beneath the covers making a sound.

Neah crept closer, the plush rug beneath her feet muffling her steps until she stood over the bed and found Zennon safe.

Then she clamped a hand over her best friend's face to muffle any noise she might make when she awoke. Zennon had a tendency to swing first and think later.

Brown eyes flashed open, alarm making the whites of Zennon's eyes stand out before recognition lit her face.

Neah touched her free hand to her own mouth and Zennon nodded, agreeing to the silence as Neah sat down on the edge of her bed.

"Where are your guards?" she said quietly, the words barely a breath as she murmured them into Zennon's ear. If her friend had been a shifter like Neah then she would have heard her clearly without Neah leaning down, but, as it was, Zennon was human and therefore more limited.

Zennon's dark brows drew together, telling Neah everything she needed to know. Whatever had happened to the guards hadn't been planned. Had someone known Neah was coming here and tried to head her off? But then, why wait until she was inside the house? Why not attack in the forest? Or the town?

Neah stood and Zennon started to follow, swinging her long legs out from beneath the sheets before Neah held up a hand and shook her head.

Nearly imperceptible footsteps vibrated the wooden floor and Neah slipped underneath the space of Zennon's bed as the other girl sank back down and feigned sleep.

The door opened, a shadow filling the doorway visible only from the gleam of steel on either side of their hips.

What the Hel was going on?

Neah tensed, watching the figure come closer. The sing of their blade as it was removed from the holster at their side sent goosebumps over her skin and she could only assume the figure was human, otherwise they might have sensed the second heartbeat thundering in the room.

They closed the last of the distance and Neah readied herself.

The mattress moved. The figure grunted, and Neah

swept her legs out and under the assassin. She was on her feet in moments and pinned the figure to the ground by shoving their own dagger down with force until it embedded through their thigh and into the floor beneath.

They screamed, the tenor clearly male, and Neah had a moment of smugness as she glimpsed the blood crusted around the white skin of his nose where Zennon had taken him by surprised and socked him.

It was a fleeting feeling though, because that was when his friends joined the fun.

Two had swords and another favoured daggers, and Neah was baffled. Why on earth would someone send four assassins to attack a human noble?

"You have some explaining to do," she muttered to Zennon as she stripped the wounded assassin of his remaining weapons and handed them to her friend. She wasn't a shifter, but Zennon could hold her own with a sword at least.

The other woman accepted the blade with a grim nod and Neah placed a foot to the throat of the man on the floor as he struggled to get up with his pinned leg.

"Now, we can be civilised about this," Neah said, eyes on the newcomers. "Or you can die. You decide." Neah assessed the three remaining assassins as the one beneath her boot squirmed. Their faces were partially covered with a strip of cloth but their eyes were visible as they looked between each other and stepped forward as one. "Death it is," she said, bringing her foot down with force and not flinching as the assassin's neck snapped.

This particularly enraged one of the assassins with the sword and he growled, amber eyes glowing as he stepped forward and then widening as he looked down at the dagger in his chest. Neah lowered her hand and stepped forward to retrieve his sword before he could hit the ground. His eyes had been a dead give away of his shifter heritage and it was better to dispose of the biggest threat quickly and efficiently. He hadn't even seen her take his friend's blade.

Zennon traded blows with the other daggered assassin and Neah forced herself to focus on the one who had her in his sights, rather than fretting over her friend. *Zennon would be fine.*

Her borrowed sword swung effortlessly in her grip, well-balanced if a little heavier than she would have liked, and she nodded to the other assassin. "Shall we?"

He darted toward her, swinging the blade with precision and a strength that surprised her until she saw the gold of his eyes, matching her own. In the shadows of the room, she'd missed the tell-tale colour. Another shifter. Fuck.

Their blades clashed and she met him blow for blow, faltering slightly when his strength dwarfed hers and her arm shook as she defended against him. He moved with grace, his footsteps never hesitating, like he had formal training much like she did. So she took a risk.

Sword-play was clearly where he was comfortable, and so she batted his blade away and used the opportunity to move in closer and stun him with a blow to his sternum before snapping up her knee and catching him in the jaw. Swords were a gentleman's weapon, for the most part, but Neah had found that bending the rules could be just as useful as learning them in the first place.

Her borrowed sword slid cleanly through the assassin's chest, the shocked widening of his eyes visible as she pulled the sword out just as swiftly as it had entered.

Zennon cried out, the daggered-assassin having slashed across her chest. It was a nick, barely a scratch, but the sound of Zennon's pain plus the scent of all the blood in the room had her more animalistic side clamouring for revenge, to protect.

She whirled, sword flashing, and Zennon shrieked at the flash of blood that hit her skin as the assassin's head tumbled to the floor.

The part of Neah that wasn't human scanned the room, taking in the gore dispassionately as she searched for further threats.

"Stay here," she demanded, the growl in her voice a dead give away that she was losing control, and Zennon nodded, her olive skin looking pale beneath the blood spatter as Neah marched out of the room with the sword in hand.

The hall was empty and Neah opened each door on the landing in turn to check for further intruders.

In the third bedroom she found the guards, all dead. Then she turned to face the bannister that overlooked the grand entrance to the house. Neah would have used it herself if her senses hadn't alerted her to danger. It looked untouched, no signs of a struggle, so the assassins must have taken the guards by surprise.

Neah put the bedrooms to her back as she walked down the stairs, noting a smudge of blood on the white marble floor that she hadn't been able to see from up high. The drawing room was directly to her right, so Neah checked inside and found it empty before moving on to the adjoining lounge.

She focused, standing still and tasting the air with the tip of her tongue as she listened for heartbeats and movement but found none. Still, she checked the rest of the rooms opposite and ventured down into the kitchens and wine cellar and found no trace of further intruders.

Adrenaline fading, she made her way back to Zennon and found her dragging the assassins into a tidy pile in the center of the room and glaring at the large bloody stain on an otherwise pristine rug.

"No sign of anyone."

"The guards?"

"Dead."

Zennon nodded, like she'd expected as much, and Neah stretched out her tired muscles. "How did you know they were coming?"

She sat down on the ruined coverlet and shook her head. "I didn't. I was on the way to see the king but decided to stop in to give you a message for my father in case I didn't make it."

Zennon's eyes widened. "I—"

"I'll tell you all about it, but first—why would someone send four assassins after you?"

"They didn't follow you?"

Neah shook her head. "They were here before me."

"I honestly don't know, then. Nothing new has happened, it's been surprisingly quiet. I haven't heard anything from Jamison in weeks."

It didn't make sense.

"Neah—"

A faint noise tickled her senses and Neah pressed a finger to her lips. Zennon fell silent, her face still paler than usual as blood dried in the long lengths of her dark hair.

"Someone's coming," she murmured and Zennon stood. They walked to the window where Neah had entered and she relaxed minutely as she recognised the crest on the silver uniform below. "The king's guards. Why would they be here for you?"

Zennon bit her lip. "I don't know. Something is definitely—What are you doing?"

"Hiding," she said, peering into the walk-in closet space. "I don't want anyone to know I was here. Not before my father does."

"But—"

Neah doubled back and squeezed Zennon. "I'm glad you're okay." The guards below knocked at the door and voices called out when there was no response. "Do whatever they ask of you and I'll find you later."

She hesitated but nodded and Neah darted into the closet, closing the door behind her and crouching down to peer through the slats in the bottom of the door as the first of the king's guard reached the top of the stairs.

"Lady Zennon Darke?"

"In here," Zennon called, voice shaking convincingly, and it wasn't until Neah took in the destruction of the room and the bodies piled up that she considered her friend may not have been acting.

"Lady, are you—" The guard halted as he took in the scene and Neah was relieved to see his eyes were a human blue. He strode across to her within seconds and bowed crisply. "My Lady, I've been directed by the king to request your presence at the palace. It seems our enemies got here first. Are you injured at all?"

Zennon shook her head and leaned against the post of her bed. "The blood—it's not mine."

The guard ran his eyes over her small form and looked impressed, understandable given the carnage. "Will you allow us to escort you to the king?"

The king. What did he want with Zennon?

"Of course." She strode toward Neah's hiding place and Neah backed away from the door, handing Zennon her cloak and a pair of boots when she reached inside. Their eyes met for a moment and Neah nodded reassuringly. She'd give the guards a head start and follow Zennon in the morning. Whatever was going on here was bigger than she could have anticipated.

CHAPTER FOUR

NEAH

The house was still after the guards and Zennon left and Neah decided to make the most of the peace by cleaning herself up as best she could, despite the absence of the attendants that would normally have been in the house. At this late hour, they'd all left. Lucky for them, or they might have shared the same fate as the guards.

Still, Neah managed to fill a large tub half-way with steaming water that was probably a little too hot to be comfortable. But the lure of the sweetly fragranced soap was large enough that she didn't wait for the bath to cool before stepping in. Really, she just wanted to be free of the smell of horse that clung to her skin.

The water rose as she sank in, climbing up and over her shoulders, and she dunked her head while trying to ignore the way the heat made her face sting. Tension slipped out of her muscles as she rested her arms on the rim of the tub, basking in the steam for a few minutes before she set about cleaning the blood and dirt from her face, body, and hair. By the time she stood up in a rush of water, the contents of the tub were stained pink and her skin was flushed and honey-scented.

She was familiar enough with Zennon's estate, had stayed there several times while waiting for her next orders or to deliver news and gossip. Zennon acted as an intermediary, a half-way point, providing both sanctuary and plausible deniability—because who would be suspicious of one Lady visiting another? Whereas frequent trips into the palace to report to the king's captain of the guard would surely garner unwanted attention.

It did feel strange, though, being there without Zennon. Her presence was soothing, her countenance calm, and after the day Neah'd had she could have used a little of that. Instead, she was left to borrow some of Zennon's clothes and cobble together a sparse dinner with what was left in the pantry. Mostly bread, cheese, and dried meat.

A generous helping of honey wine helped quiet the buzz in Neah's mind as she rummaged in Zennon's closet. It was lucky that she and Zennon were similar in size, though Neah had more of a lean musculature than Zennon who was soft and curvy, otherwise Neah might have been stuck putting her dirty clothes back on.

She carried her finds to the bedroom next to Zennon's and laid them out on the perfectly-made bed before slipping on a simple nightdress. It wasn't often that Neah managed to sleep well, but she would try to get a few hours of rest before following her friend to the palace.

Maybe it should have bothered her that there were dead guards in the room down the hall, or that she'd killed four people that night, but she could only feel relief that Zennon was safe and that tomorrow she'd see her father and explain what she'd learned.

The bed was soft and she sighed as she sank into the mattress, pulling up the heavy covers and wriggling into their depths until they started to warm against her. It was a bed too big for one person, but she didn't mind. It gave her space to roll around. Regardless, it was much more comfortable than the bed she'd been staying in previously at a noble's estate in the north east of the kingdom. Lord Pembroke was known for his disdain for the current monarchy and so it seemed as good a place as any to linger in an attempt to glean any plans that might be being hatched by the king's enemies.

Her father always said that a good spy was merely in the right place at the right time, so she endeavoured to be in as many of those places as possible. So far, she'd managed to foil a number of small plots against the king and his allies, but they were nothing compared to what she'd heard at Pembroke's party at the beginning of the week.

Neah rolled and tucked one leg out of the covers, folding it back into the cool outer top of the coverlet as she tried to empty her head of the worries that had pursued her across her three-day ride. She would never be able to sleep at this rate. Maybe it had something to do with her animal form, locked away and prowling under her skin but unable to escape for whatever reason, but sleep was a luxury that often eluded her until she was so exhausted she could drop at any moment.

But she made do, and she needed to have her wits about

her when she travelled to the king's palace if she was to keep up the pretence of nobility. Or, at least, that nobility was the sum of her parts rather than the shallow surface.

She rolled again, her skin feeling too tight, like her nerves were buzzing. Was this just anticipation? Or more worry for Zennon, mysteriously spirited away into the king's clutches? The palace was where her father lived, where Neah had grown up for the most part before she was sent away to train in the less lady-like arts of violence. So Neah hadn't actually seen the king since he'd been crowned, though their paths had occasionally crossed while he'd been a prince.

Zennon would be safe there, doubly so when Neah arrived.

Neah squeezed her eyes shut, trying to focus on the comfort of the bed and the soft honey smell of her clean hair. Instead, she saw blood on the backs of her eyelids, the gleam of steel in the dark.

Sleep, as usual, didn't come easy.

At dawn, the staff returned to the estate and Neah was waiting for them already dressed in Zennon's finery.

Most of them knew who she was, even if they didn't know the truth of *what*, and were excited by the prospect of Zennon's stay at the palace. They readied a horse and carriage for Neah with an enthusiasm that only dulled when she informed them of the clean-up waiting inside in the form of the guards and assassins. Though, as best Neah could glean from eavesdropping, most of them felt that a little gore was worth the potential elevation of household that would come if Zennon married the king.

The idea shouldn't have surprised Neah as much as it did, but it was atypical of a king to send for a bride rather than hosting a ball for the purpose of courtship. No, Neah would find out what was happening for herself soon enough.

A scant hour later, the carriage set off and the gentle rocking motion had Neah's eyes drooping. She'd tossed and turned for most of the night, managing a harried couple of hours of rest before giving up and preparing herself for the day ahead. At least she'd managed some sleep, a small miracle likely a result of the post-battle crash that left her feeling drained.

She caught her head as it bobbed down once more, shaking herself and pulling open the brocade lace of the curtain that covered the small window. Travelling on the open road through the forest in this part of the kingdom wasn't typically too dangerous, but it was still better for her to remain alert. You could never be too careful.

The dirt path they rode was worn smooth from frequent travel, vendors to and from the local towns and villages or passing through on their way to Tarrow in the east where large markets congregated and festivals and celebrations often took place.

Either side of the road stood trees, mostly oak, their trunks nearly triple the width of her body and their height impressive as they curved in from either side, as if they were ushering them ward the palace.

The king lived centrally, just slightly closer to the south of the kingdom than the east, under the guise of accessibility to all the provinces within his land. Personally, Neah thought it more likely that the monarchs simply enjoyed the balmier heat the south offered to the lighter spring sunshine in the north.

Neah had wished more than once that she might get to travel outside of Valeneos, to see other continents, but in her heart of hearts she secretly knew she would miss her home too much. The leaves in the south were a myriad of orange and reds year-round, glimmering like jewels in the cooler months when frost tipped their edges, and nothing compared to the annual lunar festival celebrating the goddess Selene—the moon swelled to triple its size and shone amber instead of its usual silver glow. It was like living in a world of gold and most believed it to be good luck to sit beneath the golden light—some even believed the goddess granted wishes during the small window.

Neah wasn't sure what she believed, but the goddess had never seemed to answer Neah's prayers or wishes. Not when it came to setting free her inner shifter at least. The only thing she longed for more than to see the world, was to experience it anew as her animal-self. Maybe it was foolish to wonder, to long, but Neah often played a game with herself, considering whether she would have wings, or paws, or hooves, or maybe even gills. Something about running in the forest on all fours with nothing but the wind and the taste of the trees in her mouth appealed immensely, but she wouldn't know for sure what form she took until she shifted. *If she ever shifted.*

She sighed and let the curtains fall closed, leaning back against the cushioned seat. Her arse was beginning to go numb. For all the pomp and decoration in these tiny boxes, they were awfully uncomfortable. Though, not nearly so much as riding—her inner thighs and back still ached from the punishing pace she'd set before, but she could be glad of it now for it had allowed her to reach Zennon in time to save her life. Perhaps the goddess hadn't given up on her just yet.

By the time the sun shone high and bright in the sky, they arrived at the palace. She'd brought no bags and so merely thanked the driver and approached the gates of the king's palace with a grace that anyone would have recognised as nobility if they'd bothered to look.

Guards stood to attention outside the open gates and let her pass with only a brief look and nod. She was a familiar face around here, even if it had been a while since she'd been back, mostly because she was the spitting image of her father. If she'd needed it, she could have provided the seal to the guards that signified her access to the court, but she was relieved she didn't need it because it was tucked inside her corset and would likely have drawn attention if she'd had to remove it from the brassiere.

The palace was structurally similar to a castle, with turrets and spires that arched towards the blue sky, but was made of a white rock that looked nice in the day but transformed in the light of the moon to become a glowing beacon of resplendence. Ostentatious? Definitely. But it was undeniably a sight to behold.

A long line of steps in the same material as the palace held another set of guards that nodded as she passed and began the long climb. Her thighs were complaining and sweat beaded along her hairline under the tenacity of the sun by the time she made it to the top. She took a second to regain her composure and smiled when the guards at the next set of doors swung them open with ease to reveal the hustle and bustle inside.

Some nobles chose to live in the palace, many had their own wings—an honour granted to those who pleased the king or otherwise held high status. Others stayed in the rooms used for travelling visitors, of which there were many.

Neah had her own room in the palace, though it likely needed airing out by now, but that wasn't her destination. No, she needed to find her best friend and warn the king of the plot she'd discovered at Lord Pembroke's party. Before they all ended up dead.

CHAPTER FIVE

WREN

His mate was in the palace. *His mate was in the palace.* His mate was *in* the palace.

It was all Wren could think about. Somewhere within these walls was the person who completed his soul, who called to the tiger beneath his skin, whose heart beat in time to his.

And he was fucking terrified.

Lady Zennon had arrived with the dawn, while Wren had been sleeping. The ritual Sonnet had performed had taken a lot out of him. More than he'd expected. He'd slept for a full day and had risen to the news that his mate had arrived.

The relief was tempered by nervous anticipation and then soured further when he learned of the brutal attack Lady Zennon had faced—and thwarted.

Wren smirked into his tea as he lifted the cup to his lips. Of course his mate had taken on four assassins and lived to tell the tale. She would be a match for him in every way.

His mother sighed and patted the hardwood of the table between them, snapping his thoughts away from Lady Zennon and back to the present where the late queen had clearly been speaking while he'd daydreamed.

"I'm glad to see you looking well, darling."

"Thank you, Mother," he murmured, replacing the cup in the delicate saucer gently so as not to cause a clatter. He couldn't say he particularly cared for the beverage, but it was what was expected, a genteel drink to mask the wild nature of the beast-king.

The urge to smirk rose again and he barely quashed it as his mother continued talking.

"Nasty business about the attack, has there been any luck in finding who is responsible?"

He frowned and shook his head. "Not yet." Even if there had been any information, he wouldn't have told her. His mother was a beautiful woman, as elegant and graceful as the swan form she sometimes inhabited, but she was also a gossip. While he'd have liked to believe that in a matter as serious as this she would have held her tongue, he couldn't be sure. Not when someone at the ceremony had to have been responsible for the attack. Nobody else had known of his intent to retrieve Lady Zennon.

A circle of his closest confidantes and family members, and yet someone had tried to kill his mate before the guard could reach her—and likely would have succeeded if not for Lady Zennon's own prowess.

The betrayal cut deep, like a physical wound that pulled when he moved and rubbed against his clothes. Or maybe that was just his tiger, prowling below the surface, half a heartbeat away from exploding from his skin to hunt down those who were responsible.

Soon, he consoled himself. When he found out who had done this, they would wish for death.

It would not come swiftly.

"Have you seen her yet?" The words were casual, but the interest gleaming in his mother's amber eyes was unmistakable as she feigned nonchalance by tucking a strand of blonde hair behind her ear.

"No." The short response didn't invite further questions, not that his mother cared. "She had a busy night, despatching our enemies," he continued, the amusement he felt colouring his voice just slightly, but it was enough for his mother to award him with a look of disapproval. "I imagine the Lady is still resting. Are we going to talk about the obvious?"

She sighed. "And what's that, darling?"

Fortuna Ainsworthy was no fool, and Wren resented his mother for making him pull the words out of her. "That we have been betrayed. I would appreciate any insights you have for me."

The chair scraped across the wooden floors of his mother's parlour as she pushed back from the table and stood in a huff. "I don't like what you're insinuating."

"Then let me speak plainly." Wren stood too, his height dwarfing his mother's impressive stature. "The only people who knew of Lady Zennon's import and location were with us during the ceremony. Someone orchestrated this attack, probably in an effort to claim the throne after I fail to break the curse and am driven quite mad. Do you know anything about it?"

Perhaps he would later regret the ice that coated his words or the harshness in his eyes as he pierced his mother with his questions, but in that moment it was all he could do to keep his beast at bay when he knew that his mate had been targeted.

Fortuna stiffened and drew herself up to her full height, her head barely in-line with his chest as she bit out, "I know of no such machinations and you would be wise to hold your tongue before levelling accusations of that manner at family, my king." Then she turned on her heel and marched away, the swaying of her purple silk dress wafting the familiar scent of his childhood in his face until he took a breath filled with temporary shame.

But it was a necessary evil. It had been entirely possible that this betrayal was not evil in its intentions. The wrong word whispered in the wrong ear could spell disaster, even when intentions were pure. Typically his union would be cause for joy, but it also put a target on his back—and his mate's—until their bond was accepted and celebrated under Selene's gaze.

Plus, there was still the small matter of informing Lady Zennon of *why* she'd been escorted to his palace. It was rare for mates to be rejected, but not impossible, and if that happened... Well, Wren would be well and truly fucked.

He'd checked on Sonnet not long after he'd awoken from the day's rest and Gabe had told him that Sonnet had mostly slept the whole time too. No harm had come to her, which was good because he would need her for the bonding ceremony if Lady Zennon was receptive.

He found Skye outside of Sonnet's room with his arms crossed and a scowl on his face, magic rolling off of him in waves that prickled Wren's skin.

"Everything… okay?"

Skye grunted. "See for yourself."

Worry swirling, Wren knocked on Sonnet's door and waited for her to call him inside before opening it and finding her lounging on a small sofa with Gabriel.

The two were laughing, Sonnet practically breathless as Gabe wiped tears from his face and attempted to catch his own breath.

Wren stepped inside and approached before looking between them, bemused. "Is this why Skye is outside, sulking?"

Sonnet shrugged. "I told him he could come in." She peered into the space behind Wren and called, "This nasty little witch doesn't bite. Unless he wants me to."

If he didn't know better, Wren might have thought Sonnet was enjoying taunting Skye—a thought that was evidenced by the smugness on her face when Skye growled from the hall.

"Where are my manners?" Sonnet stood and curtsied. "How are you, my king?" The words had an undercurrent of humour, like she was placating rather than respecting him. The witches mostly governed themselves, having a hierarchy separate to Wren's crown, but it still felt a little like being mocked as a child playing at power rather than having it.

And *that,* his beast did not like.

He let his tight control slip for half a second, stripes rippling along his skin and claws showing at his fingertips before he let a mask of civility fall back into place.

Sonnet paled but stood her ground and Wren could admire that tenacity even as he demanded obedience.

"I'm well, thank you. I hear that you slept for nearly as long as me?"

"The spell took much from me," she said, nodding and Skye snorted from the hall, making her eyes narrow. "Oh for the Goddess' sake, either get inside or close the door. You won't become affected by my dirty magic just by standing here."

Skye's form filled the doorway, his blue eyes practically beacons as they fixed on the witch. "You're lucky I let you live, that Wren needs you alive."

"Indubitably," she said, pressing her hands together and widening her eyes. "My gratefulness knows no bounds. Would you like me to get on my knees to show you my gratitude?"

Magic sparked at Skye's fingertips and Wren watched, intrigued. He'd never seen much active magic from his friend, but this witch knew how to push his buttons.

"You dare—"

"That's quite enough," Wren said mildly and Skye fell silent. "It's not polite to threaten our guest," he continued and Skye's jaw clenched. "And you should know better than to taunt *your* king," he added to Sonnet and saw the first trace of true anger on her face at his insinuation that she owed Skye her fealty.

"He is no king of mine."

Sensing they stood on a precipice that could implode at

any second, Wren decided to change the subject. "Close the door, would you, Skye?" He sat down in the armchair that faced the sofa where Sonnet and Gabe had been laughing only moments ago. "My mate is here," he said quietly, as soon as the door shut.

"You seem surprised," Sonnet remarked, settling back down onto the sofa at a less than demure distance from Gabe. "Was that not the point of the ceremony?"

Wren ignored her sarcasm as he cast his eyes over the room. It was plain, compared to his anyway, but likely better than any bed she'd have slept in for a long time. Unlike the suites reserved for high ranking company, Sonnet's room was a parlour and bedroom all in one. A hearth sat opposite the bed, with the sofa, two armchairs and a small ovular table surrounding it. It was clean, comfortable, and warm. It seemed unlikely that they were qualities Sonnet had found much time for while in hiding for her survival.

"Yes," he allowed, and said nothing more on his nerves. Not while Sonnet was there, anyway. "I have a proposition for you," he said, the idea forming slowly as his gaze came back around to the witch's. Skye had lowered himself into the armchair opposite Wren but his eyes didn't stray from Sonnet's, as if he expected her to pounce at any moment. "You must be tired of running all the time."

Suspicion made the witch's nostrils flare, but Skye had caught on far quicker to Wren's intentions and was now glaring at the king. "No. Absolutely not."

Wren ignored Skye's protests. He could say what he wanted, but this was still Wren's palace, his kingdom, and unless Skye was willing to fight his oldest friend it would stay that way.

"What are you saying?"

He smiled at Sonnet. "I want you to help me find a way to break this curse on my bloodline. Permanently."

The witch's eyes gleamed. She was interested. Good. "And in return?"

Wren shrugged, leaning back casually and crossing one leg over the other as he spread his arms across the back of the chair. "Safety. You may stay as long as you wish and, for so long as you remain, no harm will be allowed to befall you."

"Wren—"

"What if I can't find a way to break it?"

"*Wren*—"

"Well, let's cross that bridge if we come to it."

Sonnet grinned and stood, shaking his hand firmly. "I accept."

"No! Wren, I cannot allow this." Skye had stood when Sonnet had and Wren looked up at his friend calmly. "Her magic… It is dangerous. Unnatural. I will help you break this curse, I swear it, but—"

"Excellent," he said smoothly. "You can work on it together." Now they both looked horrified, mouths dropped open in protest even as no words escaped their lips. "We have bigger problems than magical bickering and, frankly, *you* do not allow anything, friend."

Dominance. His beast would accept nothing less.

For a moment, they watched each other, eyes held, until Skye nodded. "As you wish."

Only then did Wren stand. "Good. Now, I think it's past time that I meet my mate."

CHAPTER SIX

NEAH

Walking through the palace was strange. The flurry of activity in the corridors was the same as it always had been and already she could hear the gossip stirring about her presence. Though, interestingly enough, many of the gossipers had no clue who Neah was and instead ruminated on her mysterious identity—she'd been gone for too long. While it was true that she'd changed a lot since she last spent time in the palace, now more woman than girl, it felt odd to have been so thoroughly erased from the minds of the court.

At least it made it easier to waltz through the halls without interruption.

Neah was debating whether to attempt to find Zennon or her father first when she spotted the familiar garb of the king's guard. The silver-grey of their shirt, emblazoned with a crown and a moon, was unmistakable and Neah pivoted to approach.

The windows that ran intermittently on one side of the

palace's walls made her nervous, the light catching on the deep blonde strands of her hair and highlighting it in gold and red, a constant reminder of how open the space was as she moved. From a security standpoint, the windows were trouble. Easy to scale, or blast open, though the stained glass effect was rather pretty.

"Excuse me." Neah pitched her voice low and the guard looked up at her in surprise before interest flared in his long-lashed brown eyes. "I'm—"

"Oh, I know exactly who you are, Lady," he said, surprising her even as relief made her throat tighten momentarily. She hadn't been *completely* forgotten, then. "Please accept my apologies that I couldn't be there myself to escort you this morning."

She raised her brows but accepted his apology with a smile. "Not at all. I was perfectly safe."

"I'll say." The guard grinned, his teeth even and white and she found herself smiling hesitantly back. "I imagine you're looking for the king?"

Perhaps the guard was right, it would be better for her to approach the king directly with information this potentially time-sensitive. "I—yes, actually."

"Come. It would be my honour to take you to His Majesty."

It was a pleasant but not unwelcome surprise to be granted such a courtesy and she inclined her head in thanks. Playing the part of Lady came naturally to her and, in truth, she enjoyed the freedom it gave her. Not for the privilege and monetary benefits, though they were helpful, but the freedom to be underestimated was intoxicating. The court looked at her and saw a woman, a delicate noble with the power and prestige of a shifter beneath her skin. They didn't see the strength in her lean frame, the cunning in her eyes—nor did they know her shame, that she was almost as much a shifter as the humans among them, given that she'd never shifted.

But to be unremarkable was the gift of a talented spy, one she had subverted with her reputation. After all, who expects the life of the party to be reporting its every facet?

Her chivalrous escort garnered further whispers but she paid them no mind, most of her attention was focused on keeping the train of her borrowed dress out from underfoot. It was long and green and not at all something she would typically have worn. She loved dresses, but more often than not they were a hindrance.

Lady Neah wouldn't care about that though. Lady Neah didn't need to know how to fight or hide daggers on the inside of her thigh. Lady Neah had time for dresses and pinning her hair just-so.

Neah the spy? Well, she was becoming frustrated with the mass of forest material even as she admired the way the gold thread design on the skirt glimmered in the sunlight.

"I'm sorry," she said after a moment, their pace slow due to the volume of her skirts. "I didn't ask your name."

"Dean Grandy." He gave a short bow that revealed the top of his close-cropped dark hair. "And it's no bother, Lady. I understand wanting to make a good first impression."

First impression? She smoothed her brow and nodded, even as she turned over his words in her mind while they walked.

They rounded a corner and she was relieved when the

windows were replaced with art and tapestries. The palace wound inward in a spiral formation meant to confuse intruders, though Neah knew it like the back of her hand. She'd expected Dean to lead her toward the King's quarters, or perhaps a banquet hall as it would soon be nearing supper. Instead, they continued on to the center of the spiral and the formal viewing chamber. Typically it was used for ceremonies, trials, or other matters of importance. Why would the king be there? And why would Dean think she would be welcome to interrupt what was likely a closed and exclusive meeting?

It had grown darker when they walked, the natural light mostly disappearing as they moved into the depths of the castle, but toward the viewing chamber they approached the far side of the palace walls once more. She'd only been inside one other time before and knew that a large stained glass window took up the majority of the back wall, the effect both grand and foreboding all at once much like the carved entrance doors that were double her height.

"Perhaps we should wait outside until the king is done?"

Dean frowned, thick brows drawing together tightly. "Don't be ridiculous, Lady."

The use of the honorific as he gently berated her made Neah's lips twitch but the humour faded quickly when the solid oak doors swung open and four unfamiliar sets of eyes swung her way.

"Your Majesty," Dean boomed from beside her, making her jump, "may I present to you, your mate, Lady Zennon?"

Neah froze. Then the terrible urge to laugh swept over her, barely restrained, as she met the final set of eyes in the room. Familiar brown irises that swam with a mixture of worry and amusement.

"What is the meaning of this?" The words came not from the king, but the tall shifter at his side—Gabriel, if she remembered correctly. "The king's mate is *here*, you idiot."

Dean spluttered, looking between Neah and Zennon with mounting confusion. "I—"

"My apologies, Your Majesty," Neah said smoothly, stepping further into the room and walking to Zennon's side before she curtsied deeply. "It seems there was some confusion, but I have ended up where I intended to be."

Eyes a gold so deep they burned watched her with a cat-like intensity from the dais where he sat, and the king's mouth curled as he took her in. "Is that so?"

Zennon cleared her throat, causing all eyes to shift to her. "Yes, quite."

Dean shuffled awkwardly in place before bowing his head to the king and making a swift retreat, closing the doors behind him. The room was large and the sound of his exit echoed, the smell of oak overpowering almost everything else in the room as dust motes drifted lazily in the beams of sunlight that cascaded in through the large window behind the king.

"I know you," he said suddenly, standing from his seat and descending the small set of steps from the raised platform to stop inches away from her. "Who are you?"

"Most certainly not your mate," she said, attempting humour and letting it fade when the intensity of the king's stare only increased. "I am Lady Neah Fallon. Lady Zennon sent word to me of what transpired at the Midmyr estate and I came as quickly as I could."

"Fallon?" Gabriel breathed and Neah slid him a bored look. "But that would make you—"

"Yes," she said, cutting him off but keeping her gaze on the king. "My apologies for barging in, Your Majesty."

His eyes stayed on hers even as he addressed Zennon. "Is this true?"

"Yes, Your Majesty."

The king nodded once, the motion powerful, final. "I'm glad to know you have allies, Lady Zennon."

Zen smiled, but Neah barely saw it. Instead, she was caught on the way the king inhaled sharply, like a predator catching the scent of prey. "Me too. Though, I'm afraid it's still more than a little unclear to me *why* I'm here?"

The king at last looked away from Neah and she nearly slumped with relief, only to stiffen at his next words.

"Misguided as my guard appeared, he was not entirely incorrect. It is time for me to take a wife, to secure the future of this kingdom, and who better than my mate?"

"How could you possibly know—" Neah fell silent when Zennon nudged her in the side and the king turned his hypnotic gaze back to her.

"A spell was performed that gave me the location of my mate. Midmyr Forest. Once my men drew closer, they were able to track the magic more precisely to your estate, Lady Zennon."

The bottom of Neah's stomach dropped, the sensation leaving her feeling vaguely nauseous as she absorbed the king's words. His mate was in the forest. Then at Zennon's estate.

"How do you know your mate wasn't one of the dead

guards? Or the assassins?" This time, Zennon didn't chastise Neah for the questions.

The only other woman in the room stepped forward, her silver eyes gleaming as she assessed Neah. "The magical trail the guards followed would have immediately dissipated had the king's mate perished. Instead, it remained intact and led them to your friend's door."

Sensing Zennon might say something that Neah wasn't quite ready to make known, she slipped her arm through her friend's and squeezed tightly. For now, it was better that the king not know that Zennon hadn't been the only person in the house that night. At least until Neah could speak to her father and determine the best course of action.

Zennon's breath wheezed out of her and Neah understood the feeling. "I don't—"

"You don't need to say anything right now," the king said, and the words were surprisingly soft as he reached out and took Zennon's free hand into his own. "I'm just grateful you're here, and alive, and that we have the opportunity to know one another."

The beams of sunlight illuminated the king's silhouette and wrapped him and Zennon in a glittering golden haze and Neah couldn't deny that they looked good together. Zennon was soft and dark, the king as unyielding as stone but with a softened edge made of spun bronze. A perfect balance between dark and light, soft and hard. The silver-eyed woman's gaze hadn't left Neah as she observed the king and her friend and she raised a brow in the woman's direction while the king continued to murmur to Zennon. What did the woman think she knew?

"I'll leave you to settle in, but perhaps we could have breakfast together tomorrow?"

For a second, the king looked young, vulnerable, his golden eyes wide and his long, pale fingers moved a shade too fast when he tucked a strand of chestnut hair behind his ear.

Neah nudged Zennon and she sucked in a shaking breath. "That—sounds lovely."

"Until tomorrow, then." The king bowed and they curtsied in turn, remaining in place as the king swept out of the room with Gabriel, Skye, and the silver-eyed woman in tow.

Only then did Zennon turn to Neah, dark eyes narrowed into slits. "You have a lot of explaining to do, *friend*. And is that my dress?"

CHAPTER SEVEN

NEAH

Zennon was silent for the entire duration of the walk back to her room and Neah glanced at her friend frequently, trying to assess what she was most upset about. Had the assassination attempt finally sunk in? Surely she couldn't be angry that Neah had broken into the house, considering she'd then saved Zennon's life? Or was it only that Neah had borrowed this gorgeous, frustrating dress? They'd shared clothes before, so Neah had assumed it wouldn't be an issue.

Speculation running wild in her mind, by the time they reached Zennon's door amongst the wing of guest chambers Neah was fit to burst.

The room was nice, clean, though a little small compared to what Zennon was likely used to as a noblewoman. A large four-poster bed sat off to the left, taking up the majority of the space in the room, and a quick glance revealed an adjoining bathing chamber. It wasn't Neah's first time visiting the guest chambers, but it was her first time taking them in by daylight. Dark woods and white sheets gave an impression of freshness and the air smelled faintly of cedar. The effect was pleasant, if underwhelming.

Zennon kicked off her delicate pumps and stomped over to the large window at the back of the room, the only source of natural light in the space. A small round table meant for one had been set next to the window, the gauzy curtains brushing its edges, and Neah followed the other woman and took a seat in one of the upholstered armchairs. They were a strange shape, a half-moon whose back only reached Neah's waist when she sat. Whoever had designed these chairs had clearly never sat in them—or they knew nothing of what it meant to be comfortable.

"Well?" Zennon remained standing, her arms crossed as she glared out of the window so fervently that Neah peered around her to see what she might be looking at. "Do you have anything to say for yourself?"

Neah blinked, folding her hands atop one knee as she considered Zennon. "Hello, dear friend, I'm happy you're alive?"

Zennon softened slightly. "Yes, yes, I'm grateful for your heroics—though it *is* a shame about the rug. I had that imported from the continent."

"I'm sure the king would procure you another." Neah's lips twitched and Zennon scowled.

"Finally. I'm glad you're done dancing around the topic."

"That's what your sour mood is about?"

Zennon's eyes flashed and Neah grimaced, wishing she could snatch back the words. She loved her friend, but her ire could be... uncomfortable. "Why does the king think I'm his mate? Why didn't you tell him you were there that night too?"

Neah shrugged. "You could be his mate."

A gleam of something in Zennon's eyes made Neah sit up straight, curiosity brimming. "I very much doubt that."

"Oh?"

Zennon waved the unspoken demand for answers away like she was batting an irritating fly. "What's going on?"

Neah sighed. "I was at Pembroke's, one of his parties. I overheard some information that was critical to the king, so I left straight away. I came to you so I could give you the information too, that way if something happened to me en-route to the palace..."

The grim set to Zennon's mouth told Neah she understood. "And now?"

"Well, I became a little distracted by the assassins trying to kill you," Neah pointed out, drumming her fingers impatiently on her knee. "Then, before I could speak to my father, I was mistaken for you and brought to the king."

Zennon shook her head. "Jamison is at my estate, investigating. He'll be back tomorrow afternoon, I heard."

Great. Now she would be burdened by this information for even longer. "Someone is going to attempt to kill the king."

To her surprise, Zennon didn't seem perturbed by this. "That's a little vague. I'm sure people plot to kill the king all the time. He's the *king*."

Neah rolled her eyes. "Sorry, let me be more specific.

Someone put a price on his head." *There*. Now Zennon looked intrigued. "Treason," Neah said and Zennon nodded.

"Why would anyone risk it? Why *now?*" Zennon murmured almost to herself as she finally sat down opposite Neah. "Perhaps it has something to do with this mate, business. It just seems an awful big risk to take otherwise."

"Yes… and no." Neah frowned. "The bounty was placed anonymously. It was sheer luck that I came across the information—two of the hunter's guild were discussing it in rather hushed tones. If someone is sending the hunter's guild after the king, then this is more serious than a run of the mill threat."

"I agree." They looked at each other, worry etched into the lines of their faces, before Zennon continued. "But I'm still irritated that you took my dress. I haven't even had the chance to wear that one yet, Neah."

"If it's any consolation, it's been a nightmare to walk around in."

For half a second, Neah thought she'd got away with the change in subject but then Zennon tilted her head and regarded her so shrewdly it was as if she could see into Neah's soul.

"Why?"

Neah knew what she was asking and felt reluctant to answer, even though there was a rational explanation. "Because I find it's better to keep as much information as close to your chest as possible. What people do when they think you're not watching, that they don't have to impress you, is important. Plus, if my presence at your estate were known it might raise questions that my cover wouldn't allow." It was true, even if it wasn't strictly the truth. Neah wasn't sure she knew what that really was anyway—did the thought of being someone's mate scare her? Maybe. Did it alarm her more that the someone in question might be the *king*? Definitely. She was a shifter who couldn't shift. A spy. And he was her king.

Zennon was the logical choice. The *better* choice.

"Okay," Zennon said and Neah breathed out a sigh of relief. "I'll keep your secret. For now." Neah nodded even as a sense of dread filled her and the odd and unfamiliar urge to run away and hide rose up. "But as soon as you're ready to face the truth, let me know. Because there's no possible way that the king is my mate."

She seemed so sure. "How?"

Zennon smiled and it was full of secrets. "Trust me." Neah hesitated but then nodded. "So you want a way to observe him without him knowing that's what you're doing... Want to be my chaperone?"

The laugh escaped her before she could smother it. Having a chaperone was a relatively antiquated practice. They were a kingdom of shifters and sometimes passions ran high, and hot.

"Sure," she said, though they were sure to raise a few eyebrows. "You'll garner a reputation though. The human so wild she needs a chaperone."

Zennon grinned and the look was wolfish. "Sounds about right."

They fell quiet and a sense of peace filled Neah, making her blink slowly as tiredness washed over her. She'd had barely any sleep the past few days and it was catching up to her now.

"Come on." Zennon's voice was soft and the pressure of her hand on Neah's was gentle as she guided her up from the chair and into the bed. "Sleep, Neah. I'll watch over you."

Neah was asleep before her head hit the pillow.

CHAPTER EIGHT

WREN

Golden eyes had haunted Wren's dreams. It had been a surprise to learn that his mate was human. Such matches were not uncommon, of course, but he'd been so sure that Selene had been telling him his mate would bear his stripes. Maybe the goddess had meant metaphorically. After all, Lady Zennon must have been a warrior indeed to take on four assassins and live to tell the tale. So perhaps her stripes were beneath her skin, adorning her soul.

Wren sighed, leaning back in his chair as he waited at the long table that had been laid out for breakfast.

The Lady seemed pleasant enough, attractive, he supposed, with her dark hair and pouty mouth.

So why did he still dream of golden eyes?

Sonnet, Gabriel, and Skye had joined him at his request as they awaited Lady Zennon and her companion to arrive and Wren found that he was nervous. What if they had nothing in common? What would they talk about? What if the Lady didn't want a mate?

"Are you certain the spell worked as intended?" The words slipped from him before he could think twice and even Skye looked affronted that Wren was questioning magic.

"Of course it worked." Sonnet rolled her eyes. "If it had failed, I certainly wouldn't have stuck around."

"It's just that—"

The doors to the small dining hall swung open, cutting off his words, and Wren swallowed before standing to greet his guests.

Lady Zennon was remarkable in a dress made of indigo that fluttered around her form as she walked, slits in the sleeves showing off the creamy white skin beneath, but when she smiled up at him he couldn't help the feeling that something was *wrong*.

He smiled back nonetheless and reached automatically for her hand, brushing a kiss across the delicate knuckles before withdrawing and turning to her companion.

Bright eyes ensnared his and for a second he couldn't breathe. He shook himself out of the stupor and smiled, looking awkwardly away as he accepted Lady Neah's hand and pressed a similarly chaste kiss to its back. Except, it felt less like a kiss and more like the exhilaration of paws hitting the ground beneath the moon, the thunder of his heartbeat so loud he was surprised nobody else remarked upon its echo in the room.

Wren relinquished his grip and took a large step back. Whatever kind of shifter Lady Neah was, it called to him— but Zennon was his mate.

He pulled out her chair and reclaimed his own in time for the servers to bring out platters of fruit and oats, cooked meats and eggs, and honey wine which he declined. He needed his wits about him.

"Thank you for joining me," he said once everyone's plates were full. "Dig in."

A murmur of chatter broke out as cutlery scraped across plates but Wren found his appetite had largely vanished. He poked half-heartedly at the sausage on his plate and instead watched the two women interact at the opposite end of the table. They seemed close, sharing looks and quiet whispers that spoke of friendship and the kind of comfortability he felt around Gabe and Skye.

Speaking of which, the two were at odds sitting opposite each other. They almost never fought, though it was clear to Wren what—or rather *who*—had come between them. Yet, the silver-eyed witch watched them with worry, as if dissension had never been her intent.

Wren was so lost in his thoughts he nearly missed the question that Lady Zennon posed to him and even so, it took him a second too long to respond.

"My apologies, Lady, my mind was elsewhere. What did you say?"

Zennon smiled and it was graceful, patient. "Not to worry, my king. I only asked if you enjoyed your breakfast."

"Please, call me Wren." He smiled and she inclined her head. "Truthfully, though the spread is fantastic, I find my appetite somewhat reduced this morning."

A throaty chuckle made his body perk up, alert, and he wanted to curse when he realised who it came from.

"I think you make him nervous, Zen," Lady Neah said in a mock-whisper and Wren scowled.

"You do realise that's your king that you're speaking of?" The words were haughty and he was surprised by them. He didn't mind good natured ribbing, but something about this woman... she pushed his buttons in all the wrong ways.

"Goodness," Neah said, eyes widening with fake surprise. "I suppose I am as unobservant as I am forgetful, Your Majesty."

Something told him that Lady Neah was neither unobservant or forgetful.

Warmth stained his cheeks as he fought the urge to bite back, to squabble like a twelve-year-old pulling a young girl's hair, and so he settled for mumbling, "That's quite alright."

Thankfully, Lady Zennon didn't seem off-put by the turn of the conversation. "You'll have to forgive Neah, she's spent some time in the north recently and, as such, has forgotten all manners."

Neah rolled her eyes and speared a sausage with her fork, biting into the end with such vigour that he knew he wasn't the only male at the table wincing. There was a sparkle in her eyes that irked him, like she was taunting him on purpose and, for reasons he couldn't fathom, it was *working*.

"Well, we can't help our friends," he said, and even he could recognise the snide quality to the words. Still, Lady Zennon just kept smiling like she was in on the world's funniest joke but had neglected to share it with the rest of them.

"I take personal offence to that," Gabriel muttered and Skye nodded in agreement.

"So many fragile male egos," Sonnet remarked, sighing, and Neah chuckled.

"You took the words right out of my mouth. I'm sorry, I don't think we've been introduced."

Sonnet smiled. "A deliberate oversight, I'm sure. Wouldn't want us ladies getting together and putting all sorts of thoughts in each other's heads, would we?" Neah laughed and Lady Zennon giggled alongside her. "I'm Sonnet."

"Pleased to meet you."

How was it that the witch had made a better first impression than he had? At least Skye's feelings towards Sonnet hadn't shifted, judging by the glare he had levelled on the witch at any given moment.

"And you, Lady Zennon? Did you enjoy your breakfast?" Why did he suddenly feel so awkward? Like he was grasping at straws to maintain the barest hints of dry conversation.

"Very much, thank you. It was a strange day and a half, so the normalcy was refreshing."

"Did you really take on four assassins?" Gabriel took over the conversation and Wren felt relieved and then profoundly guilty.

All first meetings are awkward, he reasoned. Just because he didn't immediately click with Lady Zennon didn't mean he wouldn't ever do so.

The two women on the end of the table glanced at each other and Neah waved her friend forward, as if encouraging her to tell the tale.

"Truly, it was nothing exciting," Lady Zennon said, glancing down at her silverware and jumping when Gabriel let out a laugh that echoed even in the relatively small dining room. It was only for Wren's personal use, for more informal settings than that of the banquet hall, and he liked to think it was cosy—for a palace, anyway.

"Nothing exciting? Do you frequently conquer your enemies so easily, then?"

"Oh, no. I just mean that I was very lucky. They weren't very good assassins."

Wren's brows scrunched together as he tried to puzzle the Lady out. Was she merely being modest? Or was she hiding something? But what? And why?

"And, well, my guards did some of the work," she continued and Wren relaxed. Her guards. Of course.

"Speaking of assassins," Lady Neah said and Wren nearly groaned. "Do you have plans in place to keep Zennon safe in the palace?"

Skye raised a brow at Neah. "In the palace? There are guards everywhere, nobody would dare attack her here."

Neah looked unimpressed. "Complacency is death. You may as well swan around the place with a target painted on your chest."

Wren tried to hide a laugh behind a cough and was sure he didn't succeed when Neah gave him a look of surprise and Skye scowled. "We can, of course, provide a personal guard for you, Lady Zennon."

"I'd also like her to be moved to my room," Neah continued, as if he hadn't spoken. "Safety in numbers," she added when she noticed their quizzical looks.

"You have a room in the palace?" Sonnet asked and

Neah's face shuttered. *Interesting. So she didn't like to talk about her father.*

No. It wasn't *interesting*. Nothing about her should intrigue him. Not when his *mate* sat on her left.

"Yes," Neah said, the word not inviting further questions. Her eyes caught his and held, a challenge flaring there that had his instincts sitting up and paying attention. This woman may be dressed as a noble, but everything inside of him told him what really lurked below the surface: *predator.*

CHAPTER NINE

NEAH

Breakfast had been an odd affair that morning. She'd expected it to be a private audience between the king—or *Wren* as he'd insisted Zennon call him—and Zen, so she'd been taken aback when Zennon had insisted that Neah join them.

She wasn't sure what to make of the king yet. He was petulant one moment, magnanimous the next, and the way he'd watched her…

Neah shivered. It wasn't right. There was too much in his gaze for a man who believed he was mated to another and, despite Zennon's protests, likely truly was.

The halls of the palace were relatively quiet and Neah felt more alert than she had in days, thanks to the long sleep she'd managed the night before. She barely remembered drifting off before Zennon had woken her for breakfast. It had been needed. Tired spies were sloppy spies, and sloppy spies ended up dead.

She passed by several windows before turning a corner

and walking a path she knew well. It was the corridor of her childhood and she hadn't seen it in many years. She wasn't sure if it had always been so small and narrow or if she'd just grown up since last she'd walked the hall.

Before long, she'd reached the familiar arched door and used the metal knocker above the handle to signal her presence, smiling when a deep voice called for her to enter.

Golden eyes, a match for her own, widened beneath the short dark hair, stubborn chin, and strong brows of the Captain of the king's guard. Full lips that closely resembled her own pushed into a grin as he saw her standing before him.

"Neah."

"Hi, Dad." Her smile made her cheeks ache but she couldn't help it. She'd seen very little of her father since she'd become his spy. Most of her time was spent travelling or lingering at other estates around the kingdom. What she had seen of him had been harried, information given first and pleasantries exchanged after if they had time.

They often didn't.

Her resemblance to her father was obvious if you knew him well enough and particularly evident when they stood together, making some of the particulars of her job difficult—but, for the most part, if she showed the world a Lady then that was all they saw. Not the daughter of the famed Captain Jamison Fallon.

Jamison rounded his desk and engulfed her in an embrace that lasted forever and also nowhere near long enough. He pulled back and cupped her face between his palms as he looked her over, scanning for injuries, and then her dad faded away and the captain stood before her.

"You're here."

She nodded. "I have urgent information to share. I was on my way here when the assassins attacked Zennon."

"I assumed as much." At her surprised look, some humour bled back into his face. "You think I wouldn't recognise my own daughter's handiwork?"

Her laugh was quiet and he softened hearing it. "I'm worried for her."

He nodded. "I am too. If someone attacked her once…" He pulled away and reclaimed his seat behind his desk, gesturing for her to join him in the chair opposite. "You'll keep an eye on her?"

"Of course. What are sisters for?"

Jamison smiled but there was a weariness to it that Neah hadn't seen on him before. Zennon's connection to their family was a closely guarded secret, one Neah had killed to protect despite her being the youngest child. Zennon had been born out of wedlock, a result of a young soldier's fling with a noblewoman looking to take a walk on the wild side. Her father hadn't even known of Zennon's existence until she was five and her mother ran into some trouble only Jamison could solve. The truth, as it often did, came out, but their father agreed not to claim Zennon as his own so that she could keep her title as the noblewoman's only heir.

Neah wasn't sure if the noblewoman's husband had known that Zen wasn't his. Not that it mattered now, seeing as Zennon's parents were both dead.

Jamison switched gears, the tiredness fading behind the strong persona of the captain. It was a shift that never failed to amaze Neah, the way he could compartmentalise the different facets of his life. "You were with the Pembrokes?"

She nodded. "Someone was willing to pay a fool's worth in coin to the hunter's guild for a hit on the king."

His brows rose and she understood the sentiment. The king had allies of his own within the guild of assassins, no hit placed there would ever reach his door, but that someone had tried… "Bold."

"Yes. And if they're willing to do this through official channels then I'm nervous about what they may be offering those who operate under the radar."

Jamison grumbled his agreement, displeasure sharp on his face as he pulled a stretch of parchment towards him and dipped a quill into a pot of ink. "I'll take care of it."

"How?"

The sudden darkness in the bright gold of his eyes was disconcerting as he considered her over the top of the quill's tip. "The guild has authority over its own. They will be best placed to hunt the hunters."

She shivered. She couldn't help it. Neah was good at what she did, there were not many people she couldn't outfight or outwit, but some of the monsters caged within the confines of the guild made her look like a Goddess-blessed priestess. To have those people on your trail was a terrifying enough thought that she felt a moment of pity for anyone who might have taken their enemy up on the offer of gold.

"What I don't understand is why Zennon was a target," Jamison muttered, blowing gently on the ink and folding the paper into quarters that he sealed with wax and his ring. "Do you think someone knows of her connection to me?"

Her teeth worried her bottom lip as she considered his question. "I think it has to do with the king. He's under the impression that Zennon is his mate."

Jamison froze and then pushed to standing in a move so fluid that she recoiled, the beast locked beneath her skin recognising the power of a fellow predator. "Of course. Midmyr Forest. I should have realised."

She hesitated and then decided he deserved to know the full truth. "Zennon doesn't believe it to be true." The lump in her throat felt impossible to swallow as she gulped. "Because I was there too."

The confession seemed to suck the air right out of him and Jamison slumped back into his chair, deflated. "And you? What do you think?"

"Zennon is the more logical choice for a mate." Neah looked away, glancing around the room and inspecting the new piles of books and scrolls that had crept into the space since last she'd visited, illuminated only by the streams of light that came in through the small circular window set high in the wall. "But she does seem certain."

"This is not a fate I would have chosen for either of you."

"Why? One would think we could do worse than a king. Unless… is he an unkind man?" Her thoughts were bordering on treasonous, but Neah couldn't help it. If the king was a threat to Zennon, then she would deal with him. Treason or no.

Jamison waved the words away. "No, nothing like that. It's complicated. For now, you will observe. I will investigate Zennon's estate further, perhaps there was someone else there that night that the king's spell detected," he added the last in a mutter but her heightened hearing caught the words all the same.

"And if it's true? If the king is mated to one of us?"

He wouldn't meet her eyes, glancing around the room and eventually settling on a point just beside her head. "Then we'll deal with it as best we can. But being mated to the king brings more danger than you could know. His enemies will become your enemies, and there are many."

This, she knew too well. "You would have us refuse the bond?"

He hesitated and then sighed deeply, as if the weight of the world rested on his shoulders and she'd only added to the load. "It is not my decision to make, my darling. For now, let's focus on finding whoever placed the bounty. Once the guild takes care of its own, they may try again— perhaps within these very walls if they hold the influence that I suspect they do."

"I'll have Zennon moved to my room." She stood and then faltered, her roles blurring until she asked in a small voice, "How is she?"

Jamison brightened, the weight of his years lifting. "Your mother is fine. She misses you. Both of you."

Neah's throat tightened but she nodded jerkily. Her mother might not have been Zen's by blood, but she loved Zennon all the same. Neah's parents were both shifters and so benefited from the extended lifeline that came with their nature but Zennon was more human than shifter and likely wouldn't live as long as they did. It made the time they could spend together all the more precious. "Can we see her?"

The softness to her father's face had returned as he stood and reached her in two steps, wrapping his arms tightly around her and squeezing until she could hardly breathe. "Of course. I'll make the arrangements."

Neah squeezed him back almost as hard and then released him, spinning away before he could see the dampness in her eyes. It wasn't weak to cry, but she didn't like to worry her father and if he knew how much she'd missed this, missed *them*, he might not forgive himself for keeping her active in his network of spies.

"I'll keep you updated," she said tersely and didn't wait for his reply as she strode out of the room and back into the corridor. Only then did she allow the tears to slip free.

By the time she reached the more populated area of the palace, her eyes were dry and her mask was in place once more.

She'd left the palace's keepers instructions to air out her chambers before she'd gone to meet her father, and was pleased to find they'd worked quickly. As daughter of the captain, she was afforded a suite much more luxurious than the guest suite Zennon had been allocated and even with the chill air from the open windows, it was comforting to be back in the familiar space.

The set-up wasn't too different from the guest room, only Neah's was bigger and came with an adjoining parlour area as well as a bathing chamber. She'd chosen the tapestries on the walls herself, sweeping landscapes hand-painted featuring the forest below throughout the seasons, as well as the leather armchairs in front of the hearth in the parlour. There was also a small row of bookcases, filled with books on martial arts and sword play as well as romances that she'd snuck into her bedroom as a teen.

It was like returning to a version of herself she'd nearly forgotten had existed.

But here was the proof, the ghost of her soul spread about the room freshly dusted and polished, like it had been waiting for her all along.

Zennon had opted to stay in her chambers for the next few hours with a guard posted outside of her door but would be coming to see Neah soon with options for what to wear tonight. They'd received word of a feast that evening that the king had organised and, despite her weariness, Neah knew they had to go. Not only did she need to protect Zennon, but Neah was also keen to keep an eye on the king. For Zen's sake, she needed to know what kind of man Wren truly was.

What about for your own sake?

She pushed the thought away, taking advantage of the momentary privacy to strip off the oppressive dress she'd worn for the sake of breakfast and padded over to the adjoining bathing chamber to find a bath already waiting for her. Goddess, but the palace keepers were *good*.

It had been a while since she'd had the time to soak and she took full advantage of it then. At Zennon's, her bath had been perfunctory, necessary to remove the traces of blood from her person, and less than skillfully drawn seeing as she'd been the one to throw it together.

But this? Bliss.

Her worries, and thoughts of Zennon, and the king, and her father's beleaguered state, all fled her as she breathed in the steam and stretched the full length of her body out beneath the water. For now, without prying eyes and court expectations, she could just be herself.

Breaths slowing, she relaxed incrementally until her limbs floated weightless in the water. Her skin smelled like the cinnamon soap she'd left behind that had been her favourite growing up and it wasn't until her fingers and toes started to wrinkle that she reluctantly stood and climbed out of the tub.

Unlike the freestanding bath Zennon had at her estate, this one was built into the wall and the water drained away with ease as she towelled herself off and added another old favourite to her skin and hair—golden honey oil with added jasmine. The scent was sweet and fresh at the same time and she inhaled deeply as she combed it through her long hair, focusing on the lightened ends that sometimes dried out in the summer.

After the oil had soaked in, leaving her skin shimmering and smooth, she made use of the chamber pot and approached the armoire in her bedroom. She'd filled out since last she'd seen these clothes, her breasts fuller, her hips rounder, and she was a good amount taller too. It was likely that nothing in there would fit.

As if she'd heard the thought, a knock came at the door to her chambers and Neah smiled. Zennon's timing was impeccable. Neah slipped on a silky robe that just reached the tops of her thighs and walked toward the parlour. It was only Zennon, who had seen Neah in worse states of undress than a too-small robe.

Except, when she opened the door it was not to the sight of familiar brown eyes.

Instead, golden ones widened as they took in her scantily clad form and Neah cursed under her breath. "Your Majesty. I'm sorry. I was expecting someone else."

The king hadn't looked away from her, his eyes dropping to the damp spot her hair was making on the material above her breasts and then lower to the peaches and cream of her long legs. He swallowed hard and a muscle in his jaw ticked, as if her words irked him. "Please, call me Wren."

"Wren," she allowed, curiosity rearing its head as his eyes did their best to swallow her up. "Are you looking for Zennon? She should be here any moment."

Was that relief that flitted across his face? Had he thought she'd been expecting a different kind of company? Why should he care?

"No, actually I was looking for you. I wanted to apologise for my behaviour at breakfast. I was a little out of sorts." He ran a hand through his chin-length hair and appeared to be doing his best not to let his eyes slip down past her chin. "But I fear I've made a bigger mess of things now by bothering you while you're..." He swallowed. "Indisposed."

A smirk tugged at her mouth and she did her best to hide it as he sucked in his bottom lip and let his eyes flick down just once before he screwed them shut.

"Not at all." What was she saying? Why was she torturing the poor man? King or not, he was clearly uncomfortable. "I was getting ready for the feast. I appreciate your apology, though I don't feel it's warranted. Zennon tells me I can be abrasive in my protectiveness."

"Right. Well, I'll just leave you to–to *that*." He waved a hand towards her body and then looked pained, as if this were not at all how he'd imagined this conversation going. "And I'll see you at the feast." She nodded, amused when he turned around so quickly he must have been dizzy, and then hid her smile when he glanced back at her. "Oh, and wear comfortable shoes. There will be dancing afterwards."

Joy. "Thank you for the warning."

He chuckled and the sound was pleasant, warm and deep, and the animal inside her seemed to stretch languidly in response, watching through her eyes like the king was prey she wouldn't mind tasting.

Neah closed the door sharply, uncomfortable with the way her beast reacted to him. Normally she experienced small twinges every now and then, but beyond her heightened senses she could have passed for human. But something about the king and what lurked under his skin called to the part of her trapped beneath hers—and that worried her more than the depth of his laugh or the gleam of hunger in his eyes. She'd given up on ever being able to shift, what would it mean if he was the one who brought it out of her?

This time when the knock at the door came, she called out first and was relieved to hear Zennon's voice through the wood. As soon as she stepped inside, Neah vowed to forget the encounter with the king and instead focus on getting through the night.

CHAPTER TEN

WREN

*W*as it possible to be haunted by someone who wasn't dead? That was how Wren felt, haunted by the scent of jasmine and tortured by a long length of leg. It was ridiculous, but more than that—it was *frustrating.*

Objectively, Neah was an attractive woman. But Wren had met plenty of attractive women in his time, had slept with a good share of them too, and yet none of them had occupied his thoughts quite like the shifter who sat demurely sipping her wine at the long table across from his.

She hadn't even glanced his way when she'd walked in, wearing her own version of the dress Lady Zennon had worn to breakfast. On Zennon, the dress had been floaty and dreamy. On Neah? It was pure temptation, the gauzy movements of the high slit in the side of the gown luring him in with the promise of a glimpse of the lightly sun-kissed skin beneath. The dress felt like more of a suggestion of material than anything else, like if he looked at it the wrong way he might see more than he'd bargained for—except, he found he couldn't think of anything else.

And still she sipped her drink, primly dabbed at her mouth with a napkin after she ate, and flawlessly selected the correct silverware for each course of food. Not so much as one look at him. Her *king*.

"You're staring," Gabe muttered and Wren blinked, wrenching his stare away from the woman who shouldn't have held so much of his attention. Perhaps he'd been mistaken for looking at the woman on Neah's left, the one who was supposedly his mate.

He'd heard the same stories they all had of fated mates finding one another, of puzzle pieces slipping into place and other halves fitting an empty hole, but with Lady Zennon... There was no spark. *Yet.* It could come with time, maybe.

"I'm the king. I can stare if I want to," he griped, but looked away and refocused on the final course in front of them. The chef had outdone themselves that evening, each dish exquisitely prepared and beautifully seasoned, but dessert had always been Wren's favourite.

Crumble was no exception and he dug in with gusto, savouring the tartness of the apples and plums mixed with the sweet oat layer atop, smothered in a thick creamy sauce. It was the perfect late-summer dessert, in his opinion. He would eat it for breakfast, lunch, and dinner if it had been deemed *appropriate* for a king to do such a thing.

Most of the court was in attendance, the room filled with those seeking attention from the king, or even his favour, plus many a suitor who hoped to catch his eye. They'd kept his mate ceremony quiet, for the most part, with only a select few knowing who Lady Zennon was and why she mattered, but it was common knowledge that the ruling monarch often wed around their twenty-fifth birthday. Of course, the court didn't know that the real reason was because of the curse that plagued his family line.

Once dessert was over, Wren stood and a hush fell over the room nearly instantly as all eyes turned to him. Well, almost all eyes.

What could be so interesting to her? Once again, Neah was preoccupied by chatting to the male shifter on her right and her undivided attention on the young member of the court made Wren's skin prickle.

"Thank you all for joining me tonight. I'm sure you'll all agree that Chef Markhane did an incredible job feeding us all. Now, if you'll follow me, the festivities will truly begin." He tried hard to keep the irritation out of his voice and thought he'd been successful until Skye leaned in to murmur in his ear.

"You okay? You're looking a little… orange."

Fuck. "Fine. Too much wine," he muttered and vowed to get himself under control—the last thing this feast needed was a tiger on the dance floor.

The doors at the back of the room swung open and the string quartet immediately began playing. Beckoning the crowd inside, he strode across the room and immediately grabbed a glass of silver fizzy wine, downing it in one gulp.

"Whoa, easy tiger."

Wren rolled his eyes as Skye placed a heavy hand on his

shoulder. Where Skye could be found, Gabriel usually wasn't too far behind and, lately, where Gabe was Sonnet often followed.

Sure enough, by the time Wren turned both Skye and Gabriel were standing beside him with Sonnet lingering just behind Gabe—or maybe it was more accurate to say that Gabe was standing in front of Sonnet, easily adjusting when she moved, almost protectively.

The witch huffed under her breath when Gabriel repeated the movement, keeping himself between Sonnet and Skye, and Wren couldn't help but find that *very* interesting. Not much came between those two—let alone a woman. They were more inclined to share than bicker.

Wren took another glass of wine and raised a brow at the disapproving look on Skye's face. "What? It's my party isn't it?"

"What's got you all broody?"

Long legs. Damp hair. Parted lips and the scent of honey. "Nothing," Wren growled and Skye raised his hands, palms up. Sonnet, however, smirked. "Do you know something?" He stepped forward, eyes intent on the witch, and was surprised when Gabe blocked his way. "If she knows something—"

Sonnet stepped out from behind Gabe, dodging him effortlessly as she sized up Wren. "I know a great number of things. I imagine we'd be here all day if I had to recount every single piece of knowledge I possess that you do not."

Had… Had she just called him stupid?

"Sonnet," Gabe muttered, looking pained as he reached for the witch's arm, and Wren decided right then and there that he was better off not knowing whatever was going on between them.

"Do you know anything pertinent to me and my mate?" Wren said, attempting a calmer tone of voice even as his vision shrank down to capture every twitch Sonnet made.

"Everything I *know*, you know." The words were confident, but measured, and Wren didn't like the way her eyes sparkled, like she'd hidden some clue within the response that she knew he wouldn't decipher.

Wren huffed, turning away and sipping the second glass of wine. "Fucking witches," he muttered and his lips twitched when both Sonnet and Skye protested.

"Hey," they said, and then grimaced at one another.

The moment of awkwardness was luckily averted by the presence of his mother and his uncle, stepping into their little circle with proud smiles. His uncle shared only a passing resemblance to his father, but it was enough that seeing his face was still a gut punch since his father had died on a hunting expedition with his brother. Wren didn't hold it against him though, Castor couldn't help the family resemblance, and he'd been nothing but kind to Wren his whole life, stepping up when he needed advice, supporting him when being a king felt impossible.

Wren smiled, reaching out to clasp his uncle's hand. "Your arrival is a gift."

"Oh? Trouble in paradise?" Castor grinned at Skye and Sonnet who blanched, looking impossibly more horrified than before. "No matter, let's let absence make his heart fonder, my dear." He winked and led Sonnet away with an arm around her shoulders, pausing at the buffet table filled with wine and nibbles just a few paces away while Gabriel watched them intently.

"You look lovely, darling." His mother kissed each of his cheeks and beamed when she pulled away. Her face was already flushed from the wine at dinner and when he caught his uncle's eye he nodded minutely toward his mother, relieved when his uncle nodded. He would keep an eye on her.

"As do you, Mother."

The music shifted, signalling the beginning of the first dance of the night, and Wren drank the last of his wine. Typically, it was tradition for him to hold the first dance and he knew the court, as well as his mother, would expect nothing less that night too. He cast his eyes around while his mother chattered, and then paused.

Lady Zennon and Neah stood off to one side, sipping their flutes of wine and ignoring the looks they were garnering from interested suitors and gossiping nobles. The young shifter from dinner had spotted them too and when he began to approach, Wren didn't think. Just moved.

His long legs ate up the short distance between them as he kept his eyes on Lady Zennon, barely noticing when the young shifter faltered at the sight of his approach. And yet, when he arrived, his hand sought out another. Lightly calloused, long fingers that looked like they could play the pianoforte, and golden eyes.

"Dance with me." The words were more demand than request and Neah blinked at him, looking down at the hand he had clasped in his.

"But—" She looked to Zennon and he felt a momentary flicker of hesitation before pushing it down and squeezing her fingers lightly as the young shifter regained his confidence to approach.

"Now."

Neah thrust her glass at Zennon, who looked only amused as Wren practically dragged Neah into the centre of the room. His hand found her waist, her skin burning hot through the wispy material, and one of her hands fell to his shoulder, and then they began to move.

"Shouldn't you be dancing with your mate?" The words were sharp and Wren cocked his head, leading them effortlessly as he tried to make sense of the look on her face. Was that concern in her eyes? Fear? He couldn't be sure.

"I may dance with whomever I please," he countered and she frowned, a flash of anger in her eyes that he attributed to protectiveness for her friend until she replied.

"Even if your dance partner is unwilling?"

He dropped her hand so quickly that she startled. "By all means, walk away."

Her jaw clenched, mouth hardening into a fierce line as he waited for her to make her choice. She glanced around them at the shocked onlookers, but for once he didn't care. *Let them watch.*

She slipped her hand back into his and their dance resumed, her dress fluttering about his legs as they twirled silently, eyes locked in a battle of wills despite his being none the wiser as to what they were fighting about.

"Zennon—"

"Does not seem to mind that we are dancing."

This time she growled. "Are you going to keep doing that? Cutting off what I say?"

He let her finish speaking and then smirked. "No."

"But *why* are we dancing?" Her brows furrowed and he missed a step, so focused on the minute movement.

"Why not?"

"But—"

"You seem awfully preoccupied by it," he mused. "Why is that? We're dancing, *caritas*, yet you act as if we were being seen doing something far more primal." The rasp of his voice surprised him and when she shivered, he knew it wasn't from cold. "Who are you?"

At that, she blinked. "You know who I am."

"I'm not so sure," he murmured and wariness made her mouth flatten as he spun her around to the song's final crescendo. Her hair was a wash of gold tumbling around her shoulders as she followed the movement effortlessly and curled back into his arms for the final beat.

Their breaths heaved, her scent invading his senses, and for half a second they didn't move. Until a titter broke out and Neah yanked herself away before dipping into a shallow curtsy. "Thank you for the dance, my king."

He inclined his head as the dance floor filled in around them, other couples flocking to the scene now that Wren had done his duty in opening the dance. He remained silent as Neah walked away, not sure what he might say if he opened his mouth, nor did he trust the way his body responded when she'd called him *my king,* as if the words were a claim rather than an honorific.

Following Neah at a more sedate pace, he noticed her spine straighten when she sensed his pursuit and then relax when he turned his attention to Lady Zennon.

"May I have this dance?" He held out his hand and his

mate took it, a small smile on her face as they walked to the centre of the room. "I hope you didn't mind me dancing with your friend. Only, she is an intriguing character and as she is close with you, I find myself wanting to know her better."

"Of course, it's no trouble, my king."

"Wren," he corrected and she smiled as he guided her into the first steps of the dance.

"Wren," she said, and her smile was pleasant, sweet, and she was malleable under his palms. He felt overly aware of every step, every breath, not wanting to crowd her, or lead her too strongly as he felt her delicate form.

The dance was over quickly and he found that he'd spent more time concentrating on his footwork than he had appreciating the woman in front of him. But his nerves made sense—this was his *mate*. He wanted to make a good impression. Of course things had flowed easier with Neah, his steps coming easy and sure, the space between them warm and fraught, the stakes were different.

He bowed his head and Lady Zennon smiled. "Save me another later?"

She nodded. "It would be my pleasure."

His eyes found Neah, watching them closely even as her face was inscrutable. "The pleasure is all mine."

CHAPTER ELEVEN

NEAH

The night had been warm, almost uncomfortably so, especially with Zennon sharing the bed. Neah felt like she'd spent the majority of the night tossing and turning rather than sleeping, which might account for her grouchier-than-normal attitude.

Well that, and Zennon hadn't stopped needling Neah about the dance she'd shared with the king two nights ago. Since then, Neah had done her best to avoid the king and fade into the background when Zennon spent time with him. It wasn't hard—their conversations seemed dry and silence often pervaded the air until one or both of them attempted to speak. Neah couldn't deny that there seemed to be a lack of spark between the two and it wasn't often that the Goddess chose poorly when it came to matching fated souls.

With the dawn came a break in the heat at last, but the attendants woke Neah not long after she'd managed to doze off. They'd fled quickly when she'd quite literally growled at them. It was a sound she'd never made before, more animal than human, and her hand had flown up to cover her mouth. Maybe once she'd have taken it as a sign that her long-awaited shifter side might make an appearance, but she'd lost that hope several years ago. Now, she took it as an odd curiosity potentially brought on by stress.

Two strong cups of tea later, Neah was feeling slightly more awake as she made her way down to the courtyard the king's guard often used to train. The king had invited Zennon there, which surprised Neah. Though she supposed it made sense for the king to know how to fight and do battle. However, Zennon hadn't received the same training Neah had so she wasn't sure what the king was expecting from her sister.

The breeze was nice on Neah's skin as they walked across the green toward the small group gathered opposite the archery targets. Her father had designed the training course that they stood in the middle of and Neah felt her tension drain away. This, at least, was familiar territory.

The king looked up and spotted them at that moment, lifting a hand in greeting that Zennon reciprocated. Gabriel, Skye, and, to Neah's surprise, Sonnet, stood with the king, the latter looking bored.

"Good morning!" Zennon called and when she sank into a short curtsey Neah followed suit.

"Just about," Sonnet muttered and Neah fought back her smirk. Zennon, with her human hearing, didn't catch the words and the king shot the witch a frown before turning back to smile at Zen.

It was true that they were a little late, but Wren didn't

seem even slightly perturbed by this which shot him up in Neah's estimation. Punctuality had its place, of course, but flexibility was important too.

Neah's eyes ran over the king's form, trying to keep thoughts about his *flexibility* out of her mind as he gave her a polite inclination of his head.

"I thought it might be fun to shoot this morning." The king swept out his hand to indicate the archery range and it was only because Neah knew Zennon so well that she could see her nervousness.

"I've never shot before," Zennon said hesitantly and Neah tensed, prepared to defend her, when Wren smiled.

"That's okay, I can teach you."

Several bales of hay had been set up in line with each target, a bow and arrow supplied on top of the bale. Wren guided Zennon over and began explaining how to hold the bow and Neah watched from her place one bale over as Wren guided her hands into position. He was a good teacher, patient and calm, even if his technique was somewhat lacking.

"He's a good man," a voice said to her right and Neah smiled, having heard the witch creep closer. "A Lady could do a lot worse."

Ignoring the subtle dig in the words, Neah hummed her agreement. "He may be a good man, but I would wager he's a lousy shot."

Wren's head shot up and Neah bit back her smile at his wide eyes as they narrowed.

"Now you've done it," Gabriel said, shaking his head as he came up to stand next to Sonnet. "Don't you know that a man's ego is fragile?"

"Like a baby bird," Sonnet cooed and Neah looked between them with a raised brow. Were they an item? Everywhere the witch moved, Gabriel seemed to follow and Skye watched, scowling.

The twang of the bow in Zennon's hands had Neah's attention moving back to her sister. The arrow fell short of the target, but it had at least left the bow which was no easy feat for a first try. Neah smiled, thinking about when she'd first shot her bow. Her father had shown her the basics and then let Neah make her own mistakes before stepping in— her wrist had been black and blue from the bowstring by the time she'd been done that first day.

"Well done, Zen!"

Wren murmured an equal amount of praise, sending a warmth rushing over Neah's skin and for the first time she felt a small stab of jealousy toward her sister. The king's palm curled around Zennon's hip, adjusting her stance, and then he nudged her arms higher. *Too high*, Neah realised, and was moving toward them before she could second guess herself.

"Don't," she said, as Zennon prepared to let the arrow fly.

"Neah?"

Her eyes locked on the king's and she huffed impatiently. "Excuse me, Your Majesty."

He stepped back slowly. "Wren is fine."

Neah didn't reply, just set about readjusting Zennon's stance with her back to *Wren*. "If you had shot that arrow, you likely would have broken your wrist."

"That's not—"

Neah turned around in a movement she recognised as

too fast and, sure enough, the king's skin rippled, his shifter responding to the threat of another predator. Neah nearly laughed. Little did the king know, this form was as dangerous as Neah got. "I'm willing to bet that I have a little more experience with archery than you, my king." She kept the words calm, her tone polite but firm, and when the twang of Zennon's bow rang out Neah smiled. The arrow had made it to the target, embedded in the bottom corner.

"I hit it!"

Neah laughed, hugging Zennon tightly and feeling the familiar twinge of sadness as she thought about the childhood shenanigans they'd missed out on, not being able to grow up together. Sure, they'd spent time together, summered in the same place, but it wasn't the same as living together day in, day out. "Well done, Zen."

As if she could sense Neah's melancholy, Zennon squeezed her tightly.

"She would have been fine," the king insisted and Neah ignored him until his hand fell onto her shoulder. *Then* she reacted, the movement of her body pure instinct and the shouts of Gabriel and Skye sounding far away as the king landed on the grass on his back, face pale with shock, and Neah immediately released her grip on his throat.

Fuck. He could have her executed for that.

Then, to everyone's apparent shock, Wren began to laugh. Neah hesitantly offered him her hand and he gripped it tightly as she helped him up from the ground.

"I'm sorry, my king. It was instinct—"

"The fault was mine. I should have known better than

to lay hands on Jamison Fallon's daughter while her back was turned."

Apparently realising that Neah hadn't meant any harm, Gabriel and Skye's hands fell from the swords holstered at their hips.

The king's hand was still in hers, warm and calloused like he was used to hard work, and Neah dropped it quickly, warmth pooling in her cheeks.

"Well, I, for one, think archery is a waste of time." Sonnet broke the tense silence that had fallen and Neah watched in amazement as Sonnet waved a hand almost lazily and a bolt of silver lightning left her palm and hit the target dead centre, leaving behind a scorched black mark.

"Remind me not to get on your bad side," Zennon quipped and Sonnet grinned. "But by all means, why don't you two settle this?" It took Neah a second to realise the words were directed at her—and the king. "Best of three?"

Neah never had been able to resist a challenge.

She raised an arm, sweeping it out to the range in an 'after you' motion that made Wren smirk. He stepped up and took the bow from Zennon's outstretched hand, his form long and lean as he reached for the quiver of arrows. He took his time, measuring up the shot before letting his first arrow fly. It hit the target in the innermost circle and Neah smiled.

Wren picked up the next arrow and released it quickly, looking pleased when it landed just below the first arrow. His third landed in similar proximity. He was good. But she was better.

She accepted the bow from him and considered letting him win for the sake of diplomacy. He cocked one brow, like he could see the debate in her mind, and the taunt in his eyes was enough for her to make her decision.

The quiver was still mostly full and she let her lips part, tasting the air and wind. How much did she want to show off? Three arrows fired at once in a row? Or, maybe...

Thunk. Thunk. Thunk.

Someone loosed a long whistle and Neah smiled, eyeing her work appreciatively. Three arrows shot perfectly one after another, the next splitting the one before as they landed precisely in the exact centre of the target and trembled from the force with which they had struck the board.

Neah bowed her head to the king and handed him the bow. "Don't feel bad, Your Majesty. I was taught by the best."

Wren didn't look at all chagrined, a satisfaction on his face that surprised her as he ran molten gold eyes over her trouser-clad form. "Remind me not to piss *you* off," he murmured, repeating Zennon's earlier words, and Neah flushed. Because the way he looked at her... He wasn't fooled by the airs she put on. No, the king was looking at her like she was the most dangerous thing he'd ever seen, and that pleased her more than it should have.

"Haven't seen anyone shoot like that in a long time!"

The voice was unfamiliar but Wren looked relaxed, so Neah assumed it was welcome. When she looked, she realised she recognised the man who had spoken. He bore a passing resemblance to the king and had two guards behind him that signified he was someone of importance. Neah smiled, recognising one of the guards as Dean who had mistaken her for Zennon when she'd arrived.

"Uncle," Wren said, walking forward to shake the man's outstretched hand. "Yes, Lady Neah is quite the talented marksman."

"Finer even than your father," Castor said, eyes going soft at the mention of the late king. "Of course, even a perfect shot couldn't have saved him."

Wren's face seemed to close down, his grief practically tangible in the air. "Indeed."

The late king's hunting accident was a well-known tragedy at this point, though bringing it up so out of the blue seemed somewhat callous to Neah.

"Well, I'll let you kids get back to your fun." Castor smiled and Neah bowed her head to hide her expression. There was nothing particularly wrong with the words, but something about Castor's tone felt condescending—Neah had committed enough treason for one morning, though, without adding an insult to Castor to the list.

"Another round?" Wren said quietly as he watched his uncle's retreating back. "Perhaps you can give me some pointers this time."

Neah smiled. "Of course, Your Majesty."

CHAPTER TWELVE

WREN

"Something doesn't feel right." Wren pitched his voice low and Skye looked at him in surprise.

Their footsteps were soft as they walked through the forest, petrichor filling their senses. Not long after their impromptu archery session, the sky had darkened and the air became heavy and then the heavens opened. The smell of the rain and damp earth was soothing, clarifying, and Wren breathed it in deeply as they walked their usual route through the trees.

"What do you mean?" The concern in Skye's eyes was cold, assessing, and Wren fought back a grimace. Skye looked ready to face a legion of assassins, but this enemy was far less tangible.

The forest floor gave beneath Wren's feet as he walked, soft from the heavy rainfall, and mud covered their boots before long. "I mean exactly what I said, something just doesn't feel right." He had deliberately waited until he and Skye were alone to have this conversation, not wanting

Gabriel there listening while his motives were in question. "I think something went wrong with Sonnet's spell." Skye may have had his own biases against the witch, but Gabriel... Well his vision had been clouded in a different way. At least Skye would hear him out, even if what Wren was saying felt wrong—like a betrayal.

"The spell definitely worked, Wren. You know I'd be the first to tell you if it hadn't." Skye seemed surprised by the turn in the conversation and his eyes scanned the trees around them as if checking for prying eyes or ears. "What exactly do you think went wrong?"

Wren sighed and his skin prickled like the beast beneath his skin was aching to be released. "Maybe it's nothing." Wren bit his lip as golden eyes flashed in his mind's eye. Why was he questioning his instincts? Because of propriety? Social expectation? *No.* He knew what he felt, pretending otherwise wouldn't help anything. "No—there's definitely something wrong. It's Zennon."

"The Lady seems a good match, doesn't she?" Even Skye sounded unsure as he spoke the words.

"Does she?" Wren looked away from his friend, letting his gaze wander amid the oak trees surrounding them. In a week's time, they would be out amongst these trees again for the traditional lunar hunt. Typically the hunt was nothing to worry about, but with the Goddess' involvement in his mating ceremony and Wren's fresh doubts, it was all too likely that Selene would be paying very close attention to what happened beneath the leaves once his beast was unleashed. "When I was at Temple and I spoke to the Goddess, when she gave me her blessing... I would've staked my life that my mate was a shifter. Like me. Someone strong, fierce, a protector." He glanced at Skye and found his friend already watching him. "Does that sound like Lady Zennon to you?"

"Perhaps her strength is less obvious. She could be fierce of heart, strong of soul. What more could there be?"

Neah, he thought but didn't say. Instead, he spoke hesitantly, "I feel a strong connection to another."

At the words, Skye's mouth dropped open. "You don't think Zennon's your mate." It sounded more like a statement than a question, but Wren nodded all the same.

The soft patter of rain began once more, dripping onto the leaves in the canopy above them, and Wren and Skye paused for shelter beneath a valeneos' thick branches.

"Have you seen anything?" Wren didn't mean with his eyes, and Skye understood. He shook his head and Wren wasn't sure if he was relieved or disappointed. On the one hand, a lack of pressing visions seemed to indicate that everything might turn out fine. Alternatively, it could just mean that the magic from the ceremony was too strong for Skye to see past.

"Maybe both things are true," Skye said slowly as the rain came down harder. "It's possible that something's not right, as you say, *and* that the spell worked as intended."

"How?" Wren frowned. The two statements seemed completely at odds.

"I find it impressive how quickly Lady Neah arrived after Zennon sent for her. Don't you?" Skye raised a brow and Wren's heart thumped harder, his mouth running dry. He hadn't even mentioned Neah's name, so if Skye thought it was suspicious, it had nothing to do with Wren's intrigue with the woman.

"You think she was there that night? In Midmyr Forest?" It would make sense, he realised, even if it was more than he dared to hope for—that the connection he felt to her was not something for him to be ashamed about. Neah was certainly capable of taking on four assassins,if her skill with a bow spoke anything of her proficiency in battle.

Skye lifted a shoulder and let it drop. "I think it's worth finding out where exactly the lady was when her friend summoned her to court for her to arrive so quickly."

"I think you may be right."

Wren felt ridiculous. He'd taken Skye's advice... in a roundabout way. It felt too strange to just come out and ask Neah where she'd been when she'd received Zennon's summons—too accusatory.

Following her around the palace felt worse, somehow.

He remained out of sight, the hood of his cloak draped in his face to hide his identity from curious passersby who otherwise might have cornered him for chit-chat.

So far, Neah hadn't done anything untoward. She'd accompanied Zennon to tea with a retinue of ladies—since Wren had danced with them both at the feast, they'd drawn a good amount of speculation as to their familiarity with the king.

Neah had expertly dodged all prying questions while effortlessly appearing charming, it was a masterclass in etiquette if ever he'd seen one.

Then, the two had returned to Neah's room and had left

in fresh dresses several hours later. Nothing was outwardly strange about their ensemble, but the tension in Lady Zennon's shoulders made him wary. The corridors were much quieter in the early evening and Wren had to work harder to avoid notice, dipping into the occasional alcove where possible to avoid being seen.

To his surprise, they turned away from the main corridor that led to the hall where dinner was served nightly for the court. Instead, they wound around the outside of the palace until they approached a small doorway that led to the keeper's quarters.

Neah glanced over her shoulder as they nudged the heavy door open and Wren ducked back around the corner, peering out only when he heard the door shut and then following.

They hadn't gone far, but the corridors in this part of the castle were narrower, more winding, and he would have lost them completely if not for him being able to follow their scent.

He hurried along, careful to keep his steps quiet lest Neah sense his approach. A door opened down the hall to his right and Wren paused in place, hidden around the corner, as Neah greeted the person waiting out of his line of sight.

A familiar smell tickled his nose and Wren frowned, trying to place it before recognising the soft floral scent. It had been present a few times when he'd spoken to Jamison, his captain, but he wasn't sure why it would be here in the keeper's quarters. Jamison certainly had his own rooms, as did Neah, so why—

Wren peered around the corner in time to see Neah

step inside with Zennon on her heels. She paused to hug a small woman with hair the same honeyed shade as Neah's. Jamison's wife.

Things started to fall into place in his mind. Neah's protectiveness of Zennon, the secrecy of this visit... Jamison had long been protective of his wife, and mate, guarding her whereabouts fiercely to prevent her from being a target for the king's enemies.

It wasn't until Zennon pulled back from the woman that it all clicked, though. "Mama, I've missed you."

The door closed and Wren forgot how to breathe for several seconds. *Mama.* Zennon and Neah were sisters? Jamison had never mentioned a second child, why hide one and not the other?

Nothing made sense, but at least Wren now knew that there was more to the both of them than met the eye. However, he also knew that in this exact moment in time it was none of his business. Their secrets were of no pertinence or danger to him, so what right did he have to poke around further?

Satisfied that his spying had yielded nothing that pointed toward a deliberate deception, beyond familial ties that Wren would wager had been hidden by Jamison rather than his daughters, he decided to give up and return to his rooms. Maybe he *would* have to confront Neah directly in order to get answers to his questions.

Or, perhaps... *Zennon.* She seemed more unused to court games than Neah, who had grown up in the palace for the most part, so maybe it would be easiest to extract the information he wanted from her. It would save him from an awkward confrontation if he could instead subtly coax the truth from Zennon—plus, he wasn't sure he'd come out on top in a conflict with Neah. Whatever manner of animal lurked beneath her pretty exterior, Wren was certain that coming face to face with it might spell his death.

CHAPTER THIRTEEN

NEAH

"Tell me you didn't." Her father's face was aghast as Zennon and Mother gasped around their laughter. Zen had taken great pleasure in recounting the incident on the training concourse that morning, much to Neah's chagrin.

"She's exaggerating, Dad." Neah rolled her eyes, the lie sounding smooth until Zennon found her voice again.

"Nope, he was in the air for a solid five seconds." Zennon giggled and Neah begged her with wide eyes to shut up. "Ahem, I mean. It was more of a love tap than anything."

Fuck. That was worse. After their last conversation, Neah didn't want to put thoughts in her dad's head about her and the king *love tapping*.

Ever the diplomat, her mother changed the subject effortlessly by setting a plate of food down in front of Jamison and another two for each of her daughters.

Despite Zennon only being Neah's half-sister, Darwinia

treated her as if she were her own—especially once Zen lost her own parents so young.

The smell hit Neah a second later and her thoughts faded as her stomach growled. Her mom's chicken and potatoes were famous in the family and Neah hadn't realised how much she'd missed them until her first bite made her groan.

Darwinia laughed. "Enjoy, my love."

"I'm literally salivating," Neah mumbled, trying her best to savour each mouthful even as she shovelled it in. In truth, her eyes felt suspiciously damp too. The nostalgic flavours, her mom's smile and the sparkle in her eyes... It had been too long. "Did Zennon tell you she shot a bow?"

"It hit the target," Zennon said, beaming and their dad softened, becoming gentle in the way he only seemed to do around the three of them. "Wren—the king, nearly made me break my wrist."

"*What?*"

If Wren wasn't the king, Neah might have feared for his safety at that moment. "It was an accident, he had the bow lodged too high for her, the string would have snapped back against her tendon."

"Neah saved me," Zennon added, and the pride in her voice made Neah grin. "Though if *someone* had already taught me, she wouldn't have had to," she grumbled and Neah grimaced. It was a point of contention between Zennon and their father. Neah couldn't say she disagreed with Zennon, and she'd given her some rudimentary lessons in self-defense when she could, but the truth of it was that Neah was hardly ever in one place for long and Zennon didn't spend much time with their father either given the secrecy of their relationship. In fact, Neah realised, Zennon likely didn't see much of anyone at her estate in the forest. For the first time, Neah wondered if her sister was lonely and that was why she was enjoying court so much.

As if he'd come to the same conclusion, Jamison just sighed. "Maybe Neah can help train you while you're both here. Show you the basics."

She shared a look with Zennon and cleared her throat. "Sure." It never hurt to brush up on the basics, not that their dad knew Neah had even shown Zennon that much.

"So, your father tells me you don't know which of you is fated to the king?" The sparkle in Darwinia's eyes made Neah roll hers. "Come on, girls. It's not often we get to gossip together."

That was true, and Neah felt a stab of guilt for her gut reaction being exasperation.

"Well, Neah might not be sure but I am." Zennon folded her cutlery back onto the plate with ease and dabbed at her mouth primly. "I have no interest in the king. Good thing too, because those two are one spark away from an explosion."

Jamison grumbled something under his breath and pushed up from the table abruptly, stalking the short paces away to the kitchenette and clanging around seemingly randomly to avoid the conversation.

"Zennon," Neah complained. "Where do you get this stuff? I've read just as many romance novels as you and yet—"

"You lack imagination, my dear sister." Zennon grinned and turned to Darwinia. "Mystery solved."

Neah opted to ignore her sister's ribbing in favour of soaking in the sight before her, the two of them giggling and whispering together while Jamison stomped around in the kitchen.

"I missed this," she said quietly and didn't resist when her mother lifted her hand and brushed a kiss to its back.

"So have I." She smiled and a hint of the same tiredness Neah had seen on her father's face appeared. "My girls." She stroked a strand of Zennon's dark hair back from her face.

"It's getting late girls," Jamison said, voice gruff but face soft and Neah nodded. She knew he didn't like having his wife in the palace walls for long if he could help it, there were too many potential spies and enemies on the grounds and his family was the one thing she knew her father wouldn't risk. It was part of the reason why he hadn't claimed Zennon publicly, why he'd sent Neah away when she was a teenager to train elsewhere, and why her mother was never in one place for long.

She had to wonder if the price they paid was worth it, even if she couldn't fault him for his sense of duty and devotion to the crown. He'd encouraged the same loyalty in her, too.

"So soon?" Darwinia sighed and for a second the tiredness from before seemed to sink in a little deeper. "I'll be with you in spirit, my darlings."

Jamison pressed a kiss to her cheek and then looked at Neah from across the table. "Before you go, I have information for you. Or, rather, information I want you to get."

Pushing her doubts aside, Neah nodded. "Where and when?"

"Valena, I've heard whispers of a benefactor looking for help." He kept the details vague, but she knew what he was telling her. The same person who'd tried to place the hit on the king before was ready to try again, this time closer to the palace. They were getting bolder. "Three night's time, at the Crow's Nest."

Neah nodded and stood, pushing back her rickety chair easily and guiding Zennon to standing at her side. "I'll let you know if I see or hear anything interesting."

"Good." He hesitated and then walked forward quickly, wrapping the both of them into a quick, one-armed hug. "Be safe."

"You too," Zennon whispered and Neah nodded before hurrying around the table to hug her mother.

They left as quickly as they'd arrived and the palace was quiet. The candles in the sconces had started to burn low and she knew that if they were to come back in a few nights time they would have been replaced with soleil magic—most places throughout the kingdom were in the midst of swapping over to the cleaner, longer lasting energy source. Well, those that could afford the witch-fee to have the orbs of light installed. Other places, like the palace, were using up what they had left of traditional light sources and phasing a little at a time.

Zennon was quiet at her side as they walked, but when Neah glanced over there was a peacefulness on her sister's face that put her at ease. Family time was rare, but maybe it was time that changed—it was clearly weighing heavily on them all.

She understood her father's concern, but fear couldn't rule them forever. Not at the expense of their lives, they'd spent far too much of it apart.

"I meant it, you know," Zen said quietly as they walked the halls back to Neah's room. "I knew before that the king was not meant for me, but seeing the two of you together… It's obvious, Neah." She snorted and Zennon frowned. "Why are you resistant?"

"I'm not resistant."

"Could have fooled me."

Neah continued on in silence, trying not to let Zennon's words burrow into her mind. It was true that she was nervous about having Wren for a mate, not only because of his position and her… defects, but because she wasn't sure she could trust the Goddess to make this decision when it felt like Selene had botched so many others in Neah's life.

Neah had lost some of her faith in Selene over the years and now, she had to just trust that Wren was the person best suited for her, the other half of her soul that she'd be stronger with than without. It seemed unfathomable. The Goddess hadn't cared before, Neah still couldn't shift, and now she had to just *trust* this deity to know what was best for her?

Fuck. Zennon had got in her head.

The walk back to her rooms felt shorter than before, maybe she was hurrying, trying to outrun her thoughts. It was no use though, when she wasn't ruminating on the goddess she was thinking about Wren. Like she'd given her brain permission to consider him in a way she hadn't been allowing before, but now she couldn't hold back, her imagination running wild as she considered the ways that things could have been different the night of the feast, when he'd found her half-naked and then danced with her. Or even out in the field, with her hand around his throat—

"Night," Zennon chirped from the other side of the bed and Neah's voice was hoarse when she replied.

"Goodnight." Now she just had to convince her subconscious to behave. The last thing she needed was Wren in her dreams as well as on her mind.

CHAPTER FOURTEEN

WREN

Getting Lady Zennon alone felt like an impossible task. Wherever she went, Neah followed. It offered him no opportunities to pry for information, not when Wren had seen how effortlessly Neah had charmed and eluded the ladies of the court. She would see right through him in an instant.

But he could be patient, waiting and watching for the right time to strike. His chance came late in the afternoon, the day after he had spied on the girls inside the palace, while they attended an afternoon gathering. The rain had been annoyingly persistent, though he knew he'd be glad for this rainfall early next week when the lunar hunt was due to take place in, hopefully, drier conditions.

Neah had walked away from her sister in order to talk to a young nobleman across the way and Wren had seized the opportunity while she was distracted.

"Lady Zennon! It looks as if the rain has eased. Would you care to take a turn with me around the gardens?"

Zennon smiled and nodded, relief sharp on her face as she left the clutches of three Ladies who were likely intent on prying information out of her. Not that Wren was any better.

"Thank you," she said a few moments later as he led them out of the room and toward a hidden exit that opened straight into the gardens. "The offer of fresh air couldn't have been better timed."

"You're not enjoying your time at court?"

Pink stained her cheeks and her fingers tightened on the inside of his arm as they walked at a sedate pace. The wet grass dampened the hem of her dress from blue to indigo, but Zennon showed no sign of caring. "I like court very much, Your Majesty. But, as you might have guessed, I don't have much experience with the intricacies of court machinations."

He chuckled, unable to help himself. "If by that you mean that the court is full of incorrigible gossips, then I agree." A cool breeze drifted over them, lifting the ends of Wren's hair. "They have their uses though."

"Oh?" Brows scrunched together, it was clear that Zennon couldn't imagine how that could be the case.

"Allies," he said, matter of fact. "Take Melinda Bashwather, for example. An odious woman, but a rich one. Where she spends her coin, others tend to follow."

"You're the king, what use could you have for coin?"

He shrugged. "Sometimes it's less about what I do or do not lack, and more about what that support could do for our enemies."

They paused by a row of bushes decorated with tiny lilac flowers, droplets of rain caught on their petals.

"You know, I have quite a lot of money."

Wren bit his lip to hide his laugh. "Humble, too."

Zennon laughed and it rang high and pure, like the wind chimes at his father's hunting cabin. "I only mean that I am a less odious woman than that of Melinda Bashwather. And yet, until now, you have made no requests of me."

This was true, but largely because money didn't always equal influence and, for the most part, Lady Zennon was an unknown. She kept to herself on her estate and lived a quiet life—or, that's what he'd believed until he'd seen her with Neah the night prior.

"What about your family?" He hoped the transition was smooth and breathed easier when she seemed unalarmed. "Must you split your many coin with them?"

She laughed but the sound faded quickly. "No. I am the last of my mother's line and my parents have been gone for quite some time now."

Given that Jamison and his wife were very much alive, Wren could only assume she referred to the parents from whom she claimed her name. Wren sniffed delicately but couldn't detect even a faint trace of shifter or magic on her. Either she was being cloaked by someone, or some*thing* powerful, or Zennon truly was human.

"You and Lady Neah are very close," he said carefully, keeping his tone light and smile unconcerned. "How did you cross paths?"

To his surprise, she grinned. "You know, I can't remember the exact moment we met. Sometimes it feels as if I've known her forever."

He understood the feeling. "I'm the same way with Gabriel and Skye."

"Not Sonnet?"

They turned away from the flower bush and continued walking, doing a loop of the stone fountain up ahead and coming back the way they came. "No, Sonnet is a more recent and temporary addition to our group."

Zennon hummed, the sound amused. "She may become more permanent than you realise."

"Oh?" Wren frowned and followed the direction of Zennon's gaze when she nodded to the shrubbery to their left where Sonnet and Skye stood beneath a leafy canopy, arguing by the looks of things. Although...

"It's strange, isn't it? How attraction can blur the lines between hatred and desire."

Desire. Skye didn't desire Sonnet, did he? And Sonnet... Well, there was clearly no love-lost between the two of them. But the way they stood, their eyes wholly focused on the other, Skye's large form bent over Sonnet's, her hands curled into fists that occasionally sparked silver... It was enough to make a king doubt himself.

Wren looked away, unsure what to make of the tense altercation, and Zennon chuckled quietly.

"Do you believe in honesty, my king?"

The question startled him and Wren looked up at Zennon in surprise, taking in the warmth in her brown eyes and the gentle kindness of her face. "Yes. In fact, I prefer it. As king, I'm too often capitulated to—it's infuriating."

She nodded, her dark hair falling into her face. "I believe in honesty too. But please know that it brings me no pleasure to say this to you." She took a deep breath and Wren's mouth ran dry as she took his hands in hers and pulled them to a stop, facing one another. "Your spell is inaccurate. I would be glad to consider you a friend, but I feel nothing more for you than that—and I never will."

Wren recoiled, his hands slipping out of her soft grip. "But—"

"You can't tell me that you truly believe *we* are fated." She laughed and patted his shoulder. "We have about as much chemistry as a wet log in the mud."

He knew she was right, had said almost the same thing to Skye himself, but to have it confirmed... to know for certain that he was back at square one... It was more than he could take. His face crumpled and he dragged a palm over it, not wanting Zennon to think his despair was caused by her.

"Oh," she said softly. "I–Um, I'm sorry, Your Majesty. I had thought you felt similarly to me. Perhaps I was mistaken—"

"No," he said, the words guttural, and he cleared his throat before trying again. "No, I believe you are right, Zennon. And please, for the last time, call me Wren." She still looked worried, eyes crinkling at the corners as her brow pinched with concern. "Sonnet assured me the spell worked—and so did Skye, there's no way he would lie to me."

Zennon looked away, biting her lip, and he knew this was his chance.

"Do you... know something? Was someone else there that night?"

Voicing the question aloud felt freeing, even as Zennon

shut down. Her face pulled perfectly blank even as a new tension settled in the lines of her shoulders.

"I don't know what you mean. There was nobody there but me."

Lie. He wasn't sure how he knew, but he would have bet his life that she was hiding the truth in that moment. The only logical reason he could think of was that she was protecting someone.

Neah, his mind supplied and he tried not to fixate on the thought or the hope it reared in his chest. But why did Zennon think that Neah needed protecting? He would never hurt her, nor blame her for being hesitant to accept the enormity of a mating bond.

Sensing if he pushed, Zennon would shut down further, he instead nodded. "Okay."

Thunder rumbled faintly and the rain began again, this time in a subtle mist that was visible only in the strands of their hair and the tips of their eyelashes. Zennon didn't seem to mind the damp though, and nor did Wren, and so they continued their slow walk back to the palace in a silence that he found comfortable. He hadn't gotten all the answers he'd wanted, but he'd learned a lot just the same. In some ways, Zennon had cut to the heart of the issue— she wasn't his mate.

The realisation brought more relief than panic the second time he repeated it, like the Goddess had been waiting for him to catch-up to what his instincts already knew.

"Thank you," he said to Zennon as they reached the arched door that would lead them back into the castle. He pressed a chaste kiss to the back of her hand and smiled. "Your honesty was exactly what I needed to hear."

Without waiting for a response, he turned away and left her in the doorway. Now that he had parsed out some of the truth, he needed time to process it, to let his mind settle the best way he knew how.

Heavy paws hit the earth with only half a thought and he heard Zennon gasp as he shook out his fur and stretched his claws.

For now, he needed to silence his thoughts. He needed to *run*.

CHAPTER FIFTEEN

NEAH

Zennon had seemed quiet all day. Neah had found her standing on the edge of the royal gardens, staring out into the forest with a layer of mist caught in the wind-blown tangles of her hair. She hadn't said much, just that she'd gone for a walk with the king, and that had been that.

She hadn't said another word about it—not through dinner, not while they got ready for bed, and by the time breakfast came about it was as if her walk with the king had never happened. The air of melancholy had faded, but Neah knew her sister well. She would tell Neah what was on her mind when she was ready.

Now wasn't the time to ruminate on it, anyway. The tavern Neah found herself in was large, but crowded. Noisy. The perfect meeting place for someone not wanting to be overhead or noticed. It was something she was using to her own advantage too, tucked in a shadowy corner of the long, square bar and observing who came in and out of the front entrance while she kept her back firmly against the wall behind her.

Jamison's intel was usually reliable, so she kept her wits about her as the evening wore on and she nursed her ale, content to fade into the background. A good spy could blend with a crowd as easily as they could command it when needed, but the lesser known skill of the spy was spotting those who *also* didn't want to be seen.

Much like the two cloaked figures who had just approached the bar, placed their drink order, and then promptly left without waiting for their ale. *A code*, she surmised, as the barkeep didn't look perturbed by their departure.

Neah slipped out after them, keeping her steps light and her hood pulled low. The darkness of the bricked passageway would have been complete if not for her enhanced vision, she could only assume that at least one of the cloaked figures was also a shifter—or they used the passage so frequently they knew it well. Neither conclusion particularly comforted Neah.

Unfamiliar territory, unknown threats… she much preferred to have all the info rather than going in blind. But needs must and if these two could help her get the information she needed about the king's enemies then it would be worth the uncertainty.

The sounds from the tavern faded as they walked the length of the darkened alley. It narrowed until it was little more than a breath between buildings and she was glad that she'd never been affected by enclosed spaces or she might have been struggling about now. A soft murmur of voices told her they were getting close to wherever they were going and Neah hung back as the alley widened, waiting to see where the two men would go next.

It looked like the alley ended abruptly in a bricked-off enclosure, and for a second she was worried she'd walked into a trap, but then one of the cloaked figures reached out and rapped his knuckles on a brick on the wall to their left. Neah blinked and where the bricks had been instead stood a door, clearly spelled to hide its existence from anyone who didn't already know it was there.

A brief flare of noise sounded when the door opened and the two figures stepped inside. She narrowed her eyes, what was this place? And how did the assassin's benefactor know about it? It had to be the meeting place, considering it also held a noise dampening spell in addition to the cloaking. Everything about this set-up screamed *off the radar trouble*.

Neah hovered in the shadows, deciding whether or not to risk following the men, when the door re-opened and they stepped back out into the dark space where Neah waited.

They didn't notice her, but they would if she remained still any longer—they had to go past her to get back the way they'd come. So, Neah stalked forward straight to the hidden door. Whether her knowing its location was enough for them or if it was the confidence of her stride, she couldn't know, but they walked away without a glance at her. Their reaction furthered confirmed her suspicions of this place: ask no questions you wouldn't answer, and the two men hadn't hung around for idle chatter.

The darkness swallowed them up and Neah lowered

her hand from where it hesitated in front of the door. If this wasn't where the meeting was, why did they go inside?

She waited half a beat and then followed the two figures back the way they'd come, unsurprised when they came back through the tavern and exited the way the regular customers did, through the front entrance.

They walked for a further five minutes, until they ducked into another alley—a less secret one this time—where another two men waited dressed in a similar garb of dark boots and cloaks.

What the Hel was going on?

All four of them held parchment scrolls, but Neah couldn't risk getting any closer to see who the seal might belong to without getting caught. Their murmurs were too quiet for even her sensitive hearing and she was just debating whether she could climb atop of the closest building, a tailors, and get closer via the roof when a hand fell to her shoulder.

She jumped, too intent on the four unknown assailants ahead of her to notice the person coming up on her from behind. *Sloppy*, she chastised herself, before grabbing onto the hand that had touched her and squeezing hard enough that she was surprised the bones didn't grind together.

"Ouch, fuck. *Fuck*. Neah—it's me."

No. She dropped the hand like it had stung her and spun to take in her attacker. *Fuck.* How did she keep beating up the king? Or, perhaps the better question was *what the Hel was he doing here?*

She asked him as much and he looked at her incredulously. "Following you." He said it as if the answer was obvious and she wasn't sure whether to be annoyed or impressed that she hadn't sensed him tailing her.

"Go home, Your Majesty." She kept the words cold, stiff and unyielding. The last thing she needed was to be responsible for the king's murder while she was actively trying to hunt down his would-be attackers. Although… he would make good bait.

She dismissed the thought as soon as she had it. Too risky.

"After you," he said, and she glared. Too loud, he was going to get them both caught.

"Shut. Up." She hissed the words and his eyes widened, like nobody ever talked to him that way, and she couldn't deny the pleasure that gave her as she turned her back on him. "Go away."

"Not until you tell me what you're doing here." He leaned in closer, the smoky warm scent of him filling her senses and, for a damning second, she enjoyed the smell of it—until she realised he was peering around her and into the alley.

"Hey!"

"Fuck." He just had to call attention to them, didn't he? "Now you've bloody done it." Neah could hear footsteps approaching, the vibration on the cobblestones echoing the pounding of her heart in her chest. Wren, for the most part, looked alarmed, more so when she grabbed him with fistfuls of his white shirt. Goddess, he wasn't even *dressed* for subterfuge. "Not a word," she growled, and then crushed her lips to his.

He gasped into her and she groaned. The rough brick of the tailor's shop bit into the back of her head as he pressed her against the hard surface, not so much as a breath between their bodies.

She had enough sense to open her eyes and check for the approaching assassins before realising if they were going to do this, they needed to sell it.

Neah yanked the side of her cloak up and, for once, cursed her decision to wear trousers as a slip of leg would have been far more effective in that moment. But she gave it her all, regardless.

One leg hooked at Wren's hip, her hands pressed into his hair, mussing it as she dragged him closer, devouring him with her mouth as she coaxed him closer with her body.

His heat pressed into her, surrounding her as one rough hand closed around her throat, cradling her with enough pressure to hold her in place but not to hurt, before his mouth coaxed hers open. Wren kissed like he was starved, desperate, and when he plundered her mouth, taking what he wanted, she melted.

"Nothing," she dimly heard the man who'd come to check on things say, "just a couple who couldn't make it back to their room." His laughter was harder to ignore and for a second it seemed like he would stay to watch the show. Thankfully, a few seconds later he walked away— just in time, because Wren had finally noticed their observer and a growl rumbled through him strong enough that she felt it as if it were her own, the sound sending a bolt of heat straight between her legs.

As soon as the man disappeared, she shoved Wren away, panting hard. He made to step back toward her, as if in a daze, and halted abruptly when she snarled.

"Enough. Let's get out of here before they decide to come back and watch us fuck." Her words were sharp, but Wren looked relaxed, at ease, like he'd just had a question answered. "We need to talk," she said, more slowly, and he nodded, stepping toward her like he might take her hand. "Let's not, okay? We did what we had to in the moment."

His nostrils flared but he maintained the distance, a smirk on his face that unnerved her. "If that's the way you want to play it, *caritas*. But I think we both know what I just smelled on you."

"Heat of the moment," she lied. "Now let's go, before I change my mind and turn you over to them."

He chuckled and she grimaced as they began the walk back to the palace. The small town wasn't too far away, about a thirty minute walk at best, she just hoped they could delay the inevitable confrontation until they were safe from prying eyes and ears.

CHAPTER SIXTEEN

WREN

By the time they arrived back at the palace, Wren's heartbeat had settled into a more regular rhythm. His mind still felt a little foggy from the drugging effect of Neah's mouth on his, but he was doing his best to shake it off, needing answers more than he needed to taste her lips again.

For now, anyway.

He'd guided her to his rooms, seeing as Zennon was staying in hers and this was one of the few places he could guarantee privacy. Skye had spelled the rooms for him to ensure that what was said inside couldn't be heard in the hall, and that anyone who entered his rooms without permission would find themselves uncomfortably detained. The spells needed refreshing every few months so they'd opted to wait and do them all in one go before the ceremony so they'd be at full strength while discussing the sensitive information.

It was strangely nerve wracking, having Neah in his

rooms, eyes roving over the design choices and widening at the vast array of books that took up one wall in his parlour.

"You're a reader."

"Surprised I know how?" he teased and her lips twitched. The small look vanished almost instantly but he'd seen it and felt suitably smug for breaking through her defences even for a second. "Drink?"

"Definitely."

He gestured to the low oak table in front of the balcony and reached for the crystal decanter while she chose a seat, pouring a healthy measure of amber liquid into a glass for each of them. "Here."

"Thanks."

For a second it was quiet while they sipped, the sweet burn helping clear his thoughts of any last lingering heat their charade had evoked. Though, he considered *charade* to be a convenient excuse. Nobody kissed like that if they didn't enjoy it.

"Why were you following me?" Neah said at last and he lifted his eyes from where he'd been gazing into his drink and instead met her golden eyes, a few shades lighter than the liquor.

"Because I wanted to know what you were doing."

The gold all-but vanished as she narrowed her eyes. "Obviously. *Why?*"

"Because I had an interesting conversation with your sister and I wanted to find out the truth for myself."

He knew the exact moment his words registered, the way she froze and slowly lowered her glass to thunk against the wood of the table. There was indecision on her face, her fingers twitching like she fought an internal battle —who would she protect? Her family? Or her king? If she was anything like her father, then her duty to the crown wasn't one she took lightly but Zennon...

As if she'd reached the same conclusion that he had, a blade appeared in her hand faster than he could track. He'd known it was a risk to mention Zennon's heritage, but Neah hadn't moved yet. Just waited with the dagger in her palm.

"How do you know?" Her voice was hoarse and her fingers were curling and uncurling around the dagger's hilt. "Let me guess. You were following me again?"

He nodded. "Are you going to do something with that?" He gestured to the dagger and his movement made her flinch.

"Nobody knows," she whispered and he watched her steadily, letting her see the intentions in his eyes. "You won't tell?"

"It's not my secret," he said simply and she exhaled raggedly. "I just thought it might help to have us on even footing."

She leaned back in the chair, her posture relaxed, but he didn't doubt that she was still lethal even in repose. "What do you want to know?"

Were you there that night? Why did you hide it from me? He didn't ask those questions though, sensing if he did that she'd run. She wasn't ready yet.

"Why hide who Zennon is to you?"

"For her safety. Next?"

"What were you doing tonight at the tavern?"

This time she hesitated before she answered. "Looking for information."

He frowned. Why would she—

She saw the dawning realisation on his face and smirked knowingly. "Yes. I'm a spy. I received a tip that important information would be exchanged at the tavern tonight."

"Information about what?" He thought back to the men he'd seen in the alley before they'd been caught—before he'd *got them* caught, he realised.

"Before I came to the palace, I was at the Pembroke's in the north east. I overheard a plot to hire the hunter's guild for an attempt on the king." Her words were even, but her eyes burned with a fervour he couldn't place. Pride? Protectiveness? "The guild takes care of their own rogues, as I'm sure you know. But whoever bankrolled the hit was liable to try again, with more underhanded measures. Hence, the tavern."

Wren sat quietly, absorbing the information and letting his mind connect dots he hadn't had before. He'd been working with only half the information. "Why didn't Jamison—"

"Nothing was confirmed yet," she said smoothly and he bit down on the smile he could feel attempting to break free. She was so like her father and yet *not*. It made her a puzzle he would have liked to pull apart and rebuild. "All I gathered tonight was that the prospective assassins met in a hidden room and emerged with the same scrolls that the other two men had in the alley where you found me."

"Someone has been trying to cause unrest within the court," he confessed. "I've been away, necessary travelling," he said, easily dodging the whole truth. "In my absence, certain... rumours were spread."

"Oh, so you're not a drunken manwhore?" This time a full smile graced her mouth. "I never would have guessed." He wasn't sure if that was a good or bad thing. "So, now you know the truth."

"Do I?" he murmured silkily, taking a mouthful of his liquor and watching her intently over the rim of his glass. "You have a secret sister, and you're a spy. Is that everything?"

"What more could there be?" She said the words with an air of innocence that made him snort. "Is that not enough?"

She was toying with him, and the only way to get any kind of genuine reaction from her was to shake her with the truth. "You know, Zennon told me something interesting."

That same closed expression came over her face once more. "Oh?"

"She's not my mate."

The words were quiet but they may as well have been a shout for all the reaction they caused. Neah's face shuttered, an icy countenance taking over as she threw back the last of her drink and stood.

"Zennon doesn't know what she's talking about." The words were swift, confident and measured. *Certain.* "I think this conversation is over. I won't sit here while you insult my sister."

He ignored her protests. "It's funny, really. I could have sworn the Goddess had indicated that my mate would be a shifter, and there was Zennon. Fully human. I assume that means she's your half-sister at best?" Neah said nothing in response to his probing, just waited like she knew he wasn't done. "What form do you take when you shift, Neah?"

At that, she jerked. It was a fair response, it was considered beyond rude to ask such a thing. But it could also be very telling, as mated shifters took on the same form.

Her father, for example, was a jaguar and so too was his wife. Wren's mother took the form of a swan, and so too had his father. Whoever Wren's mate was, they would share his tiger form when shifted.

He hadn't really expected her to respond to his digging, but he never could have anticipated her reply.

"I don't know." The words sounded like they'd been pulled from somewhere deep down inside of her. "I've never been able to shift."

Never been able to shift.

It was unfathomable.

His mouth dropped open and she must have mistook whatever shock he wore on his face for shame because her eyes lowered, shoulders rounding, and then she walked to the door without another look at him.

"Goodnight, Wren."

"Wait—"

The door closed and he jolted. *Never been able to shift.* Whatever lurked beneath her skin responded to him, he was sure of it. It didn't matter to him that she had never shifted, but he was also certain that Neah was powerful and whatever form she took... It wouldn't be held at bay for much longer.

CHAPTER SEVENTEEN

WREN

Three faces stared at him from around the table, all with varying degrees of solemnity. Skye looked concerned as he watched Wren pace, his eyes tracking his movements as he wore a path in front of the balcony. Gabriel looked interested, eyes bright, like he was waiting to hear how he could help. And Sonnet…

Well, Sonnet mostly looked amused.

"Are you going to tell us what's going on in that head of yours?" Gabe leaned back in his chair much the way Neah had the night before, the contrast striking Wren dumb for a moment. "Or do you want us to just watch you brood in silence?"

Wren scowled and Skye threw Gabe a look that typically translated to *behave*.

"I have been doing some… snooping." The statement received quizzical looks from all three of them. "Spying," he clarified. "On Neah and Zennon."

Only Sonnet looked unperturbed by the news. "And? What did you discover, my king?"

He paused in his pacing to fold his arms across his chest and level her with a look that he hoped communicated his ire. "I suspect you know."

"Well don't keep the rest of us in suspense," Gabe protested and Wren sighed as he dropped into the empty chair in the centre of the group.

"Zennon is Neah's half-sister and Neah is—Neah is a spy." The words left him in a rush that felt a lot like relief and the bright sunshine behind the balcony doors caught in Sonnet's eyes as she watched him closely.

"Interesting," she said slowly, consideringly, and Wren narrowed his eyes. "I can assure you, Your Majesty, I knew of no such duplicity."

"It gets better," he continued. "Or worse, depending on how you look at it. Neah uncovered a plot. Someone tried to hire the hunter's guild to kill me."

That, at least, got more of a reaction from his friends.

Skye whistled. "That's some fucking nerve. Don't they know the guild answers to you?"

Wren shrugged. "If they didn't before, they do now. Whoever placed the bounty tried again last night, in town."

"You think it's someone in the palace," Gabe surmised and Wren nodded. "A shift from politically fuelled rumours to murder?"

"Maybe," he murmured. "Oh, and Zennon confessed that she doesn't think we're mates and that she feels nothing for me beyond a budding friendship." Skye and Gabriel gaped at him but Sonnet looked unsurprised at the deluge of words. "I don't suppose you'd know anything about *that*?" He directed the question to the witch and watched her intently for even the most minute of expressions that might give her away.

Sonnet shrugged. "I told you already. The spell worked as intended."

"Must I remind you that if I don't find my mate and complete the bond, I'll become quite insane? My offer of sanctuary will be no good to you if I'm trapped as a mindless animal."

Sonnet frowned, like the thought of his impending doom was a small inconvenience. "I provided you with a location. You knew that was all the ceremony promised when I performed it. If you're certain that Zennon isn't your fated, then there must have been another there that night."

He and Skye shared a look and Wren nodded. It was as they'd suspected.

"But I can see you already knew that, you just wanted my confirmation." Sonnet rolled her eyes. "It seems you won't be rushing toward madness just yet then, Your Majesty."

Wren ran a hand over his face, rubbing his eyes until they burned. "I wouldn't be so sure."

"Who would deny a king?" The look on the witch's face was coy but there was a real note of surprise to the words that made Wren sigh. Even if she was right, he wanted to be desired for *him* not his title.

"Neah," he said, deciding there was no use in tip-toeing around it. "She's not ready to accept it. Accept *me*," he muttered. "She told me she's never shifted before."

Skye raised an eyebrow. "A shifter that can't shift?" He

looked at Sonnet, almost begrudgingly, before asking, "Have you ever heard of such a thing?"

Sonnet shrugged. "I'm not well-versed in shifter magic. But perhaps you are not the only thing she's not ready to accept, my king. It's possible the bond may bring her other form to the surface."

"Tiger," he murmured. "If she's my mate, then she'll be a tiger like me."

Sonnet waved a hand. "The point stands."

He swallowed hard, looking past his friends to the sky outside where a bird flew in lazy circles amid the clouds. "I don't know what to do. I can't force her to accept the bond, or to even acknowledge it."

"But you can't let yourself succumb to the curse either," Gabriel said, voice stern and Wren didn't know how to respond. Neah, from all that he'd observed, was strong of conviction and loyalty. If he asked this of her... She might agree only out of duty and that felt untenable to him.

"Perhaps we should make plans," Wren said slowly. "I cannot and *will not* force this upon her. We keep the curse to ourselves, for now. If she chooses this, it should be of her own free will and not out of a sense of misplaced duty."

"But Wren, the kingdom—"

"Will survive," he said gruffly, standing up and resuming his pacing. "We will make provisions so that things are taken care of if the worst does come to pass."

None of them looked particularly happy with the plan, and Wren couldn't say that he blamed them.

"So what I'm hearing is, you need us to help you woo Neah?" Gabriel smirked. "Easy." Wren raised a brow and his friend continued. "Well, obviously you've got the power and station. You're a tiger shifter which is pretty impressive. If none of that does it for her, just take off your shirt."

Sonnet was staring at Gabe with fascination. "It is truly enlightening seeing how your mind works. *That* is what you think women care about? A pretty crown, some claws, and a few muscles?" Sonnet rolled her eyes as Gabe spluttered. "The odds are in your favour, my king. At the end of the day, if Neah is truly your mate she will be drawn to you. Spend time with her. Get to know her. Let her soul do the rest."

Skye looked as doubtful as Wren felt. "Let her *soul*—" Skye shook his head. "Lunar witches," he said disdainfully. "She's your mate," he said to Wren, "show her."

"I may be a *lunar witch*," Sonnet said with a sneer, "but I'm *also* a woman, in case you forgot."

"I didn't forget," Skye growled and Gabriel watched them with a sense of satisfaction that was mystifying for Wren. "But the hunt approaches and it's the perfect opportunity for you to bait her instincts. If her mind is the problem, then let her body make the decisions until her mind catches up."

Maybe he was just tired and frustrated, but it felt like what Skye was suggesting actually made sense. Sonnet clearly disagreed, muttering under her breath about the foolishness of men, but Wren liked this plan—what happened during the hunt was blessed by the Goddess herself. It would allow Neah the perfect excuse to give in to the pull between them. It wasn't one sided, that much he knew. He'd felt the way she'd responded beneath him, the way her mouth and hands had grasped at him like she couldn't get enough.

"This could work," he said slowly and Skye nodded, pleased.

"Imbeciles," Sonnet muttered and Gabriel watched the group with a smile on his face.

"See? Teamwork," he said and Sonnet rolled her eyes.

CHAPTER EIGHTEEN

NEAH

It had been two days since Neah had spoken with the king, and she was still furious. Not just with Wren, but also herself. He had spied on her, and she'd been none the wiser. It was infuriating, *embarrassing*. And it didn't help that Zennon had gone rogue and rebuffed the king.

Two days of stewing had left her foul tempered, and it appeared that Zennon had finally had enough of Neah's sulking.

"*Must* you scowl every time I enter the room?"

Neah grunted in response and ducked when Zennon reached for a nearby slipper and launched it at Neah's head. "Really?"

"Oh, I'm sorry, was that *immature*? I thought that was just the way we did things now, or are you finally going to tell me what happened?" Zennon folded her arms across her chest and Neah huffed, turning back to her book from her place where she lounged on the bed. "Clearly something is on your mind."

Neah threw the book down, a little irritated when it flopped closed and lost her page, and growled at her sister. "Do you have something you want to tell me?"

Zennon looked wary. "Your eyes are glowing." *What?* Neah blinked and Zennon shook her head. "Still glowing. I'm not sure I've seen them do that before."

"Stop trying to change the subject," she said stiffly, bending to retrieve her book from down the side of the bed. "You told the king you weren't his mate."

"Oh, that."

"Yes, *that.*" Neah gaped. "What on earth is wrong with you?"

"It seemed unfair to let him court me, Neah. He took it rather well. In fact, I'd say he was relieved." Neah swallowed, willing away the heat that rose to her cheeks as her mind flashed back to the way he'd kissed her. "You're blushing. But, because I'm a nice person, I won't pry."

"Nice is not the first word that comes to mind," Neah muttered and caught the next slipper Zennon threw in mid-air. "The king has been spying on us."

This seemed to only intrigue Zen, rather than piss her off like it had Neah. "Oh? Has he learned anything of interest?"

"Too much," Neah growled and then shook her head. "He knows you're my sister, and that I'm a spy."

Zennon walked over and sat down on the edge of the bed next to Neah. "Does he know you were in the house that night?"

"No." She hesitated. "But I think he suspects."

"Well, this is good, right? He *is* your mate after all—"

"We don't know that," Neah protested. "I'm just supposed to take his word for it? That he cooked up a spell with Sonnet and the Goddess and that's that?"

Zennon patted her hand. "Of course not. But you can't tell me that you don't feel the connection between you—I've seen the way you watch each other, the way you move when you're together. But by all means," Zennon continued, eyes not missing a thing as she narrowed them on Neah's face, "live in denial."

It wasn't denial, Neah reasoned. Just... caution. Rationality. Why would the Goddess choose a shifter that can't shift for the *king*? And even if she had done just that, she and Wren were all wrong for each other. Neah was prickly, impatient, and occasionally bad tempered. Wren was the opposite of those things, if a little pompous at times—but that was to be expected given that he was royalty.

"Though, you do realise that the lunar hunt is next week? The Goddess has a funny way of getting what she wants, especially during times like the hunt."

Neah's mouth went dry. Zennon might have a point. She'd never participated in a hunt before, but she'd heard plenty about them. Something about the fullness and brightness of the moon lowered the inhibitions, creating and cementing connections that were previously denied or unknown. Wild things occurred during the hunt, all of it sanctioned under the light of the Goddess.

"I see no reason for me to attend," Neah said, hoping Zennon wouldn't push the issue.

Her sister laughed, flopping back against the sheets and

stretching her arms above her head. "For someone so intelligent, you say some very curious things—especially where Wren is concerned." When Neah didn't reply, Zennon continued. "Anyone of importance will be invited to the king's hunt, Neah. It's considered an honour, and if you decline…"

She sighed. She hadn't missed court politics a bit, even if she did thrive playing their games. "And you're so sure the king won't be guided to you under the moon's light?"

There was a beat of silence, as if Zennon was making some kind of decision, before she sat up and took Neah's hands in her own. "I am *certain*. I have no interest in the king… or any man for that matter."

Neah blinked. *Oh.* "The Goddess has blessed you," she murmured. "Men are nothing but trouble, you're far better off without them."

Zen laughed, her eyes bright as she pressed a kiss to the back of Neah's hand.

"Thank you for telling me." The revelation had lightened the mood and Neah found herself relaxing for the first time in days. "I suppose I understand your certainty a little more now," she mused and Zen chuckled.

"So what are you going to do about the hunt?"

Neah shrugged. "There's nothing I can do, I suppose. I'll attend the hunt if I'm asked, and let the rest fall where it may."

"Even if the king—"

"Yes," Neah interrupted, not wanting to hear the words, *chooses you*, tempt fate and their fickle Goddess. "Even then."

Neah couldn't deny that she found the insipid court tea parties fascinating. They were a spy's wet dream, full of gossip and whispers and even when words weren't spoken there was much to be said for the dynamics at play within the social circles.

For instance, Lady Fleura had apparently been sleeping with a guard well below her station and, when questioned, hadn't denied it. Instead, she'd bragged about the girth of his—

"Enjoying yourself?"

Neah didn't take her eyes off the crowd. "Immensely, Your Majesty." She'd known the instant he'd walked in the room from the reaction of the gathered crowd, a sense of smug self-importance rising up around them that the king had deigned to join them. More than that, there was a new weight in the air, like he took up space by simply existing, and while it was subtle, Neah wasn't sure she could go back to not noticing it. "And you?"

"More so now that you've acknowledged my existence."

Neah snorted. "That's very melodramatic of you. I've always known of your existence and have been a loyal, dutiful member of the court."

Wren hummed and Neah dared a glance at his face from the corner of her eye. "There is nothing a man longs for more than dutiful loyalty," he mused and her lip twitched as she fought off her smile. "I confess, I'm surprised that you enjoy these gatherings."

"In my... profession, these *gatherings* offer a great deal of information. Besides, I have a weakness for gossip and scandal. Though, I'd rather be a connoisseur than its source."

The king turned to face her fully and Neah smiled, pleased that he'd given in to their game of cat and mouse first, as she also looked him full in the face. "I came to ensure you received my invitation."

"Hm, it must have passed me by. Are you hosting a *gathering?*"

"Of a kind." His full lips tilted into a small smirk. "I'd like you to join me for the king's hunt—Zennon too, of course."

"I see." Neah kept her face impassive as she snagged a glass of something fizzy from a passing server's tray.

"It's a high honour to receive an invitation," Wren continued. "Let alone a personal invite."

"Honoured, I'm sure." She sipped her drink, eyeing him over the rim as she licked a stray droplet from her mouth and swallowed. His eyes dropped, following the movement, and Neah smirked. "I'll definitely consider it," she promised. "If no better options present themselves," she amended and a muscle in Wren's jaw ticked.

"I'm sure it'll be worth your while. But by all means, explore your options." He gave a stiff bow and then waved to a group of ladies across the room. "If you'll excuse me, I believe my presence is wanted elsewhere."

Stifling her laughter with another sip of her drink, Neah inclined her head. "Of course, my king. Enjoy the rest of your afternoon."

Wren walked away, shoulders stiff, and Neah chuckled —he would have to do better than that if he sought to make her jealous.

CHAPTER NINETEEN

WREN

The magical pressure in the air had been mounting all day and even Wren wasn't immune to its effects. Three fights had broken out amidst the court already, and one particularly amorous couple had been escorted from the breakfast hall to the tittering of those surrounding them. Nobody was particularly phased though, it was all par for the course where the lunar hunt was concerned. Even those who didn't actively participate would be helpless to resist the call of the moon, the basic shifter instincts rising to the surface until animal wants and needs were the driving force behind the urges to fuck and fight.

A regular full moon had far less effect on them than the moon that shone during the hunt. Humans and shifters alike considered it to be a holy day, the amber glow of the enlarged moon a sign that the Goddess was watching over them, ready to bestow her favour.

Wren wasn't sure how accurate that was, but he

couldn't deny that the moon was something to behold. It had been visible since the dawn, strengthening as the day wore on and morphing from its usual silver glow to the amber-gold that signified the beginning of the hunt.

It was a perfect night. The rainfall earlier in the week had ensured favourable conditions for running amid the trees. Fresh earth and magic permeated the air in a heady scent that made Wren's heart thump harder. Every hunt was unique, both in the people who attended and what transpired. Some would run, either in human or animal form, some would claim a prospective mate, and some would kill the small critters that called the forest home.

Gabe and Skye stood at his side, as was their personal tradition, and the others who'd been invited to attend the king's hunt were either fanned out along the forest's perimeter or were already among the trees. He hadn't seen Neah and Zennon arrive, but he knew Neah was out there. Could feel it somehow, like a tingle across his skin that increased the brighter the moon became until the forest was washed with golden shadows and he felt like he might burst out of his skin at any moment.

The moon reached its apex and, wordlessly, Wren shifted as Gabe did the same from his place at Wren's side. Magic rose in the air, thick and heady, and the thud of his paws hitting the ground sent sparks of feeling out from under him, rising up through his body until his head lifted to taste the night air and he released the snarl building in his chest.

The hunt had begun.

Miles of forest stretched out from the palace, surrounding the outskirts of the nearby town, and spanning the length of his kingdom. The dirt beneath him felt good, *right*, as he prowled forward and raked his claws across the tree closest to him, marking his territory.

Footfalls and soft breaths sounded in the vicinity of the tree cover and Wren paused, sinking down low and retreating into the shadows to watch the passerby.

Not her.

Disinterested, he stalked out from the underbrush and ignored the gasp of fear the human woman let out as he passed. His gait quickened, a scent from ahead catching his attention—sweet but earthy, honey mixed with the damp rain.

Was Neah hiding from him? The idea was amusing and he huffed out a laugh as his gait lengthened. The moonlight was his only guidance as he wove through the trees, the sound of breathless laughter and the grunting of an ongoing tussle mere blips that he tuned out in favour of the heartbeat up ahead.

Thump. Thump. Thump.

The world narrowed down to that sound. A sharp breath, a muttered curse, and then footsteps. Fleeing.

Was she... running from him? Claws dug into the earth as Wren pushed himself to follow, to meet her stride for stride.

Neah.

As if she could hear him, her heart sped up and her breath hitched and his body vibrated with tension as her scent thickened. The sweet smell of honey grew stronger and Wren let his tongue taste the air, a growl vibrating in his chest. She was enjoying this.

So she liked to be chased. But would she like to be caught?

Her speed was impressive, but she was on two legs and not four despite the influence of the moon. It was a mystery they could look into later. For now, he was closing in.

As if she could tell he was growing closer, a burst of speed impressed him. Had she been holding back? He could just make out her form up ahead, the white silk of her jacket and trousers a ceremonial but impractical choice for running through the forest and the colour a beacon drawing him in.

Neah's arms pumped at her side, the flash of her pale hands a blur as she ran, trying to increase her speed. It was an impressive feat, she was truly a worthy opponent, and maybe if she'd shifted she might have escaped.

But as it was...

Wren leapt, his paws hitting her back as he rolled so she was above him, taking the brunt of the impact with the leaves on the floor. If he'd been expecting that to be the end of the hunt, however, he was sorely mistaken.

A leg slipped between his haunches and before he could understand what was happening he was airborne. Laughter followed Neah's retreating back as Wren shook himself, dizzy from the flip.

No matter, he reasoned. He could just catch her again, and again, until she was beneath him and begging.

Mud sprayed as his claws dug deep into the ground, pushing off with enough force to grant him a leap of distance as he pounded after her. She was fast, but he was faster, something she had worked out, because now Neah used the trees to increase her speed, rebounding from trunk to trunk with strength that awed him. He almost didn't want to catch her, to interrupt the display of acrobatics she was putting on.

Almost.

This time, when he leapt for her he didn't hold back. They collided in mid-air and he shifted simultaneously so that his claws and fangs would'n't catch on her delicate human skin. Leaves shook as they collapsed to the forest floor and this time when she swung for him, he was ready.

She was panting, her wrists caught in his grip as he flattened her arms above her head, his body pinning her down carefully. Heat burned in her eyes, arousal pinking her cheeks, tightening her nipples through the silky, now-ripped, shirt. Even if he couldn't see the evidence of her desire, he could smell it.

"Do you concede?" The words held more than a trace of a growl and his finger elongated into claws as he held her wrists with one hand and trailed the sharp point of the other lightly down her face, across her throat, down her chest. He pressed more firmly, groaning when the fabric split cleanly under his sharp claw and revealed the pearlescent brightness of her skin beneath.

She wiggled under him, her hips pushing up in an attempt to throw him off that only teased the both of them, her hitched breath telling him she realised her mistake when his eyes shut momentarily to regain control.

His claw nicked the soft skin, a small bead of blood rising to the surface there, and his fingers returned to their normal state immediately as he looked at her, apologetic. But Neah was unfazed, defiance marking the tilt of her chin, like she was daring him to take her right there.

He chuckled at the look and leaned slowly closer, enjoying the way her eyes dropped to his mouth and the warmth that poured out of her as she became pliant under him. Wren closed the distance, holding back a hairsbreadth away from her lips and instead positioning his mouth by her ear. "Do you concede, *caritas?*"

"Never," she growled, and his laughter cut off only when she surged upward and caught his mouth with her own. For a second there was only bliss, heat and desire pooling low in his stomach as he hardened against her softness.

That lasted all of two seconds, before pain slammed into him and she fled once more.

Wren cursed soundly, pressing a finger up to his lip and shaking it off when it came away stained red. She'd bitten him.

The laughter couldn't be held back and, this time, he kept things fair. Heedless of his naked body, he gave chase. If she wanted him to prove he could best her on two feet instead of four, then he would do so.

It was cool but not cold, the leaves slapping at his body barely a hindrance as he pushed through them with ease. Neah's feet thumped rhythmically against the forest floor up ahead and Wren smirked. This was possibly the best lunar hunt of his life.

When the trees thinned, leading to an open clearing, he put on the burst of speed he'd been holding back, bolting across the open space and toward the gold lengths of hair that danced in the wind just ahead of him.

Neah glanced back over her shoulder and that was what cost her. Her eyes widened, following the broad line of his shoulders and then dropping to below his waist. She stumbled and, before she could hit the ground, his arms closed around her.

Her hair hung down in a golden sheet, her breaths warming his chilled skin as she looked up at him with wide amber eyes. The world paused in that moment, their heartbeats caught in sync until the world sped up again and her plump lips opened to whisper, "I concede."

It was what he'd been waiting for. Magic washed over him, like the Goddess herself was watching, blessing them, and the influx of power made his claws return and fangs to arc down from his mouth. His kiss turned into a bite, the mark blooming red on the skin between her throat and shoulder, the satisfaction making him growl as he tugged her closer and their lips met.

Neah may have conceded, but that didn't mean she was subordinate, a fact she proved when she took control of the kiss, licking into his mouth with a possessiveness that made his cock swell, brushing against her stomach.

Her hand closed around it tightly and he hissed at the pinch of her nails, the wicked gleam in her eyes, pulling away and using his claws to finish the work he'd started before. The silk of her shirt fell away fully, leaving the creamy expanse of her skin bared to the moonlight, and Wren swallowed hard, loving the way his mark looked against the relative perfection of her.

Small scars covered her body, battle wounds that were shaped like tiger stripes, and Wren traced each one with his mouth as he lowered her to the grass beneath where they stood.

He'd known he was right. She was his, whether she accepted it or not — the moon didn't lie and the connection that throbbed between them was as tangible as the branches of the trees a few paces away.

Impatient to see her, all of her, his claws shredded what remained of her trousers as he pulled them free from her body, wanting to see more, to feel her against him, to taste her and breathe her in until he drowned in the scent of her desire.

Strong hands threaded in his hair, tugging at the long strands until his mouth tasted her skin, licking each line of scars on her body until Wren gave in and let her direct his head as she wanted, chuckling when her thighs came up and around his shoulders.

It wasn't enough, though, so he unlocked them from his body and instead pushed them wide on either side of her, opening her up until she was spread beautifully for him, glistening with her own arousal beneath the golden moon.

He dipped one clawed finger into her, oh-so careful, and he grinned when she gasped, her hands flying up to clutch at his shoulders.

So she liked the bite of pain with her pleasure? He could work with that.

Wren withdrew, tasting her heady scent in the air as he pressed the tips of his claws into her inner thighs, keeping her spread open like a feast just for him. He lowered his head slowly, watching her above the top of her mound, loving the way her eyes glowed and her hips bucked in an effort to reach his mouth.

He gave in, taking pity on her, and let his breath coast across her engorged wet heat before closing his mouth around the sweet bud that arced upward, throbbing for his attention. Her cry made him growl, his tongue working her clit in circles that made her shudder before he stopped fucking around and *sucked*.

Neah's back arched and when she screamed his name he felt his cock dip in response, the tip growing wet as she begged him with her body, called for him with her soul so loudly that he knew anyone nearby would hear. Would know she was his.

The thought pleased him and he smiled into her pussy as he speared his tongue into her entrance, lapping at her wetness as she writhed, begging him for more. He obeyed. One finger, sans-claw, curled into her as he re-focused his attention back on her clit, sucking and licking it until she whimpered—only then did he curl the digit inside of her to rub against her sensitive inner walls.

When she came, she did so with a cry loud enough to send birds flying out of the trees, soaking Wren's face as she throbbed against him and he grinned, enjoying the way she tried to ride his face even as he kept her pinned in place.

Once her shaking had subsided and the moon began to wane, Wren released her and backed away. Their instincts had been heightened, they had acted on desires more animal than man, and now that reason would be returning to their bodies and minds, Wren wasn't sure what he'd find in Neah's eyes. Regret? Fear at what they'd just done?

He wasn't sure he wanted to wait around and find out. Perhaps she herself didn't know how to feel yet. She hadn't been ready to accept that he was hers before, but now... Well, Wren could be patient.

Under Selene's moon, he'd proven to Neah what he could offer her as a mate, in the most physical sense anyway. What he had to give her now was time.

Wren bent down, pressing a chaste kiss to the sweat-slicked skin of her forehead and then inclined his head before letting the shift ripple back across his skin and padding away into the night.

CHAPTER TWENTY

NEAH

"And then what happened?" Zennon leaned in eagerly, eyes bright like she was living vicariously through Neah.

"And then... he walked away."

"He walked—*he walked away?*" Zennon's smile folded into a frown. "Why?"

Neah shrugged, though the truth was that she suspected she knew why the king had left her naked on the forest floor after the best head of her life. He'd given her a taste, and now if she wanted more she would have to be the one to chase him—metaphorically. She tilted her head as she reconsidered, *or maybe not*.

"Well, that's still more exciting than my evening." Zennon sighed. "Gabriel hovered around me for half an hour before I gave up and went back inside."

Neah winced sympathetically. "It's for your own protection. But, hey, at least you can enjoy the post-hunt feast?"

"I know, I know." Zennon pushed to standing, her long skirts flowing around her as she stretched and then jumped as a knock sounded on Neah's door from the parlour. "I'll get it."

Before Neah could protest, Zennon was already halfway there. The door swung open and her face lit up when she saw who stood on the other side, her mouth opened before she seemed to catch herself, head bowing as she said, "Captain Jamison. You're here for Neah?"

Their father nodded, entering and closing the door behind him and as soon as the heavy wood thunked shut he drew Zennon into an embrace. "You're well?" He pulled back and cupped Zen's cheek as he inspected her face, nodding in satisfaction when she reassured him. "Neah," he said, smiling as she approached. Just as quickly as it appeared, his smile vanished behind the mask of stoicism the rest of the world saw. He was no longer her father, in his place was her spymaster, her Captain.

"You've returned," she said evenly, calling upon her own mask as she took a seat in the armchair near the hearth. "A good trip?"

He nodded but gave no details as he followed her to the seating area and chose his own chair. "Zen, a moment?"

Zennon bowed her head and left, walking into the other room to eavesdrop no doubt.

"Report."

"I followed your instructions and came across several potential assassins, but there was no sign of the benefactor themselves." She kept her tone even, measured, and was surprised when the Captain slumped, a hand coming up to rub at his tired eyes. It was a sign of weakness he'd show his daughter, but not his spy. "There's something else." Her hands fisted in the smooth fabric of her trousers, catching on the swirling designs that had been stitched onto the black material. "The king has been doing some spying of his own. He knows about Zennon, and he knows about me."

Jamison's head snapped up. "Explain."

She blew out a long breath, reluctant to meet the accusation that was likely swimming in his eyes. "He followed us the night we came to see you in the servant's quarters."

There was silence for a moment and then he cursed. "Sloppy."

"I know. I'm sorry."

"And you? How did he discover that?"

The lump in her throat was hard to swallow past but she made an attempt. "He followed me to the tavern."

At that, Jamison stood and began to pace. "I taught you better than that, Neah. Tailed not once, but twice?" He shook his head and her gut churned, acid bubbling up her throat as his disappointment crested. She wasn't sure his agitation could get much worse, so she decided the best thing to do was rip the bandage off.

"Dad."

He halted, pace faltering as her father peered out of the face of the Captain. "Yes?"

"I think he's my mate." It was the first time she'd said it aloud and the words made her head swim and her heart beat faster, clamminess clinging to her palms. "He found me during the hunt."

Neah wasn't sure what reaction she'd expected. Shock,

perhaps, that the Goddess had chosen Neah for the king. Concern that this would inevitably complicate things for them all, and cast an even closer eye on them, on their secrets, as the court scrambled to learn more about them—possibly even anger. Deep down, in a small place she'd deny ever existed, she hoped his reaction might be joy—she had found her other half. Her equal in all things.

Instead, the mask of the captain fell back into place and the ache of that pain hurt more than if he'd raged at her. "I see."

Zennon rounded the corner, hands on her hips and her mouth pressed into a straight line. Despite her bearing no relation to Neah's mother, she couldn't help but think that Zen bore a striking resemblance to the captain's wife at that moment. It wasn't often that Zennon caved to anger, but when she did her temper was white hot.

"*I see*? That's all you have to say to your daughter as she confessed, for the first time might I add, that the *king* is her mate?" Zennon stopped in front of their father and Neah couldn't help her own amusement when Jamison shrank back from his daughter. "She is not just your spy, she is a *person*, shame on you for thinking only of the ways you can use her to your advantage or in how to mitigate damage to your network."

Zennon was breathing heavily and Neah's eyes were wide. She'd had no idea that her sister felt this way about Neah's service to the crown, but her father didn't look shocked. In fact, he looked *pissed*.

"That's enough." He didn't raise his voice, didn't even snap, and yet Zennon shrank back from him, retreating into Neah's safety as she hovered just behind her chair.

"My concern is not for my *network*, or the potential loss of one of my best spies. My concern is that of a father for his daughter."

Neah frowned, running her eyes over his face and finding no untruths. "What do you mean?"

Jamison's eyes were steady when they met her own. "The king set out to look for his mate only to shore up his own hold on the crown. Nothing more."

"I don't understand," Zen said softly and Neah's jaw clenched tightly before she managed to relax the muscles long enough to reply.

"Don't tiptoe around it, father. He means that the king only intends to use me."

Zennon shook her head. "I've seen the way he watches you. This is not merely a convenience for him."

But Neah was done listening and pushed to her feet as the need to move, to *act,* rushed through her. "You think it's a coincidence that there is unrest within the court and assassins targeting him at the very same time he decides it's time to find his mate? No, Father is right. I am a means to an end. Nothing more."

"Neah—"

"At least now I know," she growled, the tone deeper than usual. Better to understand where she stood with the king now, before she got in too deep. "If he needs a mate to secure the crown and protect the kingdom, then that's what I'll be. I'll do my duty." But there would be no love between them, no pretences. Her hands clenched on the back of the armchair where she'd been sitting.

Zennon frowned. "I don't think Wren would want—"

The sound of his name frayed her control and an odd

tingling swept through her hands, the fabric dimpling beneath her fingertips. She forced herself to let go of the chair, startled when she caught a glimpse of the rips in the material in line with her fingers. Had she done that?

Her eyes darted down to her hands but found only smooth, human fingers. No claws. Pushing the strange occurrence to the back of her mind, she frowned as she debated what she wanted to do next.

The two of them were staring at her, wariness and concern mixing with pity, and it was more than Neah could take. So she turned on her heel and left without another word. Perhaps there would be time later to talk this out with her sister, but for now... Neah needed to hit something.

The rhythmic thump of her hands against the training dummy was soothing as she worked out her anger. She'd stopped only when her hands began to ache and her knuckles threatened to split, because that would be hard to hide as a Lady of the court.

So she'd switched to kicking the dummy until her hips protested and she lost her balance, landing on her arse. For some reason, the impact made her cry.

If she was being honest, the impact had likely just jolted her emotions out of her rather than being the cause of her tears. She'd fought through her rage, and was left now with only disappointment. For a second, she'd allowed herself to believe Wren wanted her—that the Goddess hadn't forsaken her—but she was a fool. What use did a king have for love? Of course even his mating bond would be about power, control. She was an idiot to have entertained any other thoughts in the moments since he'd left her in the forest. What seemed like a choice, a freedom, now seemed more like a smug taunt—*come and get me if you want, because I can take it or leave it.* She'd been screwing up ever since she'd arrived at court, letting the king tail her, failing to locate the person funding the assassins, and now this.

Neah pushed out several deep breaths, wiping away the sweat that had mingled with her tears as she pushed to standing. She was about to head for a small rack of throwing knives when her gaze caught on the wooden floor where she'd been sitting. Two round circles of small, nearly imperceptible scratches marred the floor in a perfect replica of where her hands had pressed to the ground while she'd cried, attempting to ground herself.

Her fingers looked no different, and maybe the scratches had been there before she'd sat down and she just hadn't noticed, but between this and the chair in her parlour... It seemed like too big a coincidence.

Had I... summoned claws? It was too much to hope for, but Zennon would tell her if she was being delusional.

Knives forgotten, Neah made her way to the door of the private training room. It was a hidden nook, one of many in the castle if she had to guess, that nobody knew of except her and Jamison. She'd half-expected to find it covered in dust from disuse since she'd been gone, but it had been as brightly polished and well-equipped as ever, making her wonder if her father also used it as a retreat when his thoughts grew to be too much.

Neah paused with a hand on the door, about to exit

when she sensed two passersby. She pressed an ear to the door, listening for their retreat so she could leave, and instead caught the tail end of their conversation.

"...It's not as if there aren't plenty of eligible ladies here at court," one of the women said, a voice Neah couldn't place. "Why he felt the need to bring in a *nobody* from a hovel in the forest is beyond me."

Anger made Neah's body flash hot. They were talking about Zennon, she was sure.

The other person tutted and Neah was certain this was someone she'd seen recently, likely during a gathering for tea. "Now, Fleura, let's not be petty. *I* heard that the king summoned her here with a spell." The woman's tone lowered and Neah strained to hear what was said next. "I heard that *nobody* is his mate!"

Fleura, presumably, gasped and Neah stifled the curse that nearly slipped from her lips. If these two knew, then it was likely that others at court had heard the same whispers. Of course, they were wrong—Neah was Wren's mate, not Zennon, but who had told them even that much? If not for the fact that she was exhausted and slick with sweat from her training, Neah might have followed them to see what else they knew. But as it was, the best course of action seemed to be returning to Zennon and making sure she was safe.

Neah slipped out of the hidden door and moved swiftly back down the corridor in the opposite direction to the gossiping ladies. If Wren was right, then whoever had spread this rumour, and the others while he'd been away hunting, was likely the same person who had hired the assassins. A sense of foreboding gripped her tightly as she considered the implications of their boldness.

They had left a guard outside of Zennon's guest room as a security measure, hoping anyone looking to hurt her would think she was still staying there instead of with Neah. She would have to remember to question the guards on rotation there and see if they'd seen or heard anything concerning—especially with the post-hunt feast coming up, Zennon would be exposed. Vulnerable. It was too late to quash the rumours, but she could help shore up Zen's defences in the meantime.

After a day of fasting, and with one more still to go, Neah had been looking forward to the feast and lunar ball that always followed a Hunt. Now, she only hoped they would make it through unscathed.

Zennon was waiting for her when Neah walked through the door and she didn't pause for breath as she closed the door behind her and eyed her sister sitting on a chair before the unlit hearth.

"Do you still want to learn to fight?"

CHAPTER TWENTY-ONE

NEAH

Zennon had a surprisingly strong right hook. Something she was particularly pleased about whenever Neah praised her. It was a little worrying, since the main lesson Neah had tried to drum into her sister's head is that the best thing to do when faced with a threat is *run*.

They'd been going through basic self-defence manoeuvres all morning until Neah finally called time on the whole thing so they could catch their breath. The fasting since the lunar hunt wasn't helping any with the exhaustion that bore down on Neah and she knew that Zen had to be feeling it too. It was an old ceremonial tradition that, while upheld at court, many didn't bother with any more. Supposedly, the fasting promoted balance after the wild indulgence of the hunt, the only people at court who were exempt from the fast were the king's guard —hungry soldiers were never a good idea.

The keeper knocked on the door with the juice Neah

had called for and placed the tray on the small table in the parlour when Neah let them in. They'd brought a carafe of orange juice, extra pulpy and ice cold, as well as two glasses. Liquid was a grey area for the fast, but they needed some energy after sparring all morning, so Neah had embraced it.

Under the warmth of her fingertips, the glass carafe fogged. Zennon walked over to see what had arrived and then hovered by Neah's elbow until she handed her a full glass.

Zennon bounced on the balls of her feet and Neah watched, bemused. How did she still have so much pep? Normally Neah didn't become less grouchy in the mornings until she'd eaten two lots of breakfast—but maybe she was especially cranky today because of her gruelling workout the night before.

Glass shattered, jolting Neah out of her thoughts and startling her into spilling the juice as she poured it from the carafe into her own glass.

"Gods, Zen. You nearly gave me a—Zennon?"

She was staring down at the shattered glass and remnants of orange on the ground in front of her, her hands oddly limp and her face paler than Neah had ever seen it.

"I feel strange," she murmured, and then she was falling. Neah scrambled to catch her, knocking the carafe in the process until more puddles of orange pooled on the floor, rivulets of juice running down from the table in a steady drip that sounded far away as Zennon's eyes rolled back in her head.

"Zen? Zen!"

Shallow breaths passed through Zennon's parted lips, her pulse fluttering weakly against Neah's fingers. She'd been fine two seconds ago, joking and smiling, and now—

Neah halted the thought in its tracks. Zennon would be fine. She would make sure of it.

She scooped her sister up, paying close attention to the small rise and fall of her breaths as Neah held Zennon against her chest.

"Keep breathing for me, Zennon." Her voice sounded calmer than she felt, like everything inside of her had turned to stone. Panic wasn't helpful right then. Zennon needed a healer, not a sister too busy falling apart to help.

The door to her chambers flew off its hinges as Neah kicked it, the dull *boom* not slowing her down as she stepped through the doorway, careful of Zennon's head and legs that dangled from Neah's grip.

Zennon's lips were turning chalky, a whiteness that started at their corners and inched toward their centres as Neah turned to her left and ran.

The cold skin of Zen's wrist made Neah flinch as she pressed her fingers against it, feeling for her pulse and relieved when it thudded sluggishly. The healer's wing was at the other end of the castle and even with the near-empty corridors thanks to the early morning, Neah wasn't sure they would make it.

Goddess. Selene. Do not let her die. It was more of a demand than a prayer but it helped clear her head to have someone she could direct her anger at. If they couldn't get to the healers, then they would have to make do with the next best thing.

Zennon jostled against Neah's body as she ran, pushing

herself faster until she reached a guest room she hadn't been to before but knew about thanks to her own subtle inquiries. She didn't bother to knock, instead kicking in the door much like she had her own.

Silver eyes widened as Sonnet gave a cry of alarm before she took in the situation and, to her credit, didn't hesitate. "Goddess. Put her here."

Neah obeyed, setting Zennon down on the bed where Sonnet had indicated. "I don't know what's wrong with her. Is it poison? She was fine until she drank the juice." Was she rambling? Neah couldn't tell any more as she paced at the end of the bed, giving Sonnet room to work.

The witch shook her head as she ran her hands over Zennon's body, hands glowing with faint light. "No, not poison. A spell. I'll do what I can to slow it, but we need to get her to the healers before it's too late."

Too late. The bed frame creaked under Neah's grip and she let go immediately, not wanting to cause the frame to collapse atop the both of them.

"This is strong magic," Sonnet murmured and the long white night dress she wore fluttered about her form as she began weaving her hands in the air, like she could see something Neah couldn't. "But amateur."

This was amateur?

Sonnet shuddered. "Nasty, nasty. It's two-fold," she said, more to herself than to Neah it seemed. "Unravel the soul, poison the body. I can fix the soul magic but the rest will be up to the healers. If I can just…" The witch's frame quaked and her head fell back, her hair cascading in waves that stirred in a breeze Neah didn't feel. Her eyes glowed white and etchings in silver rolled across her bare arms and down to her hands as she placed them on the centre of Zennon's chest.

So that was what it was like to be blessed by the Goddess. As long as it saved Zennon, Neah didn't care whether Sonnet summoned a demon or any other manner of evil.

The light sank into Zennon, making her chest glow for a moment before the magic seemed to expand, reaching the top of her head down to her toes in the time it took Neah to blink, before dissipating with a pop of pressure that had her flying back and away from the bed.

"Quickly." Sonnet appeared above Neah's head and offered a hand to pull her to standing. The witch was paler than usual and a sheen of sweat coated her body. "Get her to the healer now."

Sonnet looked like she could use a healer herself, and when she swayed, Neah sighed and caught her. It was times like this where her shifter strength truly was an asset.

Neah swung Sonnet up and over one shoulder before doing the same with Zennon on her other side, grunting at the weight. She just had to make it to the healers.

Then she ran, grateful for every heartbeat she could feel against her shoulder as she pushed herself harder than ever before. The corridors blurred around her and she concentrated on putting one foot in front of the other until, finally, she reached the corridor of the healer's wing and nearly crashed into Gabriel, Skye, and Wren.

Gabe took Sonnet immediately and Neah sucked in a breath, grateful for the relief, before marching through the doors and swinging Zennon down gently, depositing her on the closest bed. Five healers immediately flocked, assessing Zennon much like Sonnet had with their hands hovering over her body.

"What happened?"

Neah wasn't sure who asked, didn't want to look away from Zennon for even a second lest she miss her last breaths. "Magic. Sonnet fixed the spell that was weighing on Zennon's soul, but she said there was poison in the body."

The healer closest to Neah nodded. "You're lucky that there was a lunar witch here, otherwise there's nothing we would have been able to do."

"But now?" Neah held her breath until black spots swam in her vision.

"I've got her. I think you got her here just in time, thanks to your friend's magic."

Just in time. She was going to be okay.

"Yes," the healer said and Neah startled, not realising she'd said the words aloud. "I need room to work. Go and wait in the seating area and I'll come and get you when I'm done."

Neah's breath shook. "Okay. Thank you." The racing of her heart finally began to slow and she was grateful for the hand that wrapped around her waist as the room tilted to the left from the force of her adrenaline crash.

She's going to be okay.

"Yes, *caritas*. She's going to be okay. You did so good." The words were nonsense, soothing murmurs, the familiar scent of forest and sweetness surrounding her, and it was only when she leaned her head back that she realised they'd made it to the chairs and Wren had her cradled on his lap. His hands tightened when she moved before his grip went slack, giving her the option to leave if she chose. She didn't move.

"And Sonnet?"

"Tired, but fine. Lunar witch magic works slightly different to other witches, her magic takes a part of her when she uses it. Sometimes it's energy, like with other witches, but sometimes it's life force." Sonnet had given up some of her life to heal Zennon? The shock on her face must have been apparent because Wren chuckled. "Sonnet would never let someone die if she could help it, *caritas*."

Neah's eyes had slipped closed without her meaning to and they flashed open at his words. "What does that mean? Caritas?" She pronounced it awkwardly and Wren's smile faded, a more intense look framing his face and lighting his eyes.

"Precious, or rare." He spoke in a raw murmur and Neah didn't know what to say, so she just nodded. "I'm sorry this happened."

"How did you know?" she asked around a yawn and Wren nodded to the side where Skye and Gabriel stood at the end of Sonnet's bed.

"Skye had a feeling. A strong one. So we came."

"Thank you," she mumbled and sighed when a hand stroked over her hair, lulling her to sleep as her body finally gave out. "M'just closing my eyes. Watch her."

Neah fell asleep to the sound of Wren's answering chuckle. "Sleep, Neah."

Neah jolted awake, unsure what her body had sensed that was concerning enough to wake her. A heavy tension sat in the air and she jumped when a hand stroked gently at her hair, as if to soothe her.

Wren. She'd fallen asleep in his lap.

Neah scrambled upright, avoiding looking at the king. With everything going on, she'd forgotten what her father had told her and had instead allowed herself to be driven by instinct. Regardless of his intentions, Wren meant safety, and her body had recognised that when it needed to crash. But now, she was awake and alert and remembered that she was pissed.

She was momentarily distracted from her anger by the sight of Sonnet and Zennon sitting up in their respective beds, pale but alive. "You're awake," she breathed, immediately walking over to take her sister's hand, and Zennon's answering smile was tired. "How are you feeling?"

"Like I nearly died," she mused and then glanced at Sonnet in the bed next to her. "I'm just lucky you were here, Sonnet."

"Mm, *lucky*," Skye said, more than a hint of a growl in the words and Neah's shoulders tensed. "What?" Skye protested when they all turned to look at him. "Zennon had a soul-curse placed on her, the king of magic that a lunar witch specialises in, and we're supposed to believe that it's a coincidence that one of the only lunar witches—"

"I'm not the only lunar witch left in existence," Sonnet said, her eyes narrow and tone raspy as she cut Skye off.

Skye rolled his eyes and stood up from the chair he'd

claimed near Wren, making to step forward and drawing up short when Neah blocked his way.

"If Sonnet cursed Zennon, only to then sacrifice some of her own life force to heal her, then she's an idiot."

Skye's eyes shot to Sonnet's, looking past Neah like she wasn't there. "You used your life force—"

"That's how my magic works. You might know that if you'd bothered to talk to a lunar witch, rather than murdering them."

Skye paled. "I didn't–I've never—" He took another step forward and Neah put out a hand, pressing gently against his chest. But he got the message.

"You don't come near her, unless she says so. Got it?" The words were quiet, barely above a breath, and the obvious threat in her voice made Skye's jaw clench. But he backed down, and that was all Neah cared about. Sonnet had saved her sister, and Neah owed her a thousand times over for that.

Wren was watching her, the interaction making his golden eyes burn hotter, and Neah looked away. She couldn't deal with him right now on top of everything else.

"Your Majesty," a quiet voice said, drawing all eyes to the petite woman hovering at the edges of their small group. "I was told you sent for me?"

A low growl raised the hair on Neah's arms until she realised it was coming from her, the sound cutting off abruptly but the rage lingering. "*You.*"

Neah leapt but Wren was ready for her, catching her before she could reach the keeper who'd brought them the juice that had nearly killed Zennon.

"Let me go." The words were calm even as she thrashed against Wren's hold. "I just want to talk to her."

Wren laughed. "And you need your claws for that conversation?"

Neah glanced down at where her hands gripped his arm, mouth dropping open when she saw the sharply curved edges in the place where her human fingers should have been. The shock was enough to shake her out of her rage.

"Are you going to behave?" Wren murmured against the shell of her ear and an irritating bolt of heat shot straight to her core. He chuckled, likely able to smell the arousal on her, and released her in a slow glide that made her shiver as his warm skin caressed her.

The woman had shrunk back, terror in her eyes, and Neah sighed. If the girl had been responsible for the spell, it didn't seem likely that she would allow herself to be interrogated for the crime. Neah couldn't smell any guilt on her, just fear, strong and sour.

Skye stepped up, speaking to the girl soothingly and, when she nodded, held out his hand. She took it and Skye's eyes turned white. It reminded her eerily of the way Sonnet had looked earlier while communing with the Goddess.

"She prepared the juice," Skye said, his voice echoing strangely. "She didn't curse it though. She's human. Someone else must have got to it while her back was turned in the kitchens." His eyes returned to their regular blue and he let go of the server's hand, patting it sympathetically when he noticed the green tint to her skin. "She's innocent," he concluded and Neah sighed. They were no closer to finding whoever wanted the king and, by extension, Zennon dead.

"I'm sorry," Neah said to the girl and she nodded stiffly, bowing before scuttling away like Neah might change her mind and pounce at any moment. Then she turned to Wren and glared. "You need to do something. They're going to keep coming after her as long as they think she's your mate."

He raised an eyebrow. "You'd rather they come after you?"

Neah blinked. Did she really have to spell it out for him? "Yes."

"And you're okay with that?" Wren asked, turning to Zennon who snorted and then winced, touching a hand to her head.

"Neah can more than take care of herself."

For some reason, Zen's response seemed to infuriate him further. "You're ready to admit to yourself, to the *court*, that you were there that night? That *you're* my mate?"

She folded her arms across her chest as she looked at him. "If that's what it takes to make Zennon safe, then yes. Plus, we have to do what's best for the crown—right?" She rolled her eyes, not giving him the chance to answer as she stalked past and bent down to press a kiss to Zennon's forehead. "Do you want me to stay?"

"No, that's okay. Gabe already offered to keep an eye on me and Sonnet."

Did he, now? Neah raised her brows at the shifter. "How kind."

"Get some rest, I'll be fine."

"She'd better," Neah hissed to Gabriel as she walked

past. "Rest up. Tomorrow's the feast and the ball—what better time to get that target off your back?"

Seeing as her room was covered in orange juice, Neah decided to stay in Zen's vacant guest chamber. Her father would need to know what had happened, and she needed some real sleep to recover from the exertion of hauling Zennon and Sonnet across the castle on her shoulders.

Nobody stopped her as she left, but she could sense Wren following her as she prowled the halls. She didn't remark on it. His misguided protection was as sweet as it was insulting. Let him think she was unaware like before, but this time she was watching—she wouldn't be fooled again.

Despite the fact that she'd been expecting it, the knock at the door to her chambers still made Neah tense.

Zennon and Sonnet had come back to Neah's rooms in the morning at her request, both looking much more healthy than when Neah had seen them last night. Colour had returned to their cheeks and Zennon seemed to have nearly her normal amount of energy, but she didn't protest when Neah glared at her sister to remain seated and instead answered the door herself.

The woman waiting on the other side was full-figured with creamy white skin and red hair that gleamed brightly in the early morning light. She'd come highly recommended, despite that Neah had never really heard of her before, and Neah stepped back to invite her and her three assistants into the parlour.

"Who is it?" Zennon, apparently done with Neah's heightened caution, strolled around the corner with a swish of her skirts before halting, eyes widening. "What's all this?" she said, pulling her eyes away from the woman at Neah's side.

"This is Romi. She's a dressmaker."

The woman smiled, shrewd blue eyes running over Zennon's form with a keen eye, no doubt already conjuring up designs. "Just the two of you?"

"Actually," Neah said, glancing at Sonnet who had approached with something like curiosity and resignation on her face. "Three. If that's okay?"

"Of course!"

Neah winced at the perky tone but the surprise on Sonnet's face made up for it.

"For me, too?" she murmured as Neah led Romi and the assistants into the adjacent bed chamber. "Are you sure? I don't have much in the way of money—"

"Sonnet." Neah rolled her eyes. "Shut up." The witch still looked unsure and Neah sighed. "It's a gift. Okay?"

The soft smile that hesitantly bloomed made Neah's heart clench. "Okay," Sonnet said, the words quiet.

"I've been meaning to ask," Romi said as she helped a barely-clothed Neah up and onto a box to take her measurements. "Where did you hear about me?"

Neah shrugged and received a stink-eye for moving. "Your name was floated about at a few parties and..." She hesitated before clearing her throat and continuing, "My mother."

Romi leaned back, her cornflower blue eyes narrowing before they widened. "That's why you look so familiar. You're Winny's daughter. You know, she's the one who encouraged me to leave my job to design."

Neah nodded. "I know." In truth, she'd been a little hesitant about Romi's inexperience. While it was true she'd heard Romi's name at the gatherings the ladies frequently held, it had mostly been with a tone of derision for a keeper trying to rise above their station. But when she'd answered the door and seen the, clearly custom, dress Romi was wearing, her worries had dissipated. She had been right to trust her mother, who'd got to know many of the serving girls while she'd spent some time in their quarters.

Romi's dress was tailored beautifully, even if the all-over floral print wasn't to Neah's taste, with a sage-green corset falling over the wide skirt and off-the shoulder straps that perfectly accentuated the woman's curves. The real selling point had been when Romi had taken a tape measure out of the side of the dress and Neah had realised it had *pockets*. The possibility for hidden weapons alone was enough to excite her.

Neah stepped down from the box after Romi made her notes and Zennon stepped up clad in her thin nightdress. She looked uncomfortable, which was surprising given how many times Zennon's attendants had seen her in states of undress for measurements and then like. What was different now? Neah's brow furrowed as she watched Zennon swallow hard when Romi drew closer to measure around her bust.

"You're an idiot," Sonnet muttered and Neah snorted, glad the witch had recovered from her bout of sentimental mushiness. "I can see you watching them like you're faced with a particularly difficult puzzle. When in reality, it's very simple."

Neah glanced at Sonnet and huffed a breath at the smirk on her face. She looked back to Zennon who was doing her best to avoid eye contact with Romi, something that appeared to be irritating the seamstress.

"Lady," the other woman said, none so gently despite the respectful term, "if you object to my presence so strongly, I can leave."

Zennon's head jerked toward Romi, her eyes flying wide. "No! That is, not at all. I just—" Her cheeks pinked and Neah chuckled as it all fell into place in her mind. "I, ah, can see down your corset and, well, I just–I mean, I wanted to—"

"Is it my turn now?" Sonnet asked, apparently taking mercy on Zennon who was now quite red in the face while Romi watched with dawning realisation and more than a little smugness. Zennon stepped down from the box with enough haste that her feet tangled in her long nightdress and Romi caught her, steadying her by the shoulders, and Zennon turned impossibly redder.

Romi took Sonnet's measurements without comment but the small smile on her face made Neah smirk. Zennon had excused herself to the bathroom and emerged looking nearly normal again, elbowing Neah in the side when she laughed under her breath.

The seamstress helped Sonnet down and then began to sort through the reams of fabric she'd brought with her, muttering to herself about complimentary colours and silhouettes.

"Are you sure you'll have time to get these done before tonight?" Sonnet had wandered closer and fingered a bolt of shimmery silver fabric with interest.

"I mean, it's not my preferred timeline," Romi said dryly. "But we'll get it done," she added, nodding to her assistants. "You'll have them back by tonight."

"That's it? We don't get to see the designs?"

Romi smirked and reached out to pat Sonnet's hand. "That's not how I work, sweetie. Especially on this kind of timeline."

Neah ignored Sonnet's needling and instead strode to the locked chest at the end of her bed, opening it easily and pulling a purple velvet bag of coin out. She handed it to Romi who frowned.

"Unless you're paying me in coppers, this bag is much too heavy for the fee we agreed."

Honestly, Neah would have paid thrice just to see the look on Sonnet's face when she realised Neah was getting her a new dress and Zennon's reaction to the admittedly beautiful red-headed woman. But more than that, she had a good feeling about Romi, especially if her mother's opinion was anything to go off. "Half now, half later when you deliver the dresses."

Romi's eyes widened. "That's—No, it's too much, Lady."

"Neah," she corrected. "And you're starting a business from scratch, talent should always be invested in—plus, if you're as good as I think you are then I want to snap you up early so that all my outfits can have pockets." Neah grinned and pressed the bag firmly into Romi's hands when she attempted to hand it back. "Don't you have dresses to make?"

The risk might have been minimal, but Neah wasn't ready to sit with half the court at the feast after a poisoning attempt less than forty-eight hours ago. So, instead, they had dinner sent to Neah's room where she carefully sniffed at it and then passed it to Sonnet to test magically. Only when they determined it was safe to eat did they dive in.

They were still waiting on Romi to arrive with their dresses, which was a good thing because it allowed some time for the enormous amount of food they'd indulged in to digest before they were stuffed into a corset.

Zennon was mid-stretch when the knock at the door came and Neah snickered when her sister began smoothing down her hair.

Romi strode in, her assistants each carrying a garment bag, and Neah found that she was actually excited to see what the seamstress had dreamed up for each of them. Each assistant approached one of them, helping them out of their night dresses and into three resplendent gowns.

"Wait, don't we need a corset?" Neah raised a brow and was confused when Romi laughed.

"Only if you want one. The boning is built in for some shaping, but I prefer to let my curves breathe."

Zennon looked like she was about to choke at the mention of Romi's curves, but Neah just ran an eye over the seamstress' dress and nodded. It was the same one that she'd been wearing earlier and it worked with the swell of her hips, the softness of her belly, and full chest.

Romi insisted they close their eyes while they put their dresses on, so as not to ruin the effect supposedly, but Neah was the only one who didn't cooperate. She was sure

Romi and her assistants weren't assassins in disguise, but one couldn't be too careful.

Still, Neah dutifully attempted to keep her eyes averted from the dress as she stepped into it and was baffled by the lack of fastening. Instead, the material draped along her slim form, pooling across and over her breasts in a wide scoop that gave the illusion that more skin was on show than was reality. What shocked her more, though, was that it was absolutely weightless. If she hadn't felt the material when she'd slipped it on, she might have thought she was naked.

Gasps rang out and Neah immediately looked to Zennon and Sonnet, relieved that they were okay and instead found them admiring the dresses they'd been given. Though, dresses felt a little trivial—these gowns were works of art.

Zennon's was a blue so dark it was nearly black, the skirt full without being puffy, flaring out over her hips, and the top was a sweetheart framed corset in a contrasting gold that brought out the warmth in her eyes. She was stunning and, when Neah told her so, she beamed.

Sonnet did a twirl of her own, as if to say *what about me?*

Neah laughed and catcalled the witch, her dress only moderately more scandalous than Neah's. The material was a pale pink dusted with a silvery overlay that was nearly translucent. The neckline slashed across the tops of Sonnet's collarbones and rested on her shoulders, long strands of the material fluttering down against her bare back where the dress ebbed and came back together at the base of her spine.

They were stunning, and Neah was very glad she'd taken her mother's recommendation.

"Skye's going to swallow his tongue," Sonnet said, laughing, and Zen grinned. "Thank you, Romi. This is the loveliest thing I've ever owned. And thank you, Neah."

"Anytime," she said, and meant it.

They'd waited to do their hair and make-up until they saw the dresses, so they put the finishing touches in place and allowed Romi to do a few last minute tweaks before she nodded and declared them ready.

"Aren't you coming too?" Zennon asked Romi after Neah paid her more coin while ignoring her protests.

The seamstress' smile was a touch bitter as she shook her head. "I'm no one. People like me don't get invited to balls with the king."

Zennon lifted her chin, jaw straining, and Neah knew her sister's stubborn streak had reared its head. "They do now." She held out her hand and, hesitantly, like she expected it to be ripped away at the last second, Romi took it. "You too," Zennon added, nodding at the assistants who seemed surprised to be included. "I mean, if you want. It's not mandatory."

They smiled and trailed them as Neah ushered everyone out of the door. It was time to dance.

CHAPTER TWENTY-THREE

WREN

Wren was... antsy. It wasn't a feeling he was particularly accustomed to, especially because of a woman. Even one as exceptional as Neah.

"Do you think they're okay?" he asked Gabe for the tenth time and his friend grimaced as he surveyed the dancers twirling elegantly around the dance floor.

"Yes."

"But—"

"If you're that worried, why don't you just go and—" Gabe stopped, hand halting in mid-air before he could take a sip of his wine. "Ah. There. See? They're fine."

Wren's head whipped around, following Gabe's line of sight until his eyes caught on the gleam of fabric and the expanse of skin that begged to be made red by his mouth.

Neah, Zennon, and Sonnet, strangely enough, entered the ballroom as if they had not a care in the world. Maybe it was only Wren who could see the tension in Neah's shoulders, the way her eyes scanned the room for threats as they eased their way through the crowd.

He swallowed, eyes caught on the way the silver material draped across Neah's body, more provocative than if she'd simply been naked. It was loose but somehow clung to her curves, the shimmering material nearly looking metallic in the lights of the room.

Next to him, Gabriel cursed. A long string of muttered oaths that made even Wren blink, but he realised why when he finally pulled his eyes from Neah to glance over her companions. He did a double take when he looked at Sonnet, her dress was nearly translucent but masterfully crafted to reveal nothing.

And yet, on Wren's otherside, he heard Skye choke when Sonnet turned and her bare back was displayed.

This was more than just a late and dramatic arrival, or a display of wealth and beauty. No, this was strategy and it had Neah's name written all over it. A taunt to whoever had tried to kill Zennon, a *fuck you* in the language of the court.

"Quite stunning, aren't they?" An unexpected voice said and Wren blinked, pulling himself out of his own head to acknowledge the newcomer.

"Uncle. Yes, they are… quite beautiful." Wren wasn't sure it was a descriptor adequate enough to describe Neah. Dangerous. Fierce. Like the lick of a flame on your skin, or the first droplet of rain from a thunderstorm—Neah was the beginning and the end, and she was *his*.

Wren prowled forward, eyes locked on her from across the room, watching so intently that he saw the moment she sensed him, the way her breath stuttered, her skin flushing.

They hadn't had the chance to discuss what had happened between them in the forest, and then the poisoning had happened and derailed that conversation further. But it was time, now. He just had to hope she'd come to the same conclusion he had, that they belonged together, that they were stronger as one than apart.

Yet, when he grew close, Neah stiffened and turned her back to the room. Wren hadn't realised that Gabriel and Skye had followed him until Gabe whistled underneath his breath.

"Brutal."

Wren growled and Gabe raised his hands, palms up, even as amusement gleamed in his eyes.

Zennon and Sonnet, however, didn't seem to share in whatever had provoked Neah's ire. Zennon smiled and Wren was pleased to see that she looked far better than when he'd seen her last in the infirmary wing.

"You look lovely," Wren said and was surprised when a redhead approached the women with a glass of wine in each hand. She handed one to Zennon and Wren squinted before realising who she was. "Romi. Lovely to have you with us."

Sonnet snickered. "Next time, you should try inviting her then."

Wren frowned. "I'd thought Romi had departed from our service to escape court life, but of course you're welcome," he added and Romi smiled, seemingly unperturbed by gatecrashing.

"Zennon was kind enough to insist I accompany her—and Neah and Sonnet, of course."

"Of course," Wren murmured and bristled when Skye

knocked into his side when he folded his arms across his chest. They'd opted for their formal jackets, complete with shining buttons and frothy cravats, and Wren knew Skye hated the pomp and restrictiveness of the fitted sleeves.

"How am I supposed to fight in this?" He'd once asked and Wren had barely contained his laughter as he explained to the witch-king that generally one didn't need to fight at balls. Then again, Wren had been wrong before.

"You know," Skye said, and Wren felt the energy shift as Sonnet and Skye locked eyes. "Generally you're supposed to wear clothes to these functions."

"Don't worry, you'll only have to see me naked in your dreams, seer."

"Neah," Wren pitched his voice low, tuning out Skye's retort as he reached for Neah's elbow. "Will you dance with me?"

She looked up at him, her golden eyes blazing, and Wren dropped his hand. What had changed between them to make her look at him like that? With… disappointment, and rage?

"I will not."

Whatever this was, they needed to talk about it. Near-death aside, they'd been fine before, hadn't they?

"It's a party," he said, smiling and trying to keep his tone light. "Dancing is customary."

Her jaw clenched, nostrils flaring, and he knew immediately that he'd said the wrong thing. "If you insist." She held out a hand and Gabriel, confused and clearly not paying attention, placed his hand into the palm Neah offered him. "Thank you, Gabe, how good of you."

They made to step away and Wren halted Gabe with a

hand to the inside of his shoulder, but his words were for Neah. "What are you doing?"

"Dancing. It's customary at these events, I'm told."

He scowled at his own words thrown back at him, but couldn't stop his eyes from dropping as Neah led Gabe to the center of the room and pulled him close.

Was she trying to kill him?

Gabe, for his part, looked wildly uncomfortable and that was when Wren realised Neah had been holding back the last time they'd danced.

The dancers surrounding them began to back away, giving them space, as they began to move and Gabe glanced down in surprise to find that Neah was easily keeping up with his complicated footwork. Gabriel was an excellent dancer, but Neah might just be better. If he'd been hoping to dissuade her, Gabe had miscalculated.

They twirled, the music amping up until Gabe wrapped his arms around her, lifting Neah into the air as they spun, her arms stretched out wide and her hair a golden banner behind her.

Applause broke out as the dance finished and Neah bowed to Gabe, making Wren rankle again. She would be his queen, she needn't bow to anyone.

He stood still and her eyes didn't leave his as she stalked closer and then brushed past him without looking back.

His uncle had cornered Neah not long after she passed Wren and he didn't bother to wait for their conversation to be done before he whirled around and gently took her arm in his and tugged her with him to the privacy of an alcove on the edge of the party. "Sorry, Uncle."

"What is your problem?" Neah hissed, snatching her

arm back out of his grip as soon as they settled into the shadows. "I was having a conversation."

"What's going on? You won't even look at me, and then you dance with Gabe—"

"I'm just being a good little trophy," she spat and Wren blinked, not having a clue what she was talking about. "Because that's what I am, right? A way for you to hold onto the crown, your power? Using your mate bond to further your own status... Is nothing sacred to you people?"

Wren's mouth opened and then closed. She was right, but also so very wrong. "That's not—"

"Don't lie to me, Wren."

Was that the first time she'd said his given name? It was, perhaps, not the right moment to be exhilarated by it, but he couldn't help the curve of his mouth. "*Caritas*, please, that's not true—"

"So you don't need me to secure your position? To keep the throne?"

"Well, yes, but it's—"

She held up a hand. "I'll do this, for the crown. For the kingdom. As is my duty, but that is all our bond will be."

His face fell, anger beginning to burn within him for the first time. "If you'd let me finish a damn sentence, you'd know that this is not about power. Not entirely."

But her face had already shuttered, any glimpse of vulnerability tidied away until he was surprised a layer of frost didn't coat her skin. "As you say, my king."

Wren blew out a breath and didn't stop her when she walked away. This wasn't the time or place for this conversation. They could clear all of this up later but, for now, he was irritated and not in the mood to watch her dance with Gabe and Skye all evening.

Instead, he beat a hasty retreat, his mind already whirling with ways he could explain the situation to Neah properly. But she needed time to cool off and, truthfully, so did he. They would try this again, maybe with breakfast at hand and definitely less people around, and she would understand. He hoped.

CHAPTER TWENTY-FOUR

NEAH

To Neah's utmost irritation, she couldn't say that she was having a better time at the ball for Wren's absence. Not that his presence had pleased her much, either.

He'd left not long after they'd argued and, for some reason, that had only incensed her further. It was probably contrary, she knew, but that he hadn't even tried to go after her, had instead walked away, rankled.

Zennon, on the other hand, seemed to be having a great time—aside from the fact that she'd been rip-roaringly drunk for the past hour with no sign of slowing down.

"She's beautiful, right? And talented. I mean…" Zen gestured to her dress with an exaggerated flourish that made Neah snort. "And her name! So interesting. Rooowmi. Rowmeee."

"Yes?"

Zennon sat upright, sloshing half her drink with the motion as she looked at the seamstress with wide eyes, clearly not having seen her approach. "Oh. I, well—My dress! It's lovely. Thank you."

Romi smiled and flicked her long red hair over one shoulder. "You're welcome."

The smile on Zennon's face stayed pasted on until Romi left and then it widened, tinged with hysteria. "I saved that, right?"

Neah shrugged. "Probably. Why don't you ask her to dance?"

Zen tilted her head, accidentally timing the motion to the orchestral music, and then dismissed Neah's suggestion. "No, I couldn't. I'm a perfectly fine dancer while sober. But now…"

True. Zennon was liable to have two left feet at this point. "Breakfast then, tomorrow."

She was relatively sure that whoever had attempted the poisoning before wouldn't try again, not only because they'd been unsuccessful the first time but also because the kind of magic they'd wielded had likely exhausted them. Sonnet felt it was unlikely they would be able to replicate it so soon after the first attempt. But still, Neah felt better eating in the privacy of their chambers, where she could inspect the food and drink thoroughly before consuming anything.

Sonnet had wandered off with Gabe some time ago, with a sour-faced Skye trailing behind them like a disgruntled chaperone. It made Neah antsy to have her small group split up so widely, and even more on edge when she pondered when Wren's friends had begun to feel like *hers* too. Maybe it was the shifter in her, but she'd much rather have kept Zen and Sonnet close where she could watch for threats and reassure herself with their scents. The thought was so ridiculous that Neah rolled her eyes as Zennon continued to follow Romi's movements around the room with her eyes.

"I think I'll be too hungover tomorrow for breakfast," she said eventually and Neah hummed in acknowledgement. She'd barely touched the drinks, preferring to remain alert given the display they'd put on with their late entrance. And yet, part of her preened at the reminder, at the power she'd felt walking in with Sonnet and Zennon, daring anyone there to lay a finger on them. She'd hoped to lay the rumours of Zennon and Wren to rest that night, but it was hard to do without him present. Still, the message they'd given was clear—they'd tried to kill them, and they had *failed*.

Zennon yawned and stretched, accepting Neah's hand when she offered it and pulled her sister to standing. Catching her when she swayed, Neah wrapped an arm around Zen's waist and they began the slow shuffle back to their chamber.

As fun as it had been, getting dressed up and having fun with Zen and Sonnet, Neah couldn't deny her exhaustion. It felt like she'd been on edge ever since Zennon had taken ill, waiting for the next attack. As a result, she'd tossed and turned more than usual and now her eyes felt heavy. The only peaceful sleep she'd had was in Wren's arms and it pissed her off. She should be able to sleep just fine without him, damn it.

"Did you have a nice time?" Zennon slurred, resting her head against Neah's shoulder as they finally left the ballroom and entered the hall just outside where guests lingered. Some were as drunk as Zennon and looked to be heading out for the night, others appeared to have gone in search of privacy and given up, kissing in the halls.

Neah rolled her eyes. Some things didn't change, even at court.

A clatter to their left drew Neah's attention, her exhaustion making her slower to react than she might otherwise have been as she took in the seven guards running toward them. She even recognised one of them, Dean Grandy, as the guard she'd met when she'd first arrived at court.

That was why it took so long for her to recognise them as the enemy.

A sword swung, the sound of the metal kicking in Neah's instincts even as her brain tried to understand what was happening. She threw an arm out and across Zennon's chest, pressing her back into a dip that ensured the sword passed safely overhead.

Her dress didn't end up with pockets, much to her sadness, so Neah settled for the next best way to secure a weapon in the moment—kicking one out of the hand of an approaching unfamiliar guard and catching it in midair.

By then, the onlookers had realised what was happening and began to scream, calling for help, and Neah wanted to laugh because the guards *were* the help. Except, they were attacking them unprovoked. She sniffed gently but found no traces of magic on the air, so it didn't appear that they were being controlled, which just left...

"Traitors," she growled, eyes on Dean who raised his chin as if in challenge. Whoever was behind this had learned from their mistakes. Seven guards to do their dirty work. Four she could have taken, five at a push, but seven… They were armed and closing in and maybe she could have fought them off if she'd been alone, but the chances of them getting to Zennon, of hurting her, were too great. But what other choice did she have?

One man had stepped forward, as if to offer his assistance, and Neah would have been grateful if he hadn't been run through by a sword almost instantly.

"What do we do?" Zennon rasped, voice hoarse and pupils blown wide.

"You remember the most important lesson I taught you?" Neah asked, keeping an eye on the encroaching guards as Zennon nodded. "I'll be right behind you."

Neah didn't wait for a response, or for the guards to surround them completely. Instead, she lunged forward, striking out with her borrowed sword and sweeping her leg out and under the assailant to her right. "Go!"

Zennon ran and Neah bought her time, tackling the first guard who made to chase her sister and disemboweling the one that followed. A sword clanged against her own as she parried and knocked a guard to their back with a kick to the chest, growling when he almost immediately got back to his feet. For half a second, she thought maybe they could do this.

She was wrong.

Zennon cried out and Neah wrenched her sword free from the shoulder of the guard in front of her before spinning, eyes flying wide as she took in the scene in front of her. Zen had gotten further than Neah had hoped, but it wasn't far enough.

Her dress was an inky pool against the stone floor, her

hair spilling out around her in a fan that would have seemed graceful if it wasn't also deadly. One guard was down, presumably the one who'd brought her to the floor, but the other…

Neah shook her head, her sword clanging to the floor as she dropped it and ran, even as she knew she wouldn't make it in time. The guard's sword was already descending, Zennon's eyes were fluttering closed, and Neah's scream sounded more like a roar as she pushed herself to run faster, to leap further than she ever had before. Because if she didn't, Zennon would be dead. And Zennon *couldn't* be dead. Neah would not allow it.

Her body arced through the air, a warm tingle running across her skin as she closed the distance. Need overwhelmed her. Thoughts a confusing jumble of *protect protect protect* and *kill kill kill* and then her teeth were in the guard's throat, his body knocked to one side as she collided with him and shook him like a rag doll in her mouth.

Gasps and shouts were too loud for her sensitive ears and her muscles locked, immediately preparing for another threat, but none of the people who'd finally run out of the ballroom approached.

Green marked the floor and she sniffed at it, satisfied that the puddle didn't belong to her or hers, and when the guard Zennon had knocked down regained consciousness, his eyes widened as he took Neah in. It was the guard she'd recognised, Dean, and when his muscles twitched, preparing to move, she didn't hesitate.

Two paws hit his chest, knocking him down as her claws shredded the front of his uniform. If not for the small, human hand that touched her flank, Neah would have killed him.

As it was, she turned and cocked her head, sniffing deeply at the woman beside her who smelled like kin.

"Don't kill him. We might need him. For information."

The words felt like being underwater, muffled and warped, but she understood them and backed away from the fallen guard, the stench of his urine making her swat at her nose.

A crowd had gathered around them and Neah couldn't parse who was friend or foe, a low growl beginning in the back of her throat and slowly growing louder as they continued to whisper and murmur amongst themselves. Brightness made her eyes narrow, the glow belonging to a woman who approached slowly, her hands up as if to signal she meant no harm. Neah snapped at her, not liking the way her magic stung the air around them like tiny wasps.

The girl who was kin was speaking to the witch, the words too fast for Neah to follow, but then her attention was diverted by the arrival of a man. Familiar, and yet not. His hair was peppered with lightness and he approached without hesitation or concern, dropping to his knees in the green puddle and beamed as if death didn't surround them.

He smelled the same as the other girl, like kin, but when his skin faded away and a black panther took his place, she recoiled. Every instinct telling her to move closer to the girl, to protect. As if realising his mistake, the man reappeared in a shimmer of light.

"Go," he said and Neah tensed. He couldn't make her leave the girl. The kin.

"She is mine as she is yours," he said quietly and Neah allowed one paw to slide back and away. "I'll take care of her now. You're needed elsewhere."

She was? The words didn't seem correct, and yet a small thread inside of her seemed to throb in response. As if telling her, *yes, yes, go, run, find him.*

Another paw moved away and then another, until Neah was moving, following the thread inside that pulled her closer. Her pace increased, her paws hitting the ground with a rhythmic thump that seemed too heavy, not quite right.

People dove out of her way or shrank back against the walls even as they exclaimed their surprise, but she didn't pause. Couldn't. Just followed the call that drew her in like a siren song.

A man, human, stood outside of the door she wanted. To his credit, he didn't hesitate, just turned the handle and ushered her in as if this were a regular occurrence. She couldn't say for sure yet whether that was true. Her surroundings were unfamiliar, but the scent of the male naked in the bed next door echoed inside of her, his soul filling in the crevices of her own, the thread drawing taut as she approached the end of the bed.

As if he sensed her, the man sat up, hair mussed and sheets pooling to his waist before a slow grin curled his mouth. "There you are."

CHAPTER TWENTY-FIVE

WREN

The soft closing of the door woke him, a strange swelling in his chest making him feel light headed as he lay perfectly still. Who would come here, into his chambers, uninvited? Was this a precursor to another attack, this time on him directly?

A rumble vibrated through the air, making his skin ripple in response. He dropped the act, sitting upright and squinting into the darkness until his eyes lit on two golden orbs that pierced the shadows surrounding his bed.

He inhaled, knowing what he would scent but needing to confirm it nonetheless. His eyes slipped closed as he luxuriated in it, in *her*, before he opened them once more and grinned at the tiger in his bedroom. "There you are."

Neah growled and Wren shivered as the sound rolled over him. He needed to see her. All of her.

Matches sat on his bedside table and he struck one, the drag of the tip against the rough card too loud in the quiet of the room. He almost felt hunted, like she was watching him and waiting—though for what, he couldn't be sure.

The light flared and he ushered it to the waiting set of pillar candles before waving the stick to extinguish the flame. Gold, soft light illuminated the room, flickering against the stone walls and Wren swallowed hard as he turned slowly and drank in the sight of Neah.

Exquisite. Her fur was thick, her stripes a stark black against the deep russet of her fur. She was larger than he'd expected, he could tell despite the fact that she was hunkered down close to the floor. It was more than likely that she'd come up to his chest if they were both standing, but if he were to transform he knew he'd stand only slightly taller than her.

Wren had been so focused on seeing her, finally in her shifted form, that he hadn't noticed the smell at first.

"*Caritas.*" His eyes widened as he threw off the white sheets and darted to her side. "Why can I smell blood? Are you hurt?"

The plaintive whine she uttered in response had his heart beating wildly, unsure, as he scanned her for injuries and found only the blood he'd scented coating her paws and maw.

"It's okay," he said quietly, crouching down so he could look intently into her eyes. "Many of us lose control the first time. Everything is new, heightened. If you hurt someone, nobody will blame you."

She blinked at him and he knew that was all the response he'd get until she was able to shift back. For some, it happened almost immediately and others it took days. Wren had spent a week as a tiger before he'd managed to regain his human form none the worse for wear, aside from a craving for particularly bloody steak.

"I can have a bath drawn, if you like?" He offered this even as he pondered the logistics of getting a tiger into the bathtub in front of the hearth. Neah said nothing in response, of course, and he sighed. Perhaps now was as good a time as any to have some of the more difficult conversations he'd been avoiding—especially when she couldn't talk back or interrupt him. He chuckled lightly at the thought and Neah flexed her claws against the hardwood floor.

"You know, the first time I shifted I killed a deer and harassed the chicken coop held in the town. So really, you've done very well so far." He cleared his throat, cautiously extending a hand and smiling when her nose twitched, sniffing him, before he pressed a hand to the space just above her eyes. The fur was softer than he'd imagined and her eyes slid closed as he stroked soothingly, a purr rumbling up and through her body, startling her.

"It's okay. What happens as a cat, stays as a cat," he teased, and the growl that left her sounded distinctly Neah-like. "Do you want to stay down here? Or come up to the bed?"

He was fairly certain the bed could take her weight, he'd collapsed upon it in his own shifted form more than once, though he couldn't imagine the palace's keepers would be too happy about the blood that would stain the white sheets.

Neah stood in a fluid motion that he watched with awe, the grace in her movements surprising. She'd adapted to this form far quicker than he had the first time he'd shifted, no better than a newborn tottering around on unsteady legs at first. What he was most curious about, however, was what had triggered her to finally shift. Why now?

The tiger leapt up and onto the bed, rolling around in the sheets with her stomach bared to the ceiling and he couldn't hold back his laugh. She'd likely kill him for saying so, but sprawled out like an oversized tabby, she was unbearably cute.

Wren climbed onto the bed with her, pleased when neither the tiger nor the bed protested, and rolled onto his side in time for her to curl her head beneath his chin. He debated shifting for half a second, before deciding the bed likely couldn't take the weight of two full-grown tigers— and anyway, Neah would likely benefit more from having him in human form and able to talk her through the shift back.

"I'm sorry for what happened earlier, when we fought." The words were quiet but steady and when a growl was breathed into his throat he rolled his eyes. "We need to talk about this. Because it's not what you think. Yes, I needed a mate to help me keep my crown, but the real reason I sought you out is because I am cursed."

She fell very still in his arms, only the soft chuff of her breath letting him know she was still listening.

"If I'd had a choice, I would have done things differently. Met you under different circumstances, maybe. Instead, I had to act with the hand I was dealt. You understand?" Silence met his words and he found that more reassuring than any words she might have said. She wasn't pulling away, or trying to rip his throat out, and Wren considered both of those things a success. "My bloodline was cursed a long time ago—long enough that its origins are unknown. Some say by a God, others by a witch. All I know for sure is the consequences—without finding my mate and cementing the bond by my twenty-fifth birthday, I would be lost to my tiger form, mind shattered, no better than an animal. Forever."

Wren's breaths stuttered momentarily and, for the first time, he recognised the true fear the thought held. "It would be devastating for the kingdom, as I have no direct heirs, and leave us open to attack while we're weakest. But also…" He sucked in a breath and pitched his voice low enough that she might not have heard him if she hadn't been curled against him the way she was. "I don't want to lose myself, Neah. The thought terrifies me. My tiger is part of me, but I don't wish to be consumed by it."

She didn't respond, because she couldn't, but the fact that she was still there, pressed close against him and a small purr beginning in her chest told him everything. Or, at least, he hoped it did.

"So now you know." He'd meant for the words to be light, cheery almost, and instead he sounded resigned. "The only thing that can halt the curse is the bonding ceremony, but I don't want you to choose this out of duty. Insanity would be a kinder fate than to be with you and unable to have you. At least spare me that misery."

The warmth of her was sinking into his bones, her weight a comforting force that grounded him until his eyes grew heavy.

"Promise me," he murmured, the words beginning to slur as he fought to stay awake. "Promise me that if you choose this, it's for yourself. Anything else is…

unacceptable." Wren mumbled the last and when he fell into sleep it was with the warmth of a tiger wrapped around his heart.

He had fallen asleep in the sun again. It was warm, stifling really, and Wren found he was having trouble breathing amidst the soft fluff pressed to his face.

Fluff?

His eyes blinked open and he grunted as he rolled, sucking in a breath of air greedily as he realised he hadn't fallen asleep lounging in the sun as he so often did in his tiger form. Instead, he was sharing his bed with a tiger— one that had sprawled out to take up the majority of the bed and had even claimed the covers.

Something about the sight of a tiger tucked beneath the sheets amused him enough that he began to chuckle and once he started, he couldn't stop. One tiger eye opened sleepily and then widened in an action so humanoid that Wren knew Neah had to have been more conscious in her new body than she had been last night, driven instead by instinct.

She scrambled upright, throwing him off the bed as her claws caught in the sheets and ripped them out from under him. He hit the ground with an *oof* that had her peeking over the side of the bed at him and then whipping her head away when she realised he was naked.

A modest tiger. The thought made him laugh harder and when she dared to look over the side of the bed at him again, he smiled. "Good morning, Neah."

She yawned, showing off her impressive array of sharp teeth, and then froze when she caught sight of her paws, coated in dried blood. Movements jerky, she scrambled up and off the bed, limbs slipping in different directions on the hardwood until she got them under herself again.

"Wait, where are you—"

Neah didn't pause, just bounded toward the door and then whined impatiently when he stopped to put on trousers, too slow for her liking in reaching the door to his parlour.

"If you need the bathroom, you needn't go outside," he teased, but his smile faded when he caught the wide-eyed look in her eyes and the scent of her fear in the air. "What is it, *caritas?*"

Wren opened the door and jogged to keep up with her as she raced down the corridor, gasps ringing out as the court watched the king chase the tiger. They took familiar turnings until they reached Neah's own door and Wren knocked impatiently. Neah looked liable to knock the thing down until it was pulled open and a yawning Zennon greeted them.

Her dark eyes flew open, the haze of sleep vanishing as she dropped to her knees and wrapped her arms around Neah's neck. "You're still a tiger! I was so worried about you. When you didn't come back here... Well, I was worried we'd have to send out a search party but Dad said you would be okay."

"Can we come in?" Wren said, glancing over his shoulder to the onlookers who'd paused to take in the unusual sight.

"Oh. Of course." They entered quickly and shut the

door behind them and Wren tensed when he realised there was someone else in the room. Zennon seemed to notice because she smiled reassuringly even as her shoulders rose up to nearly her ears. "It's just Romi. After last night, she didn't want me to be alone so she came back here with me." Zennon glanced at Neah and raised her brows meaningfully. "She stayed on the chaise."

Wren glanced between the two of them and frowned. "O-kay. What happened last night?"

"You haven't heard?" Zennon grimaced. "Well, I suppose if she's been like this the whole time you wouldn't have. We were attacked by a retinue of guards. Neah shifted to save me."

Ah. Suddenly, it all made sense. But why hadn't anyone retrieved him?

"Dad—Jamison," Zennon corrected, "told me to tell you that he'd speak with you in the morning. He didn't want to interrupt your night. I guess I understand why now. Was she with you the whole time?"

Wren nodded. "Tell me more about this attack."

Zennon recounted the events and Wren kept his face impassive despite his rage growing with every word. They had been targeted *again.* He had never considered himself to be much of a wrathful person before now, but he'd been wrong. When he found whoever was responsible...

Neah's ears flattened to her skull, likely scenting his rage, and Wren took a few deep breaths. "We need to fix this." He'd meant the words for Neah but Zennon was the one who answered.

"How?"

"They're coming for you because they think you're my

mate." Wren's eyes slid from Zennon to Neah and found keen understanding in her eyes. "So we'll show them that you're not." It would mean painting a target on Neah, and announcing their bond, and he could only hope that she remembered what he'd said to her the night before.

Doing this would help Zennon, and it would help him too. But he didn't want her to do this unless she was absolutely certain it was what she wanted.

Neah's head dipped and Wren loosed a sigh of relief. They could discuss the bonding ceremony and whether it was what she wanted later, but for now this was their best option to ensure Zennon's safety at least.

"Are you ready to try shifting back?"

Neah growled, as if to say, *what the Hel do you think I've been trying to do?*

"A lot of people saw her shift last night, so the rumour mill has already been fed," Zennon offered and Wren snorted. Of course it had.

"Well then, let's show them the rumours are true." Wren pushed to standing and Zennon's brows pinched together.

"What are you going to do?"

Wren smirked. "We're going to run."

CHAPTER TWENTY-SIX

NEAH

Things felt different. Clearer than yesterday, when her thoughts had felt like a jumble of scents and sensations driven more by instinct than logic. And Wren had been… surprisingly sweet.

Now though, he was firmly in kingly plotting mode. He stood, towering over Zennon in a way Neah didn't much like, and then a shimmer of light rippled over him and in his place stood a tiger that was a larger but identical version to her own form. She'd caught sight of herself in the mirror and could hardly believe this was *her*. After all this time, she'd finally fucking shifted. Her eyes, though, looked the same. Anchoring her into this new reality.

Wren turned to her, nudging at her face with his as he sniffed at her and Zennon's laughter drew Neah's attention.

"Well, that's one way to get them talking." Zennon walked them to the door just as Romi appeared from the bed chamber, eyes widening at the two wild beasts in the foyer. "Go. Have fun. Be safe."

Neah brushed against her sister as she left and Zennon nodded, understanding what Neah couldn't say. *You too.*

If the reactions to one tiger stalking the halls while being chased by the king were shocked, then the court was downright flabbergasted to see the two of them.

Neah caught hints of conversation as they stalked through the halls, more than she was used to being able to hear. She'd thought her senses in her human form had been sharp, but this was another level altogether.

"You see? I told you it wasn't the wine! She shifted in the middle of the ball—"

"Pack up our things, Esmerelda. The king's found himself a mate and there's certainly no other men of status worth your time here—"

"The king has been blessed by the Goddess! Praise Selene! Long live the king!"

The last speaker had Neah's eyes rolling skyward as they descended the stairs that would lead them to the palace's entry way and, finally, to the forest.

Fresh air drifted in toward her on the breeze and Neah raised her head, inhaling deeply, amazed by the layers to the wind in this form. Her pace picked up, eager to see what else was different about the forest on four paws, and Wren gave a little yip that seemed ridiculous coming from an animal so large.

Before she knew it, they'd cleared the last of the stairs and were out the small side door that led to the forest, rather than the stone entryway where the carriages came and went as they ferried nobles.

The ground under Neah's feet was softer than she had anticipated, the dirt crumbling in places and slippery in others. She had assumed it would feel like walking barefoot, but the sensation was completely different. The grass tickled and droplets of dew dampened her fur, and then the wind changed and she could smell *everything*.

Wren nudged her and then bounded off ahead, as if to taunt her. But it felt different to the last time they'd been together in the forest. This felt playful.

He darted away and Neah gave chase, tongue lolling out to taste the wind as they kicked up the scents of the forest with their claws. Wren was bigger, so his stride was longer, but she had always been fast.

They collided, rolling over and over until they came to a halt on the edge of a lake she hadn't even known was there before this. Wren shook off the dirt and leaves that she'd mashed into his coat and then shot her a look that made her huff out a laugh in the form of a breath.

Their forms were one as they bounded forward together, splashing into the water with a reckless abandon that made her feel untethered, the shock of icy cold freshness pushing into her with an insistence that felt a lot like freedom as she swam in lazy circles.

Now that they'd all but announced to the world that they were mated, things would change for her. She couldn't very well maintain her cover as a spy in enemy courts as the king's mate. Her time as a spy had come to an end and, to her surprise, she was very okay with that. She'd been pleased to serve, and to travel and see the kingdom, but it had come at the expense of her family, her loneliness. Maybe it was time for a new kind of life.

Warmth cascaded over her and suddenly skin replaced fur, fingers appeared where claws had been and the cold that had felt luxurious before was piercing against her more fragile human skin.

Wren had looked up at the flash of light and from one second to the next he changed from beast to man, grinning. She started to shake and his smile faded into a look of concern as he dipped under the water and appeared at her side with his hair slicked back.

"What's wrong?" The words were quiet and when thunder rumbled overhead it felt like they were in a cocoon of safety. Nothing else besides them, at this moment, mattered. Not being strong, or keeping him at arms length to protect her heart, and Neah realised she was so tired of fighting.

"What if I can't do it again?" The words were small and she was relieved when Wren didn't mock her. Instead, he pushed a wet strand of hair away from her face and smiled gently.

"You can. It'll always be there, waiting inside of you. Like it had been from the start."

She wished she could share in his confidence.

"Thank you for last night," she said finally as their eyes caught and held, the space between them seeming inconsequential as rain began to hit the surface of the water, creating mini ripples that cascaded out until the lake appeared to have a current.

Wren's brows furrowed. "For what? I didn't do anything."

She shook her head. It wasn't true in the least. He'd done *everything*. Reassured her when she hadn't even known she'd needed it, told her it was okay to have lost herself in the instincts, to have killed, even before he'd known what had happened, and best—or maybe worst—of all, he'd sleepily told her to do the one thing she'd never done before. To choose herself. To put her wants and needs first.

It had always been the kingdom, the family, and then her own desires—in that order. And Wren had thrown all of that out of the window, like nothing else could be more important than her happiness. Maybe that was what she'd needed her whole life, for someone to tell her it was okay to choose herself sometimes.

His golden eyes had darkened, the clouds reflected in his gaze as he watched her for any indication of her thoughts. So she decided to show him what she was feeling the best way she knew how.

Their lips met and tingles zipped up her spine, spreading out beneath his touch, his mouth, until all she could breathe and taste was Wren. His lips parted and she followed his lead, tasting his mouth with a hesitancy that he ignored, devouring her like he'd been waiting for this moment his whole life.

The rain fell harder and her nipples pebbled from his touch rather than the cold as Wren lifted her from the water and her legs locked around his waist. While he had managed to reconjure his trousers with his shift, she had yet to learn that nifty ability, and so her bare skin pressed to his slick chest. Her breasts crushed against him as burning hot kisses trailed from her throat to her chest.

Neah barely noticed that they were moving until her back hit the soft grass near the water's edge. A large

Valeneos tree offered them some shelter overhead, the rain pattering softly against its leaves on the way down as Wren drank in the sight of her sprawled out beneath him.

"Beautiful," he rasped, and when he kissed her again she knew he meant it. It was clear in the delicate reverence of his touch as his hands moved down her sides, coasting across her arms, feeling out the curve of her waist, and then his mouth found the rigid peak of her breasts. She gasped and he smirked as his hot tongue worked in circles against her nipple, pleasure shooting directly to her core and making her throb as he relinquished one breast and repeated the process on the other.

Her thighs parted, welcoming him closer, and her legs locked around his hips as she tried to relieve the building pressure by rocking against him.

"Patience, mate. I've heard it's a virtue."

"You know what else is a virtue?" she growled. "Putting your mouth to good use and—"

Her moan was lost in the sound of the thunder, booming around them and making her heart jump in her chest as Wren's mouth was, indeed, put to good use.

Neah remembered exactly how talented his tongue was from the last time they'd been out here and under the influence of the moon, but this felt more measured, unhurried, like he could feast on her for hours until she was a writhing, whimpering, mess.

Wren's tongue darted against the center of her where she throbbed for him, a rumble of satisfaction vibrating his chest as he pulled back and grabbed a hold of her thighs, lifting her pussy up to his face so he could taste her.

If she'd thought she knew what it was like to be claimed before, she'd been wrong.

Her hips bucked and she cried out as Wren suctioned against her clit and then curled his tongue into her opening, licking into her in deep strokes that made her head feel fuzzy.

"You taste like fucking heaven," he growled against her flesh and she whimpered as his breath teased her sensitive skin. "You taste like *mine*."

His tongue plunged back into her, pressing into her inner walls until her cries turned to high pitched mewls. Still he continued. Two fingers pressed into her heat, curling and rubbing her into an exhausted second orgasm before he spread his fingers inside of her, adding a third and fourth and laughing when her eyes widened.

"Need to get you ready for me, mate." He pulled down his trousers, freeing himself, and she swallowed hard as she took in the size of him. "You're going to take every inch."

"I–" Neah cleared her throat and tried again. "I don't think that's going to fit." She'd been with men before, but Wren... he was bigger than any she'd had before.

"It'll fit, *caritas*. I promise." The dark heat in his voice made her impossibly wetter and he grinned, feeling it against his fingers as he worked them into her at an increased pace, the sound of her wetness lewd amid the fresh waves of rain. "You're already taking me so well," he groaned, the words guttural, and she tilted her hips, encouraging him to go deeper, to give her *more*. He dipped his head, working her clit with his mouth again, and the pulses of pleasure seemed constant as she begged him with her mouth and body. He could give her more. He could give her all of him, and she wanted it. Desperately.

"Wren," she begged, sitting up and meeting his own lust-glazed eyes as he pumped himself with one hand, smearing the glistening mess at his head across the rest of him. "Now."

The first touch of him against her made them both moan as he pushed through her wetness, nudging at her clit with each thrust, before he halted the movement, the muscles in his body standing out in sharp relief as he fought for control.

"Let go," she murmured, willing him to lose himself in her, in *them*, and with a groan he obeyed. There was no delay, no more warning, just the thick length of him filling her in one swift movement of heat.

Their pace was frenzied, the rough rhythm of his hips against hers hitting all the spots she hadn't known she'd craved until he slowed to look down at where she swallowed him whole.

"Look at you," he said, voice soft, reverent. "Taking me like you were made for me. Do you see, Neah?" She followed his gaze and couldn't help the way she clenched around him as he pushed into her, making him inhale sharply. "Fuck."

It was like the one action shattered what remained of his self-control, turning him wild, and she wanted to crow in victory. Instead, she widened her legs and pressed up to meet him mid-thrust, taking him by surprise. Wren's hands came under her, holding her in place at the new, deeper, angle as he bottomed out inside of her over and over again. One hand fell away and he maintained her position with only one arm as his other dropped to her clit, working her in circles that timed perfectly with the push and pull of his cock. She clenched around him as she increased their pace by pressing up and into him relentlessly.

"Neah—" It was a hoarse shout and she grinned as he came, feeling him pulse inside of her, and when his eyes re-opened there was a fire in them that made her breathless. "You'll pay for that, mate. You come first. Always."

"I already did come, several times if you'll recall," she tried to keep her tone even but couldn't help the way her breath hitched when he continued moving inside of her, thrusting shallowly before surprising her with a deeper plunge. Sparks of pleasure made her skin tingle and it felt like the rain should have been turning to steam what with the heat they were kicking off as Wren's hands tightened on her body.

"You know what I meant. But, I have to say, this is definitely a perk." He looked down an she glanced too, just in time to see him scoop his come up with two fingers from where it leaked out of her and press it back into her pussy in time with his next thrust. "Do you like being full of me? I think you do." He smirked when she panted, shuddering as she tried to encourage him to pick up his pace. Droplets of water from his wet hair hit her skin and she licked her lips, looking down the length of her body to catch another glimpse of him disappearing inside of her. "What do you want, Neah? Tell me."

"Faster."

"What?"

Bastard. "Fuck. Me. Faster."

He gave her no warning, just hiked her legs high and

fucked into her with enough power that she shrieked with pleasure, letting him position her however he wanted as Wren worked her into oblivion. Her orgasm crashed down around them with the same velocity of the thunder storm, her cries lost to the rain and wind as pleasure ripped through her until she was left boneless and spent in his arms.

The storm raged on, as if unaware of their crescendo, and Neah let the rain wash over her as she tried to regain her breath.

"We have a problem to consider now," she said and Wren looked at her, alarmed, from where he'd flopped down beside her in the dirt. "How, by the Goddess, are we going to get back inside without being seen?"

In the end, Wren returned to the palace in his tiger form to retrieve some much-needed clothing for Neah—seeing as she didn't have a firm grip yet on how to shift at will, nor a desire to parade through the palace naked.

To her surprise, Wren brought her back to his chambers instead of her own and had a steaming hot bath waiting, as well as fresh, unbloodied, sheets on the bed. The hot water was bliss on her muddied, chilled, skin and when he dragged a chair over to the beside the bath she glanced at him in surprise.

"What are you doing?" He'd already exhausted her in the forest, so if he was thinking about climbing in for another round…

"Taking care of you." Wren's voice was husky as he

rolled up his shirt sleeves and dunked his hands in the water before reaching for the soap. Her eyes grew heavy as she watched him work the bar into a lather and then groaned when he set about massaging the suds into her hair.

Had anyone ever taken care of her like this before? If they had, she couldn't remember it. It felt… nice. Like she was the most important thing in his world and he didn't mind showing her as much.

Wren's long fingers massaged her head from the base to her temples for several long minutes until he was satisfied and rinsed the soap away with cupped hands of warm water.

"Sit up," he said quietly and she jumped, having grown sleepy in the steam and the gentle pressure of his hand in her hair. The water sloshed as she obeyed and she shivered as her hair dripped water down her back until Wren scooped it up and over her shoulder.

He picked another soap, this one smelling faintly floral, and began to work it into her tense shoulder muscles, the back of her neck, and down her spine.

It had felt strange being back on two legs instead of four, despite that she'd spent most of her life on two legs. There was a disconnect now between her body and mind, like she half expected to look down and find fur and claws and was confused to instead find smooth skin. But Wren's touch was syncing her body back in place, grounding her with each stroke of his fingers against her spine, each press of his hand against her skin.

More scooped water washed away the suds, the water clouding with dirt and leaves, and when she stood, ready to leave the filth behind, Wren looked away from her naked body as he held a fluffy towel stretched wide. Only once she was wrapped up did he look down at her with a small smile on his mouth.

"It's nothing you haven't already seen," she challenged and he half-nodded, half-shrugged.

"True. But that doesn't make me entitled to it."

Holding his eyes, she dropped the towel and was pleased when he swallowed hard before accepting her invitation and letting his eyes roam. Each look was a soft caress that set her on fire, but she was distracted from any further thoughts of ardour when a murmur of voices sounded from the next room.

Alarmed, she snatched up the towel and was readying herself for a fight when Wren caught her hand in his. "It's okay. It's just our friends."

Our friends. She'd noted the shift yesterday at the ball and it warmed her to know that he felt the same way. At some point, their small circles had combined to become an *our* and Neah couldn't say that she disliked the sound of it. Like a family they'd chosen for themselves.

"Here." Wren strode to the bed and handed her a bundle of clothing as well as her favourite moisturiser and body oil. "I hope this is okay. I didn't rummage through your things, I promise, Zennon retrieved them when I asked and—"

She cut him off with a quick, breathless, kiss. "Thank you."

A hint of pink tinted his cheeks as he nodded. "I, ah, have another bath being drawn. You can get dressed in here if you like. There's food waiting in the next room, provided those heathens haven't eaten it all." He raised his voice at the last part of his sentence and it fell suspiciously silent next door as a result, making Wren roll his eyes.

Neah slathered on her moisturiser and oil, feeling more herself already as she slipped into a simple tunic shirt with an open collar and a pair of supple trousers she was sure were Zennon's because she didn't recognise them at all.

Attendants entered the room as she combed her hair and Neah thanked them as they set about clearing away the dirty bathwater and resetting the bath for Wren.

It wasn't until she walked into the parlour that she realised how hungry she was, the scent of roasted chicken and buttery potato wafting toward her. "You better have saved me some of that. I've heard tigers have a terrible temper when they're hungry."

Zennon looked up, a smile spreading across her face as she ran to Neah and hugged her so hard the breath was pushed forcefully out of her lungs. "You're okay."

"I am. And you?" She ran her eyes over her sister, checking for injuries, and was relieved when she found none. "You saw the healer?"

Zen nodded. "Just a few bruises." Her gaze dropped to the trousers Neah wore and she grinned. "Romi! Look, they fit even better than you hoped!"

Neah blinked as she finally took in the rest of the table's occupants. Gabriel and Skye, she'd expected. Zennon and Sonnet, she'd hoped for—but Romi was a surprise, though a welcome one.

"You made these for me?"

Romi stood from her place at the table and approached

cautiously. "I sew when I'm stressed. I made them for you last night, while I was with Zen."

Zen. So they were already close enough for nicknames. Neah hid her smile as she reached for Romi's hand. "Thank you for staying with her. And for the trousers, they're stunning."

"Oh, that's alright, I just repurposed an old pair you had that didn't look like they'd still fit and—"

"You're welcome," Zennon said, nudging Romi in the side while she smiled at Neah. "And I saved you and Wren a plate before those two could devour everything." She cast a stern glance at Gabe and Skye who blinked innocently back at her.

Neah followed them over to the table and took a seat beside Sonnet, sliding her a questioning glance and relaxing when she nodded. Everyone was okay. For now.

The sound of water sloshing in the next room made her cheeks heat as she tried to focus on her food and not the images of a naked Wren just meters away. Chatter resumed around the table but her sister watched Neah closely, as if expecting her to break at any moment.

Neah finished her chicken and had moved on to the potatoes when Sonnet spoke up.

"So, you and the king." She waggled her brows and Neah groaned. "You're accepting the bond?"

Wren poked his head around the corner, wet strands of hair leaving see-through droplets on his white shirt. "We haven't discussed it yet, witch. Butt out."

Neah smirked and opted to stay silent on the matter for now, lest she be scolded next. "What brings you all here?"

Gabe's eyes bugged out, like she'd asked something

insane, and Zennon coughed to hide a laugh. "You do remember the small fleet of guards that attempted to kill you only a night ago?"

"Mm," Neah said, tapping her finger on her chin. "And where were you for that, again?"

Gabe glanced almost imperceptibly at Sonnet before he narrowed his eyes. "Busy."

"Yes, well, luckily for you, I was around."

Gabe looked set to argue when Wren walked in, barefoot as he rolled the sleeves of his white shirt up to his elbows.

"Seven guards." There was a grim set to Wren's mouth that made Neah shift uneasily in her seat. "*My* guards. How were they turned against me? And by whom?" Silence reigned and Wren sighed as he sprawled into the empty armchair closest to the bedroom door. "Whoever it is, they knew that Zennon was here as my mate—misguided as the sentiment might have been," he added with a pointed look in Sonnet's direction. "That intel was limited to the people there for the ceremony, and the king's guards who were sent to retrieve Zennon in my place."

"And the Captain," Neah pointed out and then shrugged at Zennon's incredulous look. "I'm not saying he did it, just stating the facts."

"So who does that narrow things down to?" Skye said, brow furrowed.

Wren ticked the names off on his hands. "Me, you, Gabe, Sonnet, my mother, my uncle, Jamison, his second, my cousin, and the retinue of guards."

"And, theoretically, any of them could have told someone else," Neah added. "But that list isn't exhaustive anyway, because the assassination plot I discovered was being discussed before you retrieved Zennon. And didn't you say that rumours were spread in the court in your absence? Whoever our enemy is, they've been around for longer than just your ceremony."

"That's presuming it's the same person," Sonnet said thoughtfully. "Or that it's only one person at all."

Neah stabbed at her remaining potatoes more forcefully than necessary and chewed silently as the others shared worried looks.

"Who stands to gain the most from your death?" Romi offered and then shrank back when all eyes turned to her before catching herself and straightening her spine. "As best I can tell, the most common reasons for murder are money, power, love, and revenge."

"That narrows it down," Sonnet muttered and Neah sighed, because she was right.

"Okay, fine. Let's just let that simmer in our brains for a second. What about the curse? Have you found anything?"

Zennon frowned and mouthed, *curse?* to Neah who waved her off. She would explain later.

Sonnet and Skye shared a begrudging look of dissatisfaction. "Nothing yet. We can tell the curse is there, and it's real, but not how to remove it."

"Yet," Skye added and Sonnet slowly nodded.

"Yet," she agreed.

Wren scrubbed a hand down and over his face before nodding. "Okay. Thank you for trying."

"Hey, we're not giving up." Skye frowned. "And neither should you. Of course, this would all be a lot less urgent if Neah agreed to the bonding ceremony." Skye's arms folded across his chest and Neah raised a cool brow at him in response.

A low growl erupted from the other side of the table and Neah's eyes jerked up to find Wren's glowing irises locked on Skye. "Neah's decision is for her alone to make. Anything else is unacceptable. We'll find another way."

Skye shook his head, pushing to a stand and pointing a finger in her direction. "But she could—"

He didn't finish the sentence before Wren had shifted and knocked him down to the floor. The pair rolled, grunting and yowling while the rest of them looked on.

"Should we break this up...?" Romi winced when Skye thrust a particularly vicious elbow into the tiger's jaw.

Gabe seemed unbothered, snagging a piece of chicken from Wren's unattended plate. "Nah. Let them work it out. Wren's instincts are probably running wild with the unclaimed mating bond—no pressure," he added hastily as the tiger snapped its teeth mere breaths away from Skye's face until he conceded.

The tiger retreated and a flare of magic returned Wren to his human form. He stood and snatched his dinner away from Gabriel with one final warning look to Skye.

"It's been a long day," he said eventually. "Let's talk more about all this later?"

The group mumbled their assent and Zennon paused before she could shuffle out of the door with the others. "Oh, I forgot to mention—Jamison has organised a dinner for you both, tomorrow afternoon."

Neah frowned. "A dinner? Why?"

"Because you're mated to the king," Zennon said, a

touch of exasperation in her voice. "And your parents would like to meet their son in law."

Son in law. Neah nearly choked. "Right."

Zennon left while Neah was still contemplating the words and when she looked up, she found she was alone again with Wren.

"We don't have to go," he offered. "I'm the king."

"And he's my father." She smirked. "I think on this, he outranks you."

Wren sighed. "That's exactly what I was afraid of." They laughed and when Neah made to stand and approach the door, she halted in place when Wren's soft voice reached her. "Stay. Please."

She swallowed hard but let her hand fall from the handle. "Are you sure?"

"Yes. Although, I hope you share the covers better in this form than you did as a tiger."

"I'll try," she teased and when she followed him back into the bedroom, she was surprised to feel something she hadn't felt in a long time: fully and completely, safe.

CHAPTER TWENTY-SEVEN

NEAH

Soft morning light spilled across the sheets, bathing them in a glow that soothed her as Neah blinked open her eyes. Wren was still asleep next to her, breaths slow and even as the sunlight played with the brown strands of his hair.

They'd been too exhausted to do anything more than talk last night, meaningless chatter until their eyes were heavy and their words slurred. One of Wren's arms was flung over her waist, like even in his sleep he'd reached for her, and she couldn't resist the opportunity to drink him in while he slept on.

The smooth, pale skin of his back was a long line of muscle, as elegant as it was impressive, with small freckles scattered across his canvas that made him feel remarkably human. His lashes were blond at the tips and short, but curled perfectly against the crest of his cheekbone, fluttering lightly in his sleep, and she wondered for a moment about what it was that he dreamed about.

Everything between them had happened so quickly and, truthfully, it would have been easy for her to dismiss their connection as nothing more than the draw of the mate bond. Except, in the quiet moments like this, when there was nothing between them but dreams and warmth, Neah knew this wasn't just about the physical. The sex had been everything she'd imagined it would be, but she took just as much pleasure in seeing Wren like this: unguarded, relaxed, breathing easy at her side. It was a vulnerability, a trust, that she hadn't expected but that meant more than she'd anticipated.

Wren's hand flexed against her hip, fingers brushing a stretch of bare skin where her nightdress had risen up, and she closed her eyes, enjoying the warmth of him against her.

She knew she had important decisions to make—and soon, if they wanted to thwart Wren's curse. Part of her wished she could just jump in with both feet and trust that the Goddess had brought them together for a reason, but the other, more cynical, part of Neah couldn't help questioning if it was wise to tie herself permanently to a man she'd only truly known for a handful of weeks.

Of course, she'd known *of* the king for a long time but truly knowing him, measuring the kind of man he was, had barely been any time at all.

Her mother would have said that when you know, you know. But Neah had always preferred logic to the whims of the heart, it was why it felt so foreign for her to even be considering the bonding ceremony. Once done, it couldn't be undone. It would link them on this plane and the next, and to kill one would fundamentally break something in the other—or so the stories said, anyway.

Neah sighed and the sound disturbed Wren, his brow furrowing and his grip tightening on her hip before he relaxed his fingers and blearily blinked open his eyes, squinting against the sunlight.

"Morning," he mumbled and then buried his face in the pillow, only one eye peeking up at her amidst the cloud of white.

In spite of the logic she wanted to follow, at the sight of that golden iris Neah melted. "Morning."

Who needed logic anyway?

The door swung open and Neah smiled. "Mother."

Darwinia had the grace and gentle aura of a patient, timid woman. Of course, in reality, she could turn into a sleek black jaguar at the drop of a hat and had her husband eating out of the palm of her hand on a regular basis.

"Neah." Her eyes darted to the side and she inclined her head. "Your Majesty. Please forgive me, but for the duration of this meal you will be treated as a prospective suitor to my daughter rather than my king. I hope this is acceptable?"

Wren's lips twitched but he stood straighter and bowed with a flourish that made Neah roll her eyes. "Of course, Lady. Thank you for the invitation."

"Mama," another voice chimed in and Winny's eyes widened with joy.

"Zennon! I didn't know you were coming." Darwinia

pushed past Wren to wrap Zen in a tight hug and Neah grinned. "Jamison, set another place at the table."

Her father peeked around the doorframe and smiled at Zennon before it dimmed.

"He knows, Dad," she reminded him.

Jamison seemed none too pleased that the king was aware of his secret child, but Neah knew he wouldn't cause a scene about it here, even if he was unhappy about it.

Her mother ushered them inside and fussed over them as she led them to the table that had been laid out with plates and silverware. It was one of the very few times that Neah had eaten in her father's suite with her mother there too, and she couldn't remember a time when Zennon had also been able to join them.

"I wanted to do this properly, as a family," she murmured to Jamison as he brushed past her. "That includes Zennon."

"We'll discuss this later," he muttered and Neah cocked her head to one side.

"No," she said, loudly. "I don't think we will." She meant it as a fact rather than a taunt, but her dad's face flushed all the same. He never did like to discuss family, preferring to brush off her thoughts and concerns as the flights of fancy of a young girl who missed her mother and sister. But tonight wasn't about airing family drama, so Neah attempted to smooth things over. "Shall we eat?"

They took their places around the table and Neah smiled at her mother when she caught her watching Neah and Wren. They'd been sat opposite each other, with Zennon to Neah's left, her dad to her right, and her mum at the head of the table to Zennon's left.

"It looks lovely, Father." Zennon smiled as Jamison set down the plates in the middle of the table for them to take their fill of roast beef, fresh baked rolls, vegetables, and potatoes. In another life, Neah had always thought her father would have done well as a cook.

"So," Jamison began as their cutlery clattered against the plates and Neah did her best not to inspect the room like she hadn't been there before. Though, it had been several years since she'd been in the formal dining room last. It contained little more than a large table, a plush rug beneath, a pianoforte in the corner of the room, and an armoire that she knew to be a drinks cabinet. "You're going to do the bonding ceremony?"

Winny tutted. "Don't you have other questions to ask your future son-in-law first?"

Son-in-law. Neah threw a startled look at Wren and found only soft amusement on his face in return.

"I'm an open book, sir."

"I understand what you get from this arrangement," Jamison said and Neah's head jerked up and her gaze narrowed on her father. "But how does this benefit Neah? How will she continue her work if she's queen?"

"I won't," Neah cut in. "In truth, I am tired of the life of a spy. I miss my family, and peace—"

"And you think *peace* is what you'll get as queen?" Jamison snorted and Neah blew out a breath instead of launching her fork at him.

"I *think* that I will be too notable, too recognisable, after this to make an adequate spy. The benefit being that my sister will not be locked away alone in a house in a forest, nor would my mother have to resort to hiding in the shadows. They would have the utmost protection, and, at the very least, some damn company." She hadn't meant to raise her voice, but when Zennon touched a gentle hand to Neah's she realised she'd crumpled her fork into so much scrap metal.

There was a moment of silence before Jamison cleared his throat and said, "I didn't know you felt that way."

"You never asked."

She held his gaze for a second before turning back to her food, accepting a new fork when her mother passed her one.

"So you no longer want to work for me." Jamison nodded, like it was hard to get his head around. "What will you do with your time, then? Host tea parties? Take up knitting?" he scoffed.

Neah had expected some degree of difficulty from her father on the subject, knew what he thought about Wren's motivations for finding a mate. And yet, the sting in his words hurt nonetheless.

"She'll do whatever she pleases," Wren said, and Neah had never heard the low, dangerous tone before. "Whether that's knitting or hunting or popping out cubs, it will be her business. Her decision." Wren turned back to his food as if the whole table hadn't fallen silent while Jamison turned red.

Her mate took his time swallowing his food, taking a sip of wine, before he set down his cutlery and looked directly into Jamison's eyes.

"You asked me how the bond, being my queen, will benefit your daughter. I think that question is better left for her to decide. That's what I offer her: choice."

Neah's heart pounded and a shiver ran across her skin as Wren stared her father down. After a declaration like that, vouching for her independence once again, speaking up for her but not *over* her... How could she not love him for that?

The thought startled her and she froze with a piece of meat half-way to her mouth, lowering her fork in a daze as she stared at Wren from across the table.

"Well," her mother said. "Whatever you choose, darling, we'll support you."

Wren raised his cup in a silent toast and Zennon chuckled as she echoed the movement.

For the most part, Neah's parents seemed to like Wren and when the food was cleared away and her mother brought out dessert, Wren's eyes lit up. He won her over fully in that moment, Neah was sure.

"Is that crumble? Goddess, it's my absolute favourite." He then proceeded to tuck away three bowls of it with enough gusto that even Jamison had laughed.

She hugged each of her parents tightly before she'd left, pleased that the tension had dissipated. All she really wanted was for her family to be safe and happy, no more secrets, and it felt like maybe that could really happen.

Zennon had opted to stay behind, wanting to spend some more time with Jamison and Winny, so Neah walked the corridors with only Wren at her side.

"Will you stay with me again tonight?"

Neah hesitated and then nodded. Surprisingly, she liked waking up with Wren. The normalcy of it had charmed her.

"I like having you in my bed," he said quietly and, to her

horror, she felt a blush heating her face. He laughed in response to it, pressing a quick kiss to her cheek that startled her. "Get your mind out of the gutter. Or, wait. Keep it there, I don't mind." His smirk was far too cocky and that... Neah just couldn't take.

She tugged them to a stop a few corridors away from his chambers and instead pressed him back into the shadowy alcove that had clearly housed some artwork that had been recently moved, judging by the scuff marks on the floor and walls.

"What are we doing?" The amusement in his voice belied the heat in his eyes and it was Neah's turn to smirk as she sank to her knees. She liked the sound of that. *We.* With Wren, she was never alone.

"Surely you can guess," she teased, reaching for his breaches and working the laces free with quick, sure, tugs of her fingers until the material was tented around the thickening erection Wren couldn't disguise.

"If someone sees—" His breath stuttered when her hand closed around his cock.

"Do you want me to stop?" She leaned in to breathe the words temptingly close to his crotch and grinned when he shivered.

"No. Goddess, no."

Neah pumped him slowly, hand tight around his length as she curled around to his tip. The corridor was deserted, and wasn't one often frequented as only the king's quarters could be found in that direction, but the thrill made her heart beat quicker nonetheless.

She licked her lips and looked up at him with wide eyes as she slipped his head past her mouth. He groaned at the first swipe of her tongue, one hand pressing firmly into the wall to their right as if he needed the help remaining upright. His other fisted in her hair as she teased him, pulling away and taunting him with light licks to his shaft.

"*Caritas*—" he growled warningly and she smirked as she swallowed him down, the abrupt shift from teasing to choking on his cock enough to make him shout and she laughed. The sound vibrated through her throat and Wren's head fell back to expose the long, biteable, column of his throat as she hollowed her cheeks and tasted him.

The first jerk of his hips had her feeling smug and when he opened his eyes and she saw how they glowed, how close he was to losing control completely, she stopped fucking around.

Wren's eyes widened as she pressed her face toward his hips, gagging slightly on the considerable length of his cock even as she swallowed and milked him with her throat.

"F-Fuck."

The stutter. She rewarded his loss of control with the swirl of her tongue as she worked him, pleased when he stopped holding back and instead began to fuck her face roughly.

His hand in her hair released as he swiped a thumb under her eye, catching the tear there, the satisfaction on his face purely savage even as she reduced him to a begging mess.

"Neah," he gasped and when she looked up, eyes meeting his, he came with a hoarse cry, warmth painting her throat. She licked her lips and stood, taking his hand seeing as her knees had gone numb on the stone floor. "That was…"

Her chuckle was admittedly smug. "'You're welcome."

Wren muttered an oath, sagging against the wall dizzily for a moment before recovering enough to walk the last few corridors that led to his chambers. "A nap," he said under his breath as they walked and she couldn't help her laugh when he added, "and then I'm going to make you come so hard the walls will be forever imprinted with my name—because you're going to scream and beg for me before I'm done."

"Big talk from a man I just made stutter."

CHAPTER TWENTY-EIGHT

WREN

The door to his chambers swung open and Wren's breath whooshed out of him as Neah walked in, cheeks flushed and hair tied back into a long braid that fell over one shoulder.

Without a word, he ran to her. His arms closed around the narrow set of her shoulders and when she wheezed he realised he was squeezing her too tightly. "Thank the Goddess," he muttered. "You're okay?"

It had been three days since their meal with Neah's parents and Zennon and, for the most part, they'd spent the time together. He hadn't realised how nice it would be to return to his rooms and find Neah waiting every evening, his bed had become *theirs* and the space felt too empty now when it was only him in them.

Today, he'd had a meeting to attend with a handful of Lords who were concerned about their land boundaries and Neah had declined the invitation to join him. Instead, she was supposed to be meeting Zennon in the town nearby. He got the impression Zennon didn't get out much, so it had been a nice idea. It was sunny but not too hot outside, Sonnet was joining them, and he thought it would be good for his mate to spend some time away from him for the day, even if it was under the watchful gaze of the guards he'd sent to the tavern ahead of time.

"Of course I'm okay," she said breathlessly, pulling back to look up into his eyes and then cupping his jaw with one hand as she read whatever distress lingered on his face. "What's wrong?"

"There was another attack." How they'd known Neah was going to be there, Wren couldn't say. "In the town, at the tavern. I sent guards there to keep an eye on things—"

"Wren," she protested and he shrugged.

"They were told you'd requested a private booth, so they took their seats and waited for you."

"Yes." Neah nodded and then narrowed her eyes. "Because I was *trying* to be cautious."

"So was I," he pointed out and she rolled her eyes but looked worried when he stepped back and began pacing. "Drinks were delivered. One of my men indulged. The other survived."

Her eyes flew wide. "Poison?"

"I just don't understand," he growled, pushing a hand through his hair as his legs ate up the space between the sides of the room. "How did they know your plans to be there? Why are they doing this? Going after you and Zennon rather than me?"

A cool hand took his and Neah squeezed gently. "The important thing is that we're okay and we *will* find whoever is responsible for all of this and they will pay."

The words and her tone were grim, but the strength of her conviction unwound a small amount of his tension.

He held himself perfectly still, eyes running over her face as he tried to reassure himself that they'd failed again. Neah was here. She was safe. She was *alive*. But he couldn't help the niggling thought that next time they might succeed. "Tell me what happened to change your plans."

"I got a note from Zennon asking to reschedule. A guard delivered it. I assume Sonnet received one too. And then I got changed and headed to the captain's personal training room."

"That's where you've been this whole time?"

A slight smile curved her lips. "Yes. It's wise to keep up with my training, given all the assassins trying to kill me." When he didn't laugh, she winced. "Too soon?"

"Yes," he said, the word hoarse. "We haven't spoken about it yet, because I promised the choice of whether to cement the bond with the bonding ceremony would be yours. But I don't know if I can do this, Neah. Not if it means you'll be hurt—or killed."

For the first time since she'd walked in, Neah's jaw clenched and he knew she was pissed. "What are you saying?"

"I'm saying…" Wren sighed and paced over to the armchairs surrounding the table by the balcony doors. What *was* he saying? "I'm saying you're more important than the crown, or the kingdom. I would choose you over my sanity, over my soul, and only a small part of that is because you're my mate." His voice broke and Wren looked away, unable to meet her eyes as he scrubbed a hand over his face. "So you should go, leave while you still can. Before you or Zennon or anybody else gets hurt."

There was silence in the wake of his words and he exhaled shakily, sensing she was still standing there by the door, and he wondered if this was it, if she would leave him now. He couldn't bring himself to regret it, not if it meant she would be safe. They hadn't formally accepted their bond yet, she could still go on without him, love again—he nearly growled at the thought but managed to hold it in. She was *his*. But if that meant her death, well, that was not the fate he'd choose for her.

"Do you want me?" The words were soft, vulnerable and a challenge all at the same time as Wren heard her take a step closer.

"Yes," he choked. "Desperately."

"Your crown, the kingdom—"

"Mean nothing without you." Silence fell once more and it occurred to him that the words might be too bold, too much too soon. "If *you* don't want me, if this is only a duty to you, then I want you to go. Now. Forget about me and live your life and be happy."

Wren didn't even hear her footsteps, just the touch of her hand on his, pulling his palm away from his face.

Golden eyes stared into his very soul, gentle and fiery all at once. "I want you. I choose *you*. I can handle assassins and poisonings, and whatever else they try to keep us apart. But leaving now isn't an option. I need you. I choose *you*."

The words were his undoing.

Material creaked as he shifted his weight, knees hitting the floor as he slid from the chair to kneel at her feet. He'd told himself before that nobody but the Goddess should see the king kneel, but that was before he'd met Neah. Before he knew what it meant to truly *worship.*

Her eyes burned brighter and she licked her lips as his hands smoothed the outside of her legs, feeling her heat beneath the silky fabric that clung to her legs.

"Use me," he rasped. "Own me. I'm yours, heart, body, soul."

Neah's breath caught and he swallowed hard when her hands slid into his hair and tugged lightly, pulling his head back. "I've never had a king on his knees for me before. Let's hope you don't disappoint," she taunted and his laugh was a low, dark rumble that made her heart beat quicker.

His hands coasted down her sides, thumbs hooking into the material so he could slowly peel it off and feel her bare skin, soft under his palms.

A scrap of dark lace was all that covered her and he leaned forward, tonguing the material lightly before clasping it with his teeth and ripping it away. Neah shivered as his breath touched her skin and then gasped when he leaned in and inhaled, kissing with light suction across the smooth skin between her pussy and her thighs.

Goddess, he could drown in her, wanted to feast on her wet heat until he was covered in her scent and everyone knew she'd marked him as *hers.*

Wren reached behind her, smoothing his hands up the back of her legs and cupping her posterior, squeezing and kneading the plump cheeks there before letting a hand trail back to her front and stroking over her pussy lips with a delicate, barely-there touch.

Her light moan made him grin as he repeated the

motion with a fraction more pressure, parting her folds around the hard bud of her clit that throbbed under his touch.

"I thought I told you," he murmured, leaning in to give a teasing lick to her clit, "to use me?"

As if the reminder was what she'd been waiting for, Neah unleashed herself.

The hand in his hair became firmer and when he looked up at her, waiting for instructions, her eyes glowed. She stepped closer, her legs widening until one stood on either side of his shoulders, and when she looked down her body at him, Wren felt his cock twitch in response. "Be a good little toy," she rasped, the breathless tone of her voice making it even harder to hold back. "Let me soak your face, my king."

His nod was eager and she smirked as he reached for her, raising himself up slightly so his mouth could close around her bud and suck so intently that Neah's spine arched. He wanted to laugh. She didn't know what she was asking for. She wanted to soak his face? He was just fine with that.

His tongue swept out, pressing into her entrance shallowly as it curled up, lapping at the cream of her while she whimpered. He retreated, blowing cold air over her sensitive flesh to make her writhe and then resuming his ministrations, mouth on her clit, tongue flicking the bud with just his tip, and his fingers slicking themselves against the wetness pooling at her entrance. His first thrust felt like sin, the heat of her pussy enveloping his two fingers as they pressed into her and sank in deep. Wren twisted, crooking them against her inner walls and feeling them flutter in response before he pulled them out and repeated the process, pace growing quicker as he lavished the apex of her pussy with attention, feeling it grow stiffer the more he stroked it with his tongue.

Her hips moved against his mouth, pressing down frantically for more friction, more sensation, but Wren resisted, instead keeping up his torturous pace on her clit and fucking her with his fingers. Then, when it seemed like she'd settled into the sensations, he switched things up and pressed his tongue into her entrance alongside his fingers.

She let out a high pitched, breathy moan that shot straight to his cock and Wren wasn't sure he could hold back any longer. He pulled away slightly to look up at her, enjoying the deep pink of her cheeks and the way her head thrashed as she climbed closer to orgasm.

"Are you ready, *caritas*?"

"For what?" she whined and he chuckled.

"To soak my face."

Her eyes flew open as he dove back down, withdrawing his fingers from her pussy and replacing them with his tongue. His fingers were slick with her arousal and he pressed them to her clit, slipping it between the pads of his fingers and squeezing it in short bursts that made her cry out. *Close.* She was so close.

This time, when he pressed on her clit, he feasted on her pussy, his tongue plunging into her and pulsing against the inner wall he knew would set her off. His fingers worked her as Neah cried out, legs trembling on either side of him as he felt her first orgasm shake against his tongue. But he wasn't done yet.

Her hand tightened in his hair, as if she planned to pull

him away, so he distracted her with his other hand, slipping it down between her legs to coat the digits in her come and then trailing back around to spread her cheeks and push in one finger.

The cry of surprise that left her made him grin as she grew wetter against his mouth. So she liked that? *Interesting.* He filed the tidbit away for later and sucked her pussy into his mouth in the same thrusting motion he used on her arse.

"Wren, Wren," she begged. "I can't—Not again—"

He ignored her protests and lightly spanked her clit, pleased when she moaned loudly. So he did it again, and again, until her breaths came in short pants. Only then did he press down on her clit and stroke while his tongue fucked her until she let out a keening wail and moisture exploded from her, hitting his face, soaking his mouth and wringing out the last of her willpower as she sagged against him.

Wren pressed a soft kiss to her thigh as his hand stroked up and down her leg, comforting rather than taunting.

When her breathing settled, Neah stood up from her slump and then swayed. "Did I just—?"

"Yep." He couldn't help the smug sound of his voice, but she must have been too dazed to tease him about it. Wren didn't care, he'd made her squirt—for the first time, it seemed like—so yes, he was going to be damn well smug about it.

"Maybe I should be targeted more often," she mumbled and waved off his frown with a giggle. "I think you melted my brain."

"Anytime," he said, smirking, and winced when stood up and his knees ached. "Though, maybe next time you ride my face we can use the bed? Save my knees the agony."

Her laughter was sweet as it echoed through the chambers and he followed her with his eyes as she walked to the doorway that led to their bedroom. "Well? Are you coming?"

CHAPTER TWENTY-NINE

NEAH

Zennon and Sonnet were lounging on Neah's bed when she walked into her chambers. Zen immediately jumped up to greet her, rushing over to wrap her in a hug that surprised Neah, whereas sparks jumped at Sonnet's fingertips from Neah's sudden arrival.

Sonnet grimaced, an apology on her face that Neah acknowledged over Zennon's shoulder as she returned her sister's embrace. Sonnet had been through a lot, the majority of which Neah could only imagine. It was only natural that she'd be a little jumpy. Was this the longest she'd stayed in one place?

Zennon squeezed Neah before withdrawing and smiling. "I feel like I've barely seen you lately."

"Sorry," she said, warmth heating her cheeks. It was true that she'd been spending a lot of time with Wren, both because she wanted to get to know him further and because her acceptance of their bond had made it difficult to keep their hands off each other. Though, really, a few days of absence was nothing in the face of the long times apart Neah usually endured as part of her work. "I, um, have news."

Zennon squealed, clapping her hands excitedly as she spun to face Sonnet and bounced on the heels of her feet. "I told you!"

"I haven't said anything yet," Neah protested and the two women laughed as Sonnet flicked a coin to Zen. "Seriously? You placed bets?"

Sonnet shrugged. "Sometimes a little wager can make things more interesting—and we were getting bored watching you and Wren tiptoe around each other. You *are* doing the bonding ceremony, right?"

Neah crossed her arms and cocked a hip as she glanced between the two of them before sighing in exasperation. "Yes."

"Excellent. Congrats, yada yada. Looks like I have a ceremony to prepare for," Sonnet said, eyes going distant like she was already picturing her to-do list. "And don't feel bad about taking my money," she added, grinning at Zennon. "I stole that from Skye, so it's his problem."

A startled laugh fell out of Neah. "When can we start a wager on whatever is going on with you and those two boys?"

Sonnet sniffed. "I don't know what you're talking about." But her lip twitched and Neah smirked, deciding to let it go for now. "Did Zen tell you that Romi stayed here again last night?"

It was an unsubtle change of subject, but Neah allowed it, too intrigued to do anything else as she dragged over a chair from the parlour and plopped it down at the foot of the bed. "Oh *really?*" She narrowed her eyes on her sister, who blushed and fidgeted with the hem of her blue dress. "Kept that one quiet, Zen."

"It's not like that," she said, voice slightly too high to be believable. "I mean, do I like her? Sure. Of course. She's beautiful, and kind, and funny—" Zennon cut herself off, a red flush filling her face. "But she was here as a friend."

Neah shared a look with Sonnet, reading the doubt on the witch's face that she knew was probably on her own too. "Ten coppers say they're wed before the year is out."

Sonnet snorted. "Two silvers say within the next two months."

Zennon huffed, folding her arms across her chest. "I'm sitting right here, you know."

"We know," Neah and Sonnet returned in unison.

They dissolved into laughter and casual chatter and by the time Neah left to go and find Wren, much to the girls' teasing, she was feeling a lot more relaxed. Maybe she'd been a little more worried about public opinion to this bonding ceremony than she'd realised. The problem with marrying a king was that everyone had an opinion and suddenly felt it was their place to share it. But she and Wren had been fated, ordained by the Goddess herself. Anyone else could go and fuck themselves.

The vague mention of anyone *fucking themselves* had her overreactive instincts perking up, eager to hunt down Wren and prove just how *hers* he was. The door to her chambers had only just closed behind her when, distracted, she walked into a solid chest.

Cursing under her breath, Neah looked up and then blinked. "Castor. My apologies, my head was elsewhere."

Wren's uncle smiled. "No matter at all, the fault was mine."

She glanced behind her to the door she'd just closed. "Were you looking for me?"

"I suppose I was," he said, and the odd phrasing made her brows furrow before she cleared her expression. "I heard the good news from my nephew, so naturally I wanted to offer my congratulations."

"Thank you." She straightened, finally pulling up her composure and letting the easy mask of Lady settle over her. "That's very kind of you."

"I am a kind man," he said, a small smile twisting his mouth. "Which is why I feel the need to warn you that any... secrets you may be harbouring might not be well received by the king." He glanced at the door to her back and for reasons she couldn't quite place, the hair on the back of her arms stood to attention. "I'm close with your father, of course, and being in my position... Well, one hears things, my dear."

For a second, she could only stare. What was he trying to say? "If you're referring to my *work*," she said, emphasising the word with a narrowing of her eyes, "Wren knows all about it."

"And your sister? Does he know about that too?" Castor leaned in, as if he was relaying a secret, pity shining in his eyes.

"He does," she said slowly. "But how do *you*?" If the king's uncle knew, what were the chances that others did too? There hadn't been any more attempts on Neah's life and she wondered if it was because whoever was doing this knew that she could handle herself. So if they couldn't get to her directly...

She swallowed hard and took a step closer, invading the Lord's space as she looked deeply into his eyes. "Who else knows about Zennon?"

He shrugged, a gleam in his eye that made all her senses prickle. "I can only guess—"

Neah closed the remaining distance, shoving Castor into the stone wall to their left and fisting her hand in the front of his crisp white shirt. "Enough games. Tell me how you know about her. Who told you?"

He swallowed, eyes flashing wide. "Lady Neah, I must insist—" His words were cut off by the growl that escaped her, claws appearing at her hands and fur rippling across her skin. "The Queen Mother," he gasped, eyeing the place where her claws had pierced the material of his shirt. "I don't know who else she told, I swear it!"

The Queen Mother. But why would Wren's mother spread this information? What did she have to gain? Neah was missing something, she was sure of it.

She relinquished her hold on the Lord and stepped back as the shift she'd been holding at bay took her over. Heavy paws hit the ground and she snarled at Castor as he cowered against the wall. The warning, she hoped, was clear.

When she roared again, he fled and the door to her back creaked open. Sonnet peeked out and grimaced. "I thought you left ages ago." Neah's grumble made the witch raise her hands. "Okay, okay. Good kitty. Don't eat me."

Neah made a show of displaying her teeth and licking her lips before she nodded in the direction Castor had fled.

"Someone was here? Okay. Do you want me to—" She

made as if to step out of the door and Neah snapped lightly at the air, making the witch freeze in place. "Okay. Got it. I'll stay with Zennon." A whine escaped Neah and Sonnet's face dropped all pretenses of civility as she looked into Neah's eyes. "I won't let anything happen to her."

Neah believed her.

The door closed softly behind Sonnet and Neah was already moving. She needed to find Wren so they could discuss what was going on. Maybe he could talk to his mother and get some answers. Neah had a bad feeling that whatever they'd faced so far—it was about to get worse.

She followed the pull in her chest that she knew would lead her to Wren, stalking through the corridors of the palace without looking at the court gaping around her.

The bond was stronger in this form, pulsing lightly as a tangible thread between them, whereas in her human form it was more like a gentle pull that was subtle enough she could have missed it if she hadn't been looking for it. But after the ceremony, their bond would be full fledged, linking them together so their hearts would beat as one. Two halves united. The bond was different for everyone, or so she'd heard, with most able to sense emotions of their bonded and others were supposedly able to speak mind-to-mind.

She didn't much mind what form their bond took, as long as it satisfied Wren's curse.

After three turns in a row, Neah knew where she must be headed—the great hall where she'd first found Wren when she'd arrived at court. Passersby grew few and far between the deeper she descended into the palace's maze, until the thread between them grew taut and she rounded the end of the corridor to find Wren waiting. He looked up, as if sensing she was there, but was unable to see her until the crowd of people exiting the hall parted for her and she emerged from their centre still on four paws.

He grinned, eyes lighting up in the way that made her heart beat faster, and Skye and Gabriel shared identical looks of affectionate exasperation.

"Really? You two can't go an hour without running off to fu—" Neah nipped at the hand Gabe was waving around and he yelped, not having seen her approach. "Didn't anyone tell you that biting isn't nice? Bad kitty," he said and hissed, the words reminding her of Sonnet and making her huff out a laugh.

She looked to Wren and he frowned as he read whatever emotion was showing in her eyes. Without warning, the shift rippled over her and Wren growled as it left her naked in the middle of the room.

He whipped off his shirt, tugging it roughly over his head before dropping it down over hers, the tight set of his jaw telling her he was struggling as much as she was with this turn of events. She was barely clothed, and Wren's bare chest was just out of reach, the hard ridges of corded muscle making her swallow.

Skye and Gabriel had turned their backs to offer her some privacy and she called for them to turn now that she was covered, only to be taken aback by the snarl of warning Wren let loose when his friends set eyes on her.

"Wren," she chided and he sucked in a ragged breath.

"Sorry, sorry." His voice was strained. "Ah, maybe you could move back a bit?" Gabe and Skye obeyed, retreating a few steps, and then smirking when Wren called out, "Yeah... A bit more?"

Once they were nearly all the way across the room, Wren relaxed and Neah bit her lip to hold in her laugh. The territorial instincts when a bond is first accepted were notoriously powerful and, frankly, she was surprised she hadn't had any jealous fits yet.

Feeling more settled with the distance of the other males, Wren took a few deep breaths before looking at her. "Are you okay?"

She shook her head and regretted it when it clearly made Wren's instincts kick into overdrive again. He was there in a flash, running his hands over every inch of her skin to check for injuries until she shoved him away. "I'm fine, physically. Sorry," she said and then, after seeing the hurt on his face, added, "You were touching me and you don't have a shirt on and, well, I didn't come here for *that*."

His hurt instantly faded and was replaced by a cocky swagger that made her roll her eyes. Worse, Gabe and Skye were laughing at them as Gabe relayed what was being said to Skye, thanks to his shifter hearing.

"Your uncle was lurking outside of Zennon's door. He knew who she was, and he knew what I used to be."

That stopped the laughter and Wren frowned. "That's... odd?"

It was, but 'odd' didn't seem like a strong enough word. But this was Wren's uncle, she couldn't just say that to him because of a *vibe* she'd picked up. Just something about the whole encounter seemed off.

"I... questioned him," she said, shooting a glare at Gabe

when he laughed across the room. "He told me that your mother was the one who mentioned Zennon's heritage."

Wren's brow furrowed. "I'll talk to her. But you don't honestly think…"

She shrugged. "I don't know what to think, Wren." Obviously she didn't *want* his family to be responsible for the attacks and the attempts to weaken the king, but it had to be someone with motive and access. What better motive than to steal the crown? And what better access than already being a royal? It could explain why the attacks had all been indirect too, not wanting to risk the crown by openly committing treason.

As if the same thoughts had just occurred to Wren, he nodded. "I'll talk to her," he repeated, tone more certain. "I'm sure there's an explanation."

"I'm sure there is," she said softly, reaching for his hand and squeezing it. She only hoped that explanation had nothing to do with overthrowing a king.

CHAPTER THIRTY

NEAH

"*H*ere." Sonnet passed a silver-chained necklace to Zennon, who clasped it gingerly in her palms.

"What does it do?"

"There's a protection spell in the stone. Anyone with ill intent will be unable to touch you—magically or otherwise. It's not inexhaustible though, the idea is that it will give you time."

To get away, to protect herself. Neah's brows pinched together, wishing this wasn't necessary. But word of Zennon's heritage, and her connection to Neah, had begun to trickle out to the court. It was only a matter of time until her sister became a target, this time because of *her*.

Sonnet wore her own version of the necklace too, as the officiant for their ceremony she was equally as important as Zennon. Though, at least if anyone came after the witch she had her magic to protect herself.

"What about for Neah?" Wren asked, pacing up and

down in the small space between the chairs and the balcony in his chambers.

"Sorry, there's not much I can do there. Shifters have their own innate magic to contend with, different from that of a human or witch. One of these charms would be next to useless." Sonnet glanced at Neah, her face apologetic, but Neah just shrugged. She could take care of herself. It was everyone else that she worried about. "Maybe if I'd had more time…"

Wren and Neah shared a look before shaking their heads.

They'd decided not to waste any time in performing the ceremony—both to assuage Wren's curse and to secure the crown, deterring any further attacks. Or that was the hope, anyway.

Sonnet sighed. "As you wish."

"It doesn't give us much time to plan your party," Gabe mumbled and Skye nodded in agreement. Even Zennon looked put out.

"You have a whole week," Neah said, rolling her eyes. "Why don't we just do something all together? Right now?"

Gabriel looked at her like she'd suggested an orgy. "And do what? *Chat?*"

"As opposed to…?" Sonnet raised one eyebrow and Gabe immediately sobered, murmuring something that sounded like *dancing*. "By all means, fetch an instrument. Let's hear it, Gabriel. If you're any good, maybe we'll *dance*."

Perhaps this had been a bad idea.

"How about poker?" Zen suggested and Neah clapped. "Strip poker," she added and Neah grimaced. "Or maybe I could send for Romi?"

"Is she to be our entertainment?" Skye said dryly and Neah grinned.

"No," Zennon huffed. "You two still need your ceremonial wear, right? Well, why don't we get Romi to come and dress you while we all get shockingly drunk?"

Considering hums sounded before Wren looked around at them all. "I hate to say it, but I think that's the best idea so far."

One hour and a *lot* of wine later, Romi arrived with attendants from the palace carrying swaths of material and pins.

She'd smiled at Zennon, who'd practically melted into a puddle at the sight, and said, "You can be my assistant." If by *assistant* Romi just wanted someone who would stand there and marvel at her while she worked, then Zen was doing a fantastic job.

Wren went first and Neah shuffled up on the couch by the hearth that they'd moved to in order for Romi to have space to work. Comfortable front and centre, she snagged the honey wine from Skye's hand mid-pour and cackled when some escaped the bottle to trickle down his chin and over his shirt.

"Oops," she said, batting her eyes innocently as she swallowed her own mouthful.

"You're lucky you're going to be queen," he said, frowning, but she saw the good humoured twinkle in his bright eyes. "I've hexed people for less."

"That's because you're an arsehole," Sonnet said

cheerfully from her place on Neah's other side, taking the bottle for herself and raising it to the room before taking a swig. "You'd think royalty could spring for glasses," she muttered after swallowing the fizzy concoction.

Romi tutted from the center of the room as she circled Wren, a professional eye running over his form. Neah might have been jealous if there had been any heat in the look whatsoever, but, as it stood, the buxom redhead eyed Wren as if he were nothing more than a design mannequin.

Her talent, however, was unmistakable. She'd been pinning pieces of fabric together, making a loose silhouette, and already Neah could see the vision. The tail coats were long, the fabric a deep forest green that brought out the gold in Wren's eyes and the warmth in his dark hair, and it wasn't until Gabriel cleared his throat awkwardly that she realised she'd been staring a little *too* hard. Wren smirked as he caught her scent and Neah rolled her eyes and grabbed another bottle of wine to hide her smile.

Her mate looked good, it wasn't her fault that she couldn't hide her body's response to him. Not from shifters with their keen sense of smell, anyway.

Skye opened his mouth, likely to snap back at Sonnet, and Neah held up a hand.

"Please. Just fuck already."

Skye's eyes bugged out and Sonnet choked on her sip of wine. "That's not—"

"He wishes," Sonnet rasped, still coughing.

"You wear denial well," Zen said, looking away from Romi for two seconds to snort at Sonnet.

"Oh yeah? You really want to wade into a discussion

about *romance?*" Sonnet glared before smirking at Romi. "Don't mind us, Romi. We're just talking about Zennon's big crush on a friend of ours."

If looks could kill, Sonnet would be on her way to the Goddess from all the daggers in Zen's glare.

Romi distracted them, stepping back from Wren and admiring her work before easing the material off of him, careful not to disturb any pins, and beckoned Neah. "Up."

Amused, she stood and passed Wren the bottle as they swapped places. His gaze burned into her as she lifted her arms and turned when Romi instructed.

"Hm, I was thinking gold but..." Romi held a swatch of fabric up, the shimmer making Sonnet and Zennon *ooh*. "I think it'll wash you out. Something darker would be better."

Neah was happy to defer to Romi's expertise. "Sure."

Romi gestured for Zennon to pass over several other squares of fabric, holding up different squares to Neah's skin until she found one she liked and nodded approvingly. "This one. What do you think?" Romi grabbed a longer bolt of the fabric and presented it to Neah.

It was a deep, rich colour, not quite red but not quite orange and she knew it would pop against Wren's green ceremonial jacket.

"I love it," she said honestly and Romi beamed.

"Well I have all your measurements down, so I'll get to work and let you know when they're ready to be tried on." She began rolling up pieces of parchments, presumably where she'd dotted down their sizes, and tucking away reams of fabric so that they were folded neatly into a large chest. "Enjoy your night."

Zennon's head whipped around but Neah didn't need any prompting. "Oh! You're not leaving are you? Stay, have a drink."

Romi hesitated and then let the trunk stay where it was, hesitantly accepting a seat at an armchair that had been dragged over from the balcony area. The mood felt light as they chattered, opening more bottles of wine, and cheering when an attendant brought up snacks at Wren's request. The mood only soured slightly when they waited to test it for magic and poison before diving in.

"So how specific is this spell?" Skye was asking, examining Sonnet and Zennon's matching necklaces. "If I pinched your leg, would it react? Or does the intent for harm have to be greater?"

Sonnet's smile was sweet but the look in her eyes was wicked when she purred, "Touch me and find out."

Skye, apparently not wanting to risk life or limb, wisely kept his hands to himself.

"You really think someone will try to hurt Zennon?" Romi hadn't had nearly as much to drink as the rest of them and it showed, her solemn sobriety reminding the rest of the group of the seriousness of the situation. "Why?" The word was soft, like she genuinely couldn't fathom anyone wanting to hurt Zen, and Neah liked the other woman all the more for it.

"Because I'm easier to kill than Neah," Zennon said, tone joking but words serious. "Better to be safe, than sorry. Right?"

Romi watched Zennon for a moment, eyes dark and troubled, and Neah watched them as Romi tilted her chin and shifted her body so it was between Zennon and the door. "Right."

Neah was drawn back into the other side of the group when Gabriel placed an empty bottle of wine at his feet, joining two others, and announced, "Hey, didn't someone say something about strip poker?"

They couldn't find a deck of cards anywhere in Wren's room—though Neah did wonder if that was deliberate on Wren's part. And so, after the wine and snacks dwindled, the others left for their rooms and Neah smiled, accepting Sonnet's sloppy kiss on the cheek as she walked away, bracketed on either side by Gabe and Skye. Romi and Zen left together too, the latter glaring at Neah in a warning not to comment on the seamstress spending another night.

Finally, it was only her and Wren. His arms wound around her waist, her head fell to his chest, and when he tugged her toward the bedroom she'd begun to think of as *theirs* she fell into bed with his arms still around her.

CHAPTER THIRTY-ONE

NEAH

Five days. That was how long it had taken Romi to make this masterpiece of a dress—a wedding gown, of sorts, though the mating bond ceremony was considered far more sacred.

It was a ceremony so old that many of the rituals were observed purely because they couldn't tell what was tradition versus what was essential any more. With Wren's sanity on the line, they couldn't take any chances. And so, for the first time in what seemed like weeks, Neah found herself in her old chambers, preparing to spend the night away from Wren before the ceremony tomorrow evening.

A surprising amount of her things had migrated to Wren's room while she'd been staying there. She hadn't even realised until she now had to carry most of them back so she could use them in the evening before bed and in the morning after her bath. The thing that surprised her the most was that the thought didn't bother her. Her old room felt cold, too empty, where she was used to Wren's presence taking up space.

Romi had found Neah on her walk through the palace, a basket of things in her arms, and had joined her for the last stretch of the journey, seeing as she was there to see Neah for her final dress fitting anyway.

"Are you nervous?"

"Not at all," Neah had said. "I'm sure whatever you've created is stunning."

Romi had just smiled in response and it was only now, as Neah posed in front of the long mirror, that she realised Romi may have been talking about the ceremony rather than the dress.

"Do you think you'll get married someday?" Maybe it was prying, but Neah liked what she'd seen of the other woman so far, the way she protected Zennon, they would be good together.

"Maybe." Romi smiled, ruffling one of the dress' sleeves. "This colour was the right decision."

She was right. The burnt amber made Neah glow, her eyes brighter, her hair shinier, and that was before she'd even considered her hair and make-up for the ceremony. It was a dramatic dress, the skirt full and frothy but still lightweight and easy to move in, and Romi had snuck in pockets too. Not that Neah would be smuggling weapons into their ceremony... *or maybe just one. To be safe.*

"Thank you," she murmured and Romi beamed. "Not just for the dress. For taking care of Zennon. It means a lot."

"No thanks necessary," Romi replied, snipping a stray thread of fabric away from Neah's sleeve. "Why don't you head around the side there and slip back into your clothes? I just have a couple of final adjustments I want to make on this cuff."

Ever the perfectionist. Neah smiled. "Sure."

A modesty screen had been erected just to the side and behind the floor length mirror and Neah let Romi undo the laces on the dress' back before she slipped around the screen to shimmy the dress the rest of the way off.

"Did you finish the other dresses?" she called out and Romi chuckled. Neah had spoken privately to the seamstress, commissioning two special dresses for Zennon and Sonnet to wear for the ceremony too.

"Yes, they're perfect. Do you want to see them?" Footsteps padded softly against the floor, Romi's voice fading as she walked to the other room.

Neah grinned, hanging the dress back up and admiring it for a second. "Nope, I trust your vision completely." Romi was good humoured and quick to laugh, so the silence surprised her. Frowning, Neah stepped away from her dress and rounded the corner of the privacy screen. "Romi, is everything—"

Neah froze. Her tongue felt thick in her mouth as Romi's breaths heaved silently, her chest rising and falling too fast and her eyes were wide, the cornflower blue of her irises darkening with her panic.

A guard stood in her room. The door was closed, so Romi must have let him in—and he was in uniform, why should she be suspicious?

His chest was to Romi's back, a short blade pressed to her throat hard enough that Neah could smell the faint tang of blood amidst the sour stench of fear.

"Put down the knife," she said slowly, calmly, like she was speaking to a cornered animal. "I'll do whatever you want, but not if you hurt her."

The guard's face remained impassive, though a muscle feathered beneath the pale skin of his jaw. "I wish I could believe that. But we both know that as soon as I release her, you'll shift."

Neah tilted her head, considering. She didn't need to shift to kill this man, but one wrong move and Romi would bleed out. Zennon would never forgive her.

"I won't shift."

The door opened and closed quickly and another guard joined the first, his captain's uniform mocking her as she kept her weight balanced evenly on the balls of her feet. She would have preferred to be a little more clothed when battling her enemies, but there wasn't much she could do about it now. At least her underwear was modest, unlike the lacy scraps of fabric she often wore to torment Wren.

"You got it?"

The other guard nodded, holding out a pair of chains that made her nose wrinkle. They smelled *wrong*, like magic and death.

"Prove your word," the guard holding Romi said, nodding to the chains. "Put them on."

If that was what it took, she would do it. Being chained wouldn't stop her, but it could save Romi.

Neah offered her wrists and the guard moved closer, his dark brows furrowed as if she might snap and kill him at any given second. Normally, she would have. But now, she couldn't risk it.

The metal closed around her wrists and Neah

shuddered, immediately knowing something wasn't right. The cold of the shackles bit into her skin, causing a lurching sensation in her stomach like she was falling, and then the pain began.

She retched, bending in half as the cuffs seemed to tighten. "What the hell… did you.. do to me?"

Through her blurry vision, Neah could make out the relief on the guards faces. "You can't shift while you're wearing those. It drains your magic."

She did her best to regain her breaths but nausea still tightened her throat and black spots dotted the air in front of her. "Fine. I'm wearing them." She groaned as she tried to straighten and one knee hit the ground. "Let her go."

Sweat beaded at her temples and her hands shook, but what sent her heart jumping into her throat was the look the two guards shared.

"Sorry, sweetheart. But we can't have you raising the alarm now, can we?"

Neah lurched forward but only fell to the ground as the guard backhanded Romi, sending her sprawling on the floor. *Maybe she's unconscious. Maybe they won't kill her and that will be enough.*

But the guard with the knife was approaching and Neah dragged herself upright, her knees scraping painfully across the wooden floor as she tried to crawl to Romi's crumpled form.

A kick to her back knocked the breath out of her and Neah coughed, eyes never leaving Romi's face from where she lay still dazed on the floor.

Play dead, Neah begged mentally, hoping the other woman would somehow read the instruction on Neah's face. Instead, her eyes widened as the guard flipped her onto her back and raised the knife.

Neah didn't blink. Didn't look away. If these were to be Romi's last moments, she would be there for her and do her the courtesy of bearing witness.

Silver flashed and Neah yelled, the sound breathless and hoarse as the blade sank into Romi's chest and thudded against the floor. Her cry of pain made the guard's face tighten, as if he took no pleasure in the kill, but Neah promised herself that the guard's death wouldn't be so quick, nor merciful.

Something wet touched her pinky fingers and she flinched back, the warmth making her feel sick as she realised it was Romi's blood. Her chest still rose and fell, but her eyes were shut—unconscious, Neah hoped.

"He'll come for me," she said, the words more slurred than she would have liked, and the other guard hit her again, the kick to the ribs swift and biting. Wren would tear apart the world to find her, just as she would do the same for him. "And when he does, you'll already be dead."

A final blow landed and her world was swallowed by darkness.

CHAPTER THIRTY-TWO

WREN

The pounding at the door mimicked the ache in Wren's head and he groaned as he rolled out of bed and stepped into a pair of trousers, not bothering to lace them up before he strode to the door to his chambers.

"What?" he barked and then balked at the grey tinge to Skye's normally warm, brown skin. By the Goddess. "Sonnet?" He swallowed, trying to mitigate the thickness in his throat. Skye had been assigned to watch over the witch for the night. Technically any human high priestess or witch could perform a binding ceremony, but this one, the one that would relieve his curse, was special. He needed Sonnet for it to work.

"I'm fine," the smooth voice said and Wren peeked around the doorway to find the witch standing with her arms folded across her chest and in a similar bedraggled state to Wren. If she was okay, then why were they here?

"I had to bring her, it's my watch," Skye said, but his

voice sounded hollow and Wren widened the door, ushering the pair of them inside. "Gabe is with Zennon."

"What is it?"

Skye shook his head. "I don't know. Goddess, I don't know. But it's bad. I can't *see* clearly. Not with her magic so wrapped around everything." The words were fact rather than accusatory but Sonnet frowned all the same. "I don't know. There's a pit in my stomach and a fire in my chest and my mouth tastes like blood."

The silver gleam in the witch's eyes looked like concern and Wren understood the feeling. He'd never seen Skye quite so undone.

"Where's Neah?" Skye asked, whipping his head around to stare piercingly at Wren.

"Neah?" Wren's heart thudded harder. "In her chambers. It's tradition the night before the ceremony. You know that."

Skye jolted, a wave of magic rolling off him and rippling through the air before his eyes turned white and his voice echoed faintly. "We need to go there. Now. Before it's too late."

Too late. "What do you mean, too late?" Wren swung open the door again, marching out and trying to slow the roll of his thoughts as they began the journey to Neah's room. She could take care of herself and if something was wrong, he would know. Right?

Skye began to run and Wren's eyes pricked, burning, as panic harshed his breaths and the pain in his head grew sharper. Sonnet struggled to keep up with their pace, her pants shallow, and eventually Skye scooped her up into his arms and continued on unheeded.

Wren had seen Skye in the depths of visions, or his feelings, before, but never like this. Even when Zennon had been attacked previously, it hadn't been so eerie, like the Goddess herself moved within his body.

They rounded a corner and Wren growled, the scent of blood thick despite the ordinariness of the closed door. It burst open with a wave of Skye's hand and Sonnet cried out as they spotted the crumpled form on the floor in a widening pool of blood.

The material of her dress was stiff, having absorbed most of it, and beneath her flaming hair the pallor of her face was extreme.

Romi, Wren realised. *Not Neah.* But his mate had been here, the scent of her rage and fear potent in the room, and Wren could smell two others, males. Human.

Skye held out a hand to Sonnet who suddenly seemed very small in the wake of the room's horror. She clasped it even as her fingers shook and Skye inhaled deeply as the magic in the air amped up. The energy prickled his skin and ruffled his hair, a living breathing *thing* that was as unnerving as it was impressive. A wave of blue light streaked with silver washed out of the two witches and fell over Romi's form, the knife in her shoulder lifting out with an invisible hand and the skin knitting together.

The barely perceptible rise of Romi's chest grew stronger and Wren allowed himself one moment of relief before his worry flooded him once more.

"She's alive, but just. We've done what we can, but she needs a real healer." Skye bent in half, as if the cost of all that magic had physically weighed on him. "Good job," he murmured to Sonnet and she nodded as she reached for Romi's hand. "One last spell?"

Sonnet squeezed Skye's hand and any other time Wren would have been thrilled to see them getting along so well. "I have the energy. Use it."

Skye obeyed, his magic arranging itself into a glowing net that encompassed Romi's body, lifting her into the air and drifting ahead of them easily. The strain on Skye's face suggested otherwise, though.

"I need to talk to her." Wren scrubbed a hand over his face. "Neah was here. She wouldn't have let this happen if she could avoid it. Something's wrong."

Sonnet stepped away from Skye, his hand stretching out in the space between them before she dropped it and pressed a palm to Wren's temples and her other hand to his chest. A faint tingle of magic, far less than what he'd just witnessed, swept through him and Sonnet nodded. "She's alive. Your bond is intact. How do you feel? Any pain?"

"Just my head. And my side."

Sonnet bit her lip. "Phantom injuries. They hurt her."

Claws ripped through his skin and Skye jerked Sonnet back, shielding her with his body as Wren's vision swam red.

"This doesn't help her," Skye snapped, eyes flashing even as the lines around them deepened with exhaustion. "Let's get Romi to the healers. You find Jamison and tell him what's going on. We *will* find her. Control. Yourself." The last words were a snarl worthy of a shifter when Wren's skin rippled and he fought the shift, nodding jerkily.

"Okay. Okay." He pushed out a long breath. "I'll meet

you in the healer's wing." Skye nodded and made to leave when Wren stopped him with a quick touch of his shoulder. "And Skye? Thank you."

The witch softened, clasping Wren's hand briefly before hurrying away. They'd got there in time to save Romi. Wren just prayed they would do the same for Neah.

In less than twenty-four hours, Wren should have been curse free and tied irrevocably to the woman he loved. So naturally, everything had gone to shit.

He'd awoken Jamison, his face turning grey when Wren relayed what had happened, and he didn't need to speak the words for Wren to know that Neah's father blamed him.

Wren blamed himself too.

But guilt wouldn't help Neah. He could wallow later, for now, he needed to find his mate.

By the time they'd found Romi, she'd been close to death and had nearly bled out in the hours between her wound and their rescue. Without Skye's warning, Romi would be dead and they would have had even less time to pick up the trail of whoever had taken Neah.

When the seamstress' eyes fluttered open, they all breathed a sigh of relief.

Zennon squeezed Romi's hand, shoulders slumped forward as she watched the rise and fall of the other woman's chest. Romi's voice was weak, but clear.

"Neah."

"We know," Zennon said, voice soft as she searched

Romi's face and Wren felt uncannily like they were intruding on a private moment, but it couldn't be helped. They needed to know what had happened. "Can you tell us what you remember?"

Romi nodded and then winced, likely as the movement pulled at the spot in between her chest and shoulder where her wound had been. It had healed, but the soreness would last a few days. "It's all my fault. I'm so sorry." Tears filled her eyes, making the light blue irises look more like an ocean. "I let him in and—"

"Who?" Wren asked and then softened his tone when Zennon's head snapped up to glare at him. "You're not responsible for this, Romi. The person who took her is to blame."

She sucked in several deep breaths and when she spoke again, her voice was steadier. "Two guards. I let one in when he knocked, he was in uniform—I didn't know—I should have—" Romi bit her lip and Zennon leaned in, murmuring to her in words pitched low enough that Wren couldn't hear even if he'd wanted to invade their privacy. "The guard had a knife."

All at once, Wren knew what had happened. "He threatened you to make her compliant."

Romi nodded. "Then a second guard arrived and he had these chains, Neah put them on and she–she went completely white, like bone. They said it would stop her from shifting."

Skye and Sonnet shared a look and Wren frowned. "What?"

"It's just that, if the chains stop her from being able to

shift, it probably stops other elements of her magic." Skye's brows pinched together. "Like her ability to heal."

Wren began to pace, aware of everyone's eyes on him as he fought for control. They had nearly killed Romi. What were the chances that Neah was uninjured? Remembering the tenderness in his side and head, Wren grimaced. It didn't seem likely, which meant Neah couldn't shift and was healing at a human's speed rather than a shifters'.

He looked to Jamison, who sat quietly in a chair by Romi's bedside, and wondered aloud, "Do you have a way to account for all the guards' whereabouts yesterday?"

The captain sat straighter and nodded. "There's a rota. But the men often swap positions if they have a preferred shift or location."

In other words, useless, Wren thought but bit his tongue.

"Maybe Romi could identify the guards if we assemble them?" Gabe suggested and then balked at the wide-eyed terror that flooded Romi's face at the prospect of seeing her attacker. "Or not," he said weakly.

"No." Wren held up a hand. "That's a good idea."

"You can't be serious," Zennon stood abruptly, her chair toppling over from the force of the movement. "I want to find Neah just as much as you but you can't force Romi to—"

"Not Romi," Wren said, cutting her off. "Me."

He'd scented the men in Neah's room when they'd been there earlier and found Romi. If he shifted, he was certain he could tell which of Jamison's men was responsible. And then they would do what they had to in order to discover their allegiances.

"What makes you so sure they'll be in the line-up?

Wouldn't it make more sense for them to hide out?" Zennon frowned, righting her chair and dropping back into it abruptly.

"They have to be working for someone," Sonnet said and Wren realised the witch had been very quiet up til now. "They tried to kill Romi so she couldn't identify them, they either didn't think about a shifter being able to find them, or they thought the scent would have faded by the time anyone came to check on Neah."

"Or," Wren added, "they didn't care if a shifter could find them, because they're hiding."

"Well, it's the best shot we have," Jamison snapped. "I'll call for the assembly. Let's hope they fall on the side of stupid, rather than absent."

Wren didn't argue, just let the captain make the arrangements while Zennon spoke soothingly to Romi.

"Do you really think you can find them by scent?" Romi's words were quiet but caught Wren's attention all the same.

He nodded. "If they're here, I'll scent them. I'll shift, because my tiger's nose is sharper than mine. I'm just…"

"Not sure if you can turn back," Gabe surmised and Wren nodded, knowing his friend understood from personal experience. Wren was having a hard enough time holding his tiger at bay already when all his instincts wanted to stalk from room to room and tear the palace apart, but he needed to have control. For Neah's sake.

Jamison's messengers were sent out and before long, a parade of men stood in the corridor outside of the healer's wing.

"Are you ready?" Wren nodded and halted when

Jamison stopped his approach with a hand to the chest. "No matter what you smell on them, you can *not* lose it. We'll need to question them. Their deaths could spell my daughter's. Understand?"

"I understand." The words were laced with a growl and Wren let the change snap over him, faster than it ever had before.

Jamison led him around a corner and the men stood straight, eyes forward, open curiosity on some faces, worry on others as Wren approached them in his tiger form.

The men stood in lines facing each other, winding down the corridor that led back toward the stairs. Wren looked up at the captain and he nodded, indicating everyone was present. Then Wren began his hunt.

He walked the line, pausing to inhale deeply, searching for Neah's scent among the guards. Each guard met his eyes before hastily looking away in an effort not to challenge him, some hearts beat faster, harder, at Wren's approach, but so far there was no trace of Neah.

He continued stalking past, and had passed a guard whose sweat smelled like the trees outside when he paused.

There.

Nearly undetectable. He'd tried to scrub it away with soap, but the metallic tang of blood, Romi's Wren could tell, still lingered.

He fell still and the guard's breaths increased, muscles twitching like he longed to run but knew it would end badly. Wren turned and the man went pale.

One step. Two. The guard looked ready to bolt but fear quickly locked him in place when Wren stopped in front of him and inhaled.

The scent was unmistakable and finding it on another male while his mate's whereabouts were unknown... Untenable.

A muscle twitched and Wren waited, sensing Jamison's approach as the guard's leg jerked like his body wanted to run even as his mind told him to stand still.

Wren looked into the man's eyes, pupils blown wide, and snarled. It was a warning as much as it was a threat—if he ran, Wren wouldn't be able to hold himself back.

The seconds stretched on as the guard looked at Wren, then down the hall to where Jamison strode toward them, and made his decision.

Like a spooked deer, the guard fled. Or tried. He made it five paces before Wren's paws slammed into his back and his teeth closed around the guard's arm. Jamison had broken into a run, his footfalls loud, and he reached them within seconds and nodded to Wren, as if to praise his self-control. The man's arm was mangled and Wren spat the blood onto the floor, wanting no part of the guard inside him. But he hadn't killed him—yet. And that was a win.

"Two," Jamison said, a reminder and Wren huffed as he left the guard with Jamison while he continued his pursuit to find the second guard.

The second one was easiest to find, mostly on account of the fact that he'd pissed himself watching Wren take down his comrade. Beneath the stench he scented more blood and Neah. The smell of her fear was stronger on this one and Wren would have wagered money that *this* was the one who had hurt her. Rage made him bare his teeth, and the reflection of his fangs showed in the guard's wide eyes.

They only needed one, right? Surely this one, the one who had hurt his mate, wasn't needed.

Decision made, Wren prepared to leap and a streak of dark fur flew into him from the side. Hackles raised, the black cat snarled viciously, the sound grating, and Wren roared back before standing down. For whatever reason, Jamison wanted this one alive.

The captain returned to two legs with a flash of light and a glare at Wren. "*Alive*," he hissed. "You can have him when we're done."

Cheered slightly by the thought, Wren took one step back and then another. Jamison snapped his fingers and two other guards stepped forward and each took hold of one of the enemy's arms while another two scooped up the guard who had tried to run.

"Now, you let me do my job. As soon as I have anything, I'll let you know."

Wren wanted to protest but Jamison had already turned away and, admittedly, Wren was a liability in this form. The guards were no good to them dead, for now anyway.

Every hour that passed without news made Wren more and more restless. He'd managed to shift back to his human form after the first hour, had been ready to find Jamison and demand answers after the second, and had nearly broken Gabe's arms when he'd tried to prevent Wren from ripping apart the palace in an effort to find something, *anything,* that indicated where they had taken Neah.

By the time it hit mid-day, Wren was half-convinced that his curse had already kicked in. He felt untethered, wild, one wrong word away from murder. Thankfully, before he could take that turn for the worst, Jamison emerged from his hideyhole and found them in Wren's chambers.

Blood speckled his face and the knuckles of one hand were split and bloody. His mouth was a grim line and Wren knew that whatever the captain had to say was worse than he'd been imagining.

"Well?" Zennon demanded when the silence went on too long.

Her father glanced at her and then away, a flicker of something passing across his face that Wren thought looked a little like shame.

"Castor."

Wren waited a beat, expecting more. "What about him?"

"He has her."

Castor. Why would his uncle have Neah? "Your information is bad. This doesn't make sense.'"

The grim look on Jamison's face only intensified. "The information is sound. They knew details about the other attacks, things we kept quiet. *He has her.*"

A tremble started in Wren's hands and made its way up his arms until his skin seemed to vibrate. Why would his uncle do this? What did he have to gain?

Wren hadn't realised he'd spoken aloud until Skye answered him. "The crown." He blinked dumbly, unable to process what Skye was saying. "Without you in the way, and no heirs muddying the water, he's the next direct link to the throne. And his daughter after him."

"You think my cousin knows about this too?"

Skye shrugged. "I don't know."

"Did you get a location?" Wren said, voice hoarse, and he licked his lips as he repeated the question to the captain.

"No. They took her to another set of guards, Castor's personal ones, and they don't know where she went after that."

It had been hours. By the Goddess, she could be anywhere in the kingdom by now.

"She has to be close," Skye said, as if he could hear Wren's thoughts. "He needs her as leverage. He'd keep her close either as bait or a bargaining chip."

Wren took a calming breath and let it whoosh out when it didn't help alleviate his worry. "Search all of his holdings, as many as possible within or surrounding the palace. If Skye's right, then he'll be at the ceremony but if we can recover Neah sooner..." Wren swallowed thickly. "She's going to be okay. We'll bring her home."

They had to, Wren wouldn't accept anything less.

CHAPTER THIRTY-THREE

NEAH

"A caged tiger, now that *is* a sight to behold."

The voice stirred Neah's consciousness and she blinked blearily, wincing as the witchlight made her head throb.

Where the Hel was she? And Romi—*oh gods, Romi.*

Chains rattled as she dragged herself into a seated position, leaning heavily against the brick wall for assistance. The front and most of the side of her cage was made of solid metal bars, caked in grime and dirt and other things she didn't particularly want to sniff out.

Her eyes slowly adjusted and a snarl ripped free from her throat when she saw the smug, smirking face of the man on the other side of the bars. *Castor.* This betrayal would hurt Wren and for that, and Romi's death, Neah would enjoy ripping him limb from limb.

"Of course," she said, voice cracking until she swallowed and took a deep breath. "You *would* stand on the other side of this cage and taunt me. Cowards become so brave when their enemies are chained up and helpless." Neah laughed and ignored the pain in her ribs as rage stoked the fire in her veins."Why don't you come in here and make your threats and we'll see how well you fair."

To her surprise, Castor smiled. His amber eyes were cold, devoid of emotion, even anger or pride as she'd hoped to stoke. "I'm fine right here, but nice try. I don't have anything to prove to you, my dear. I've already won."

"So what? You're here to gloat?"

Castor stood from his crouch and sneered down at her from above. "No. I came to warn you not to try anything stupid. Sit in your cage like a good little pet, and you won't get hurt." He ran an eye over her form and tutted at the bruises on her side. "Well hurt further, I suppose. If my nephew agrees to hand over the crown, you'll be returned to him. Unharmed."

Fuck. Wren might just agree to that. "How agreeable of you."

"Mm, yes. I rather thought so."

"And you think we'll just let you live after this?"

His smile was soft, deadly. "You would threaten your king?"

Neah surged forward, the pain in her ribs burning fiercely from the sudden movement as she slammed into the bars and spat in his face. "You are no king of mine," she intoned, smiling grimly when her glob of spittle dripped from Castor's cheek to the ground. She laughed as she backed away. Would he come in now? Give her the chance to wrap her chains around his neck?

"You know," Castor said slowly, reaching into his

pocket for a handkerchief. "I half hope my nephew refuses me, just so I can have the pleasure of your death."

Neah kept her smile on her face. If she had to, she would crawl up from the depths of Hel themselves to seek her vengeance, for herself, for Romi, and for Wren.

"I suppose we'll see," he mused and she flinched when he withdrew a sword from a scabbard at his side and clanged it against the metal bars tauntingly. "I expect I'll see you soon."

She stayed silent, slowly seething. She was his bargaining chip—the crown for her life. Sadly, she knew what Wren would choose—it would bring nothing but pain to them all. Castor couldn't be allowed to become king. His flagrant flaunting of their laws was worrying at best but to betray one's own kin? If they survived through this, Neah couldn't let him remain alive. For the good of the kingdom, if nothing else.

The murmur of voices told her Castor had left guards for her and she was shocked that he'd managed to gain so much support. Was he paying them off? Were they just as corrupt as him? Neah didn't know. The one thing she was certain of was that they were what stood between her and freedom.

She focused, listening intently and then cursing when she couldn't make out how many heartbeats were past her cell. It looked like the chains affected more than her ability to shift.

It wasn't a problem, per se, but it did make things more difficult. She had no way of knowing how much she relied on her strength and senses, even when she couldn't shift, so she would just have to hope her training was enough.

Or…

Neah lifted the chains closely to her face, inspecting them as best she could with the little light that encroached on the space from the corridor. Brickwork surrounded her, but the style was familiar. They had to still be in the palace, but not anywhere she recognised, and from the colour of her bruises she assumed most of the day had already passed while she'd been unconscious. How long had Castor been planning this? She should have killed him a week ago when she'd had the chance.

Refocusing on the chains, she tested their strength and grunted when they didn't budge. But there was a gap in the manacle around her wrist, not quite big enough for her to wriggle out of because of her thumbs, no matter how much she contorted their shape. Unless…

She glanced around, finding nothing in the dank cell except dirt and what looked like a rat's nest in the corner. It would have been better if she'd had something to bite down on, that way she'd have the element of surprise, but beggars couldn't be choosers.

Neah sucked in a steadying breath and placed her hands atop each other as she felt along the dips of muscle and bone in her left hand with the fingertips of her right.

Here goes nothing.

She wrenched and the sharp crack was lost in the shriek of pain that tore from her throat. But it worked. Her thumb bent at an odd angle and she cursed under her breath as she shoved her hand out of the manacle and felt immediate relief when she shoved the digit back in place.

Voices sounded, growing closer, no doubt coming to

investigate what the Hel she was doing. She had to be quick.

Neah reached down and repeated the process, her scream making the guards pace increase and they rounded the corner just as she slipped off the other cuff and slammed her thumb back into place.

Metal hit the ground, the sound loud enough that one guard flinched, and she didn't know whether to be annoyed or flattered that Castor had left five of them to watch her.

"Oh shit," one said, eyes falling to the chains on the ground as Neah rolled out her shoulders and smiled. *Oh shit* was about right.

The reaction of her body once the spelled shackles were off was immediate. Strength returned to her limbs and her ribs tingled as her body worked to repair the damage she'd sustained.

"I'll give you one chance to run," she said, rubbing her wrists where the chains had chafed. Two guards eyed each other, skepticism in their eyes, like they couldn't believe someone in a cage would bother to threaten them. But one guard, the same one who'd flinched before, looked more wary.

He lifted his hands, showing he was unarmed, and his companions' mouths dropped open disbelievingly. "I'm sorry. I just needed the money for my family."

She didn't like it, but Neah could respect that. She, too, would do questionable things for the ones she loved. "Leave."

He left, and the remaining four guards seemed to take

that personally, as if it had been a test of their character, or strength. And it had, but not in the way they thought. Swords were drawn and she watched impassively as they directed them at her.

"Just stay where you are," one of them said, dark eyes serious. "Stay there, and you won't get hurt."

"Funny," she murmured, strolling closer to the bars and peering into his face. "That's usually my line."

If they were still inside the palace, like she suspected, then it wouldn't take Castor long to reach Wren. He had at least a ten-minute head start, plus however long it took her to get past the men he'd left behind. Hopefully that wasn't too late to prevent him from handing over his crown.

Neah slid a palm on the inside of two bars and pushed, pleased when they gave and bent. These, at least, were weaker than the chains on her shackles. Two of the swords closest to her drooped in shock as she wriggled through the enlarged gap and smiled.

"Now, what were you saying about getting hurt?"

Maybe it was the fact that she was still barely clothed, or that she held no weapon, or possibly even that they'd witnessed her bend metal with her bare hands, but the guards didn't seem to know what to make of her bravado.

The one at the front, with the dark eyes, at last made his decision and swung for her with his sword. She stepped beneath the broad stroke easily, laughing darkly when it brought her into his space and she grabbed the dagger at his belt and drew it across his throat.

They hadn't hesitated to kill Romi. She couldn't hesitate now.

Blood flashed out from the wound and she blinked it out of her eyes, disturbed by the pink tinge in her vision as the death of one of their own shook the three guards out of their stupor.

Two charged at her and she ducked before striking up at the hilt of one sword and sending it flying away as the other passed harmlessly overhead. A glancing blow to her shoulder slowed her momentarily and a second one crashed into her stomach, but she refused to let it slow her down.

A knife flew from her hand, the first guard's blood zipping through the air in small droplets as it left the blade in time for it to gain a fresh coat as it landed with a squelch into the eye of the guard swinging for her.

He dropped and the two guards left decided there was safety in numbers, retreating toward each other and then advancing with their swords held aloft. Neah bent and grabbed the sword of the guard whose throat she'd slashed, throwing it from hand to hand to test its balance before blocking the first strike aimed her way and knocking that blade free from the guard's hand. She caught it in mid-air and cocked her head as the guard gaped, his sword now firmly in her grip.

Generally, she didn't recommend throwing away her weapons, but she had no need for two swords. So she launched the one in her left hand, sending it flying toward the empty-handed guard like an arrow and watching as it hit his chest dead-centre, the force driving him back toward the wall.

The final guard had bided his time, but when he came for her, she was ready.

"It really didn't have to be this way," she murmured as she stepped over the bodies and let the sword drop to the floor, it would only slow her down. She had a ceremony to get to.

CHAPTER THIRTY-FOUR

WREN

They had searched for Castor right up until the deadline for the ceremony, when they'd had to admit defeat. He would be there, Wren was sure. But it still felt like he'd failed his mate in not being able to find her. The shackles effect on her magic had dampened the fragile thread of their bond so that he couldn't even follow that to find her. Wherever his uncle had her tucked away had to be one of the infamous, secret rooms built into the palace. Wren had found many of them over the years, but plenty still eluded him.

By now, the court would be gathered and waiting for him and Neah, ready to celebrate their bond. Except, Neah wasn't there. The breath caught in his chest and Wren coughed lightly as he adjusted the cuffs of his custom ceremonial wear and straightened his golden crown. The details were lost on him as he kept imagining the worst, Neah's body lifeless at the altar, his uncle waiting for him with a smile next to her body.

Wren shook his head, as if he could rid himself of the image by force.

A steadying hand touched his arm and he nodded when Skye asked if he was okay.

The truth was that he was a wreck. He was trying to be strong, but rage and sorrow waged a war inside of him that left him shaken.

"It's time," Sonnet said, cutting through the buzzing that had risen up around him and left him unmoored. "Are you ready?

Wren nodded. He could do this. For Neah.

He pushed a smile onto his face and let Sonnet walk into the great hall first, Gabe and Skye at her side. Waiting a beat, Wren looked to the floor and tried to slow the racing of his heart before jolting at a touch on his inner arm.

His mother smiled at him. "You didn't think I'd let you walk alone, did you, cub?" Wren's shoulders eased and he managed a wobbly smile back. "There. You see? No need to be nervous. Your other half is waiting for you."

He swallowed thickly but nodded. Nobody knew the ceremony had descended into a farce, little more than a trap for his uncle, but they would soon enough.

Wren walked into the hall with his mother on his arm and wrath in his blood.

The room had been decorated for the occasion, an arch stood at the back of the room, haloed by the setting sun through the back window. Pale flowers twined and cascaded over the structure and a white strip of material had been laid on the ground as a walkway that led to the altar where Sonnet stood. It was beautiful, and it would have been perfect for their bonding ceremony. It was a shame that fate had other plans.

His mother kissed his cheek when they reached the front and he squeezed her hand gently before she moved off to the right to stand with Gabe and Skye.

Ingredients for the spell were laid out on the moonstone altar beneath the arch, a white ribbon, white sage, and a ceremonial knife for their blood with a hilt made of jade.

Wren turned to face the crowd, his kingdom and court, and the dark expression on his face made the smiles in the rows of seats falter.

"Well, Uncle? Are you going to make me wait?"

Silence fell before a rush of murmurs swept the room like the buzz of an insect, cut only by the chuckle of Castor as he stood from his seat within the crowd and made his way out into the aisle.

"You always were a clever one. So unlike your father in that regard."

Gasps rang out and Wren was glad to hear it, to know that Castor's poison hadn't spread everywhere in the palace just yet.

"Castor, what are you saying?" His mother had moved closer to Wren, the shock on her face authentic, and he allowed himself a moment of relief to know that whatever his uncle had planned, she'd had no part in it.

"Oh hello, Fortuna dear. You deign to speak with me now, hm? It only took some attempted murder and the attention of the entire court to gain the honour, but no matter. Bygones." Castor laughed without humour and Wren nudged his mother back toward Gabe and Skye.

"Where is she?"

"Straight to business? Well, alright then. For anyone unaware of the king's current predicament, he's waiting for his mate, his *queen*. Except, she won't be arriving. Not while I hold her in the old cells beneath the palace."

Cells. Wren saw red, a growl leaving him that shook the petals of the flowers on the arch. Sonnet moved to his side and he took a breath, nodding at her in thanks. He needed to play this right, or they would lose Neah for good.

The court sat silently, shocked, though a few had started to rise and creep for the exit. Wise, if the bloodshed Wren anticipated proved to be true.

"What's to stop me from killing you and retrieving her?" He kept the words smooth, controlled, and Castor's smile was mocking, as if he could see every inch of the struggle beneath Wren's facade.

"If my men don't hear from me within half an hour, they'll kill her."

Within half hour. Wren did the math and ground his teeth. He wouldn't get there in time if he killed Castor now. The tunnels that led to the old cells were extensive. Traversing them would be faster on four feet, but he couldn't gamble. Not when it came to Neah's life.

Resigned, he took a step down from the dais and toward his uncle. "What do you want?"

"What should always have been mine." Castor's face screwed up into a scowl and oddly, Wren thought it suited him better than the faux-pleasant mask he always wore. "The crown for your mate."

"That's not—"

Wren cut his mother off, eyes on Castor. "You'll relinquish Neah, alive, to me?"

"Wren! You cannot do this. The crown was *never* meant for him!"

"Why *is* that, Fortuna? Oh. He told you didn't he?" Castor chuckled as he approached, brushing past Wren like he was little more than an irritant. "Naughty Theodore. He was supposed to take that secret to the grave. I suppose I should have killed him sooner."

Wren froze and then slowly turned, breaths coming sharp and fast. "What did you just say?"

"Ah. You hadn't put that part together yet? Surprise," Castor said dryly. "Daddy's dead and it's all mean Uncle Castor's fault."

It was at that moment that Wren realised his uncle was unhinged. How hadn't he seen the madness lurking beneath the surface before?

"So you see," Castor continued, cupping Fortuna's face tenderly enough that Wren felt sick. "The crown should always have passed to me. No pesky curse to worry about from the illegitimate brother, an heir ready to go…" Castor dropped his hand and turned to face Wren, the hatred in his eyes burning deeply as the fading sunlight cast shadows onto his cheeks, making him look hollow. "But you were chosen. *You.*"

Wren straightened, doing his best to look impassive even as internally he reeled from the truth of his father's death. "Are we going to chat? Or crown a new king?" He'd meant what he'd told Neah before. His crown and kingdom meant nothing without her. *She* was his priority.

He took off the crown and cradled it in his palms, eyes

following the swirls and knots and the roaring tiger's head that made up the carved centrepiece. Then he tossed it to his uncle.

Castor caught it, bemused. "There's a little more to it than that."

"By all means. We're all here." Wren swept his hand out to indicate the half-full room. Many of the inhabitants had stayed, out of loyalty or just curiosity, he didn't know. Others had fled the upcoming conflict.

"Here." Castor beckoned him closer and Wren didn't hesitate, showed no fear. "Kneel. Repeat after me. *I, Wren Ainsworthy,*" Castor intoned and Wren rolled his eyes as he knelt to the ground and complied. "*Do freely surrender my throne, my crown, and my title.*"

Wren cleared his throat to continue, just wanting it over with. Wanting Neah back where she belonged: by his side. "Do freely sur—"

The doors to the hall crashed open, stealing his words. Golden eyes met his own and lips he'd tasted mere nights ago tipped up in a smile. Blood and streaks of dirt covered her skin, the remnants of bruising fading before his eyes, as Neah walked into the room as if this were an everyday occurrence.

"Sorry I'm late. I seem to have misplaced my dress," she said lightly, but the look she levelled on Castor would have driven enemies from their door in fear. "Oh good, Castor. I was hoping to catch-up with you."

CHAPTER THIRTY-FIVE

NEAH

The crown clanged as it dropped to the ground, its holder's hands disappearing in favour of wings, and Neah ran, shifting mid-leap.

I made it. I made it. I made it. And just in time, too. Though, the image of Wren kneeling at his uncle's feet for *her* would not soon vanish.

Feathers caught in her mouth as she gripped the wing of the great bird attempting to flee and brought it back to the ground with a *smack* that puffed dark feathers up and around them.

Castor transformed as he hit the ground, returning to his human form and scrabbling for a sword. Neah knocked it from his grip with a careless swipe of one paw, her claws raking against his skin and making him cry out.

Neah hesitated, glancing to Wren but he just nodded, clearly happy to let her deal with Castor as she saw fit.

"This isn't over." He coughed wetly as he scrambled

back and away from her on all fours. "I'll kill you all and take what is *mine*—"

Her jaw closed around his head, the crunch satisfying as she shook Castor before flinging his detached head from his body and to the ground. Screams rang out but Neah didn't care. The man was sick. He'd killed Romi, nearly killed Zennon, and had been targeting her and Wren for weeks too.

May he feel the Goddess' wrath in Hel.

Wren dropped to the ground and cupped her maw, gazing intently into her eyes. "I love you."

She couldn't reply in this form so, instead, she licked his face and nudged his fallen crown toward him. He picked it up and smiled, setting it on her furry head before lifting it up and back onto his.

"Here." Sonnet opened the folds of her ceremonial robes, revealing the dress Romi had made for her beneath. The flaps offered Neah some privacy to shift back and Sonnet nodded off to the side, where Gabe and Skye held her dress.

"I don't want to get it dirty," she mumbled once she was back in skin rather than fur. Skye waved his hand, muttering something under his breath that she couldn't make sense of, and the worst of the blood and grime lifted away. "Thank you." The plush orange dress fell over her and pooled around her bare feet and she swallowed hard, unable to shake the image of Romi lying still on the floor of Neah's chambers, blood pooling beneath her. "How did you know to bring it?"

Sonnet smiled as she let her arms drop back down. "Skye had a feeling."

Wren took Sonnet's place and she fell into his arms, exhaustion weighing hard on her. Unconsciousness didn't equal a restful sleep, it turned out. "Shall we do it now? Or do you want to wait?"

She smiled tiredly, smothering a yawn behind her hand. "I don't want to wait another second."

He chuckled. "Come on, then." His hand clasped hers, warm and steady, and Neah basked in the simplicity of it. The smell of sage wafted to them as Sonnet walked in a circle around them three times clockwise and three times in the other direction before placing the burning sage back on the altar to continue smoking. She raised her arms and the last of the sunlight seemed to fill the gap between her palms, her own magic bolstering the light as she guided the orb back down and let it sink into the length of white ribbon atop the marble.

They turned to face each other, hands intertwined, and Sonnet wrapped the ribbon around Wren's wrist and along and around Neah's. With their other hand, they pricked their fingers on the blade Sonnet proffered and let the blood drip onto the ribbon, speckles of red marring the white.

Magic probed within her chest, searching, asking her a simple question that Neah answered easily. *Yes. I accept the bond.*

Warmth pooled in her hand, the blood on the ribbon sinking in as if it had never been there at all before the ribbon followed suit, disappearing into the skin of their hands in an intricate whorl of silver designs.

Sonnet smiled. "Your bond is complete. You have been

blessed by the Goddess. Let all who are present here act as witness to Selene's will."

They bowed their heads and when they raised them again, it was to cheers. Neah leaned in, brushing her lips over Wren's, happy to drink in the moment before more danger could strike. The ceremony had been somewhat expedited on account of her exhaustion, but it was done and Wren was safe. That was what mattered.

"Come," he said, tugging gently on her hand and leading them back down the aisle that had been decorated with a white strip of cloth.

As they got to the end, the doors opened and Zennon cried out when she saw Neah, rushing forward to wrap her in an embrace.

Neah hugged her back just as fiercely before pulling away, pain pricking in her eyes as she bit her lip. "Zen, I'm so sorry. Romi—I tried, I really tried. I'm so sorry."

Zennon shook her head, clasping Neah's cheeks and wiping away the tears that spilled over. "Don't be. She'll be out of bed by tomorrow."

She—"What?" Neah barely breathed the word, tentative joy and relief rising up. "She's alive?"

The eyes staring into her own widened. "I didn't–I thought you knew! We got to her in time. She's going to be okay."

At this point, Neah's muscles gave out on her and Wren swung her up and into his arms. "Rest now," he murmured. "You can see Romi later. Rest, *caritas*. I've got you."

CHAPTER THIRTY-SIX

When she woke, it was without an ache in her muscles and to warmth and softness. Wren was in bed beside her, reading a book with a pair of tiny spectacles balanced on the end of his nose and a slightly warm glass of water sat on the table beside her.

He looked up when she reached for it, eyes gentle, and she appreciated that he didn't immediately jump on her with a thousand questions. Despite that she had the same number for him. Was Romi really okay? What had Castor told him about where she'd been held? Were her parents alright? Had his curse broken?

Instead of voicing them all, Neah finished her water and set the glass down with a quiet thump before shimmying back down and under the warm covers. She curled up next to Wren and his arm came around her, stroking through her hair as he read his book and before long her eyes were closing again.

The next time she opened them, the sun was lower in the sky beyond the balcony and Wren's cheek rested against the top of her head. As if sensing she was awake, he pressed a kiss there and then pulled back to look at her.

"Food?"

Her stomach answered for her, growling loudly and he smirked. "Coming right up." His retreat from the bed stole some of the warmth, but she was content to stay there, waiting for him to come back. When he did, he was laden down with plates of food. Bacon, pancakes, toast and jam, sausages, eggs, and porridge and she licked her lips, wanting to inhale all of it.

"You're the best," she mumbled around a mouthful of sausage and then slapped his hand when he reached for a piece of toast. "Oops, sorry. Go ahead." It had been instinct, but she would share her breakfast for Wren. She drew the line at bacon though.

Once her hunger had been sated, she used the bathing chamber to freshen up and then climbed back into bed. She wasn't quite ready to face the outside world yet.

"Are you okay?" she asked eventually and Wren nodded and then shrugged.

"Yes. I'm glad you're okay, that my curse is broken—"

"Sonnet confirmed it?"

He nodded. "While you were sleeping. I still carry it though, in my blood." Wren licked his lips. "She's going to try and find a way to be rid of it entirely."

Meaning his children wouldn't also be afflicted. Neah smiled. "That's great."

He shrugged. "We'll try anyway."

Silence fell and Neah broke it first, tentatively reaching for him. "Are you okay?"

"I feel like I should be asking you that." Wren laughed without humour. "I'm not sure how to feel about Castor. He was… I don't know, Neah. Mad, perhaps? Feral? I think he truly hated me. He killed my father."

Neah sucked in a breath and squeezed his hand gently. "I'm sorry." There was nothing more she could say or do, time would have to do the healing of that wound. But she could be beside him while it scarred.

"Did he hurt you?" Wren looked scared for the answer, his worry coming through from their bond, and her eyes widened.

"I can feel you."

Wren squeezed her fingers and raised a brow. "Yes?"

"No, I mean, the bond. I can *feel* you."

Wonder shone in his eyes. "I can't sense anything yet."

Her smile was brief before she thought back to his question. "No. A couple of the guards were a little rough, but most of the blood I was wearing wasn't mine. He left five guards, one surrendered and I killed the other four." She said the words bluntly, keeping emotion out of it as best she could, but despite her best efforts and the knowledge that it had been necessary, she knew their faces would haunt her the same as her other victims.

"You did what you had to do," Wren murmured, seeing right through her.

Their lips met in a tender kiss that deepened after only a few seconds.

"I was so scared I'd lost you," Wren mumbled against her mouth, his breaths feverish as she reached for him, pulling the shirt from his shoulders so quickly the material ripped.

"Never," she whispered, pressing the word into his skin over and over as she tasted him, warm and sweet on her tongue. Her mouth sucked gently at his throat, nipping at the underside of his jaw, licking at his bottom lip, devouring him. She'd nearly lost him, lost everything.

"*Caritas*," the word was a whispered groan as he arched under her mouth, and she gave him more. Her hands ran down his body, tracing every ridge and every scar on his chest and stomach, loving the way he shivered at the featherlight touch.

Wren rolled, taking her with him as he hovered over her and kissed a path of heat down her neck to her chest, worshiping her breasts with lingering, wet kisses that made her gasp. The last of his clothes were shed and hers joined his, flung beyond the bed.

Then his hands were on her, roaming her body with a proprietary grip that made her rock against him eagerly. It had only been a few days, and yet she'd missed him. Missed the feel of him against her, his scent intertwining with hers, the gasp of her name on his lips.

Her thighs fell to either side of his and she lay flush against him, whimpering when he teased her with his hand and then the tip of him, slicking through her wetness. She wiggled, impatient, ready to demand more, and he sheathed himself in one long thrust that made them both groan. The relief was instant, but her pleasure was cresting to a new high, like she'd had a taste in her need for him and now she wanted it all.

"I love you," he murmured, breath warm in her ear and

making her shiver as he began to move, the roll of his hips making sparks come alive in her body.

"Wren," she gasped and his hands found her hips, encouraging her to rock against him while she squeezed her own breasts. A glance down had him sprawled out under her like feast, the lightly mussed elegance of his hair and the satisfied all-male gleam in his eyes making her pussy tighten around his cock. "I love you."

He ground up and into her, eyes dropping down to watch her taking him and when he looked back up his eyes smoldered. "Neah—"

Her head fell back and she moved quicker, needing more, hovering so close to the edge she could almost taste heaven, and then his fingers pressed into her mouth and she sucked eagerly before he withdrew and pressed down on her clit with his wet digits until she saw stars.

The pleasure rippled through her, claws forming at the tips of her fingers and sending puffs of feathers up into the air from the pillows and she laughed as their pace slowed, a languid heat filling her when Wren clasped her to his chest, still inside her.

Once their breathing slowed and the sweet stroke of Wren's hand up and down her spine had her bones feeling like jelly, he pressed a kiss to her temple. "So, mate, what do you want to do now?"

The possibilities felt endless. No more assassins, no more spying. Just family and love and maybe breaking a curse or two. Neah smiled, dipping her head for a long, lingering kiss that nipped at his bottom lip. "I can think of a few things."

Her laughter was lost in the covers as Wren rolled them over and kissed her once more.

Looking for more steamy romantasy? Check out the rest of the Romancing the Realms series of standalones!

ACKNOWLEDGMENTS

First and foremost – thank you to you, the reader. Your support means everything and I hope you loved reading Wren and Neah's story. While Courting the Tiger King is a standalone book, I do plan on writing more in this world, so keep an eye out for more news soon!

Thank you to Jordan, Michelle, Chloe, and Miranda for taking part in the Romancing the Realms collection with me, your dedication to make this project work has been incredible and I can't wait for readers to discover the series and the gorgeous Kickstarter campaign for our books!

Courting the Tiger King wouldn't be what it is right now without Selkkie, who created the original discreet cover, and Valentaine who created the beautiful illustrated edition. Thank you to Jenna Weatherwax, Callie Dahl, and Sophie Snow for reading an early draft of this book and cheering me on, and to Helena V Paris for always encouraging me! Thank you also to Brigid Kemmerer, whose Discord group helped me actually write words and bring this book to life!

Finally, thank you to my partner, Connor, for your endless support and my two little kitties for keeping me company while I write.

**Continue past the acknowledgments to read the first

chapter of each Romancing the Realms novel: five steamy standalone romantasy books!

ABOUT THE AUTHOR

Jade Church is putting the 'O' in romance with her high-heat and swoony romance books. Jade currently lives in the U.K. and when she's not cuddling her cats or writing, she spends the majority of her time reading and binge re-watching The Vampire Diaries.

LOOKING FOR MORE STEAMY ROMANTASY? CHECK OUT THE REST OF THE ROMANCING THE REALMS COLLECTION!

ROMANCING THE REALMS

JORDAN DUGDALE

COURTING THE DRAGON MAGE

COURTING THE DRAGON MAGE

My head slammed against the floor, and the shouting became distant.

Still, I'd never felt more alive.

Get up, Lyra.

"No one told me the Pit Viper was little more than a weedy little cunt. It's almost unfair, beating on a woman like that..." My opponent's words were invigorating as my anger sang through me like a numbing drug. The taste of copper was thick on my tongue as blood flowed through my mouth, and I spat it out as I forced myself to my feet. People surrounded me, shouting, though I could not discern their words. The man who had struck me waved his hands as if he had already won. I wanted to groan; the world swayed, but I refused to fall again as I launched myself at him. The people around me gasped, but I was quick and had my legs wrapped around his waist and my arm across his neck before he could turn to see me coming.

I pulled my arm taut against his neck, crushing his windpipe, and he flung us around in a panic, scrambling with blunt fingers to pry me from his back. If I could just get him to pass out…

I cried out as he threw himself back. I hit the ground hard, and my vision went spotty as the air was ripped from my lungs. Gods, had he broken my rib? No, no, I could still breathe.

"Submit," I whispered, forcing my arm to tighten around his neck. I had managed to keep my arm across his neck by Nymera's miracle. My fingers locked around my wrist, and though he struggled, his thrashing was beginning to fade. I was lucky; they'd put me against someone suited to my size in this fight.

After a few tense moments, the man slumped against me, allowing my hold on him to lessen. The fighting rings of Kraeva were not to the death, and though my blood sang for violence, I yielded. I used what strength I possessed to push the man off of me, allowing the one in charge of enforcing fair fighting to drag me to my feet. My hearing was distorted; the crowd cheered as he lifted my arm, their screams distant and too loud all at once. Still, I smiled.

This was why I came down here.

"The Pit Viper takes another prey!"

"Thank *fuck*. I put a lot of sandyms down on her victory."

"Fucking bitch cheated!"

Their words surrounded me as my head thundered painfully. The headache I was about to have would be merciless, but I won, which was all that mattered.

"A small spitfire as always, my little viper." A man in noble silks approached with a large bag of sandyms. My head throbbed again, and the motion jarred against my swelling cheek. My tongue darted out, tasting blood on my lip, which had split on the right side. My opponent had done a number on me before I knocked him out.

"Some of us have to earn our suppers." The lie came to me quickly. I had more than enough sandyms to fill my belly, but the fewer underlings who recognized me, the better. The last thing I wanted was to get my father or brother involved with the fighting pits in the belly of Kraeva. Hence, I paid a local mage handsomely for a potion that would mask my features for a few hours.

The bag of sandyms in Faeva's plump hand was for potions I could only find in the lower districts, districts my father was too proud to purchase from, even if it was for medicine for his son.

The magic was beginning to wear off, though. It prickled against my skin, a warning that if I didn't hurry away, my cover would shatter.

I attempted to keep calm as I held my hand out, hoping, for once, that Faeva would be merciful and give me my dues with little trouble.

He was not.

"Come and speak with the others. They wish to celebrate your recent accomplishments. It's not common to have someone of your stature go undefeated in the rings." His eyes raked over me, and I suppressed the urge to shudder in disgust.

"I'm afraid I have other business to attend." Now that

the fighting had won, my lust for the fight had diminished and slunk away to the hollow of my chest to slumber until it woke again and demanded blood. I had no time for the squabbles of nobles, no time to pretend to give a shit about their praises. I didn't do this for the validation. I did this to calm the ache in my chest. I did this to try to save my brother from the Blooming Dahlia, a plague that had swept through the streets of Kraeva in recent months. My brother had fallen ill with it a week or so ago, and my desire to seek his cure had consumed all of my efforts.

Faeva frowned but relented with little trouble, passing over the bag of sandyms and simply nodding. The weight felt good in my palm, and I made a mental note to stop by the bakery nearby in the morning to buy some warm gyras. They were my brother's favorite. He may be well enough tomorrow to eat one. His appetite came and went, and he hadn't been able to enjoy his favorite treat since before he got sick.

"Next time, then," Faeva said, and I agreed with a feigned smile. He said that every time. Sometimes, I indulged him, but not tonight. Not as my skin itched, and the magic began to liberate itself from my skin.

People murmured quietly around me as I made my way towards the door. Another fight was getting ready to happen, so most people paid me little mind, which I was grateful for. The room was small, and sweat collected on my brow from so many bodies pressed closely together.

The nape of my neck prickled like I was being watched. I glanced up from where my eyes had been trained mainly on the floor and met the gaze of a faerie.

She was of Eirwyn's Court. I knew that much. The fae

from Neferíl's Court did not come here, not while they warred with the humans of the north. If the fae were here, it was from the Elven King of Southern Elvira, the forest of the fae.

She stared at me, her hair almost ethereal as it wove around her, embellished with intricate braids. Her eyes were cat-like, her ears as pointed as her canines when she flashed a wicked smile my way. It wasn't uncommon for the fair folk to attend these fights; they had a simple curiosity for human affairs and could only breach the forest's edge at night.

Another faerie stood next to her, a male. He was tall and lanky, with dark hair that was longer than hers and draped over his shoulders. He was pale, eerily so, his eyes dark voids of black.

I ducked my head, ignoring the anxious patter in my chest, and strode past him.

The male faerie said something, but I couldn't understand him. Some folk from Kraeva braved the faerie food and wine to understand the fae, diluting it to avoid the consequences of too much of its consumption. I was not one of those people, and I smiled apologetically as I met the faerie's gaze.

He didn't say anything else, and I barreled into someone in my eagerness to escape them.

"*Shit.* I'm sor—" My words died as the stranger flinched away from me in disgust.

It was the crowned prince, Nasir, someone I was all too familiar with during my time growing up in the castle. His hair was slicked back, and his dark eyes raked over me in disgust. Luckily, he didn't seem to recognize me. His attention turned towards the front of his shirt, now covered in ale. I must have knocked his glass from his grasp.

What was Prince Nasir doing at the fighting pits?

"Stupid cunt—these silks cost more than your worthless life. They could throw you back in the pits, you know—all it would take is a snap of my pretty little fingers." He raised his hand, his fingers poised at the ready. Like a snake, ready to strike. "Next time, I'll see you fight someone you cannot win against."

I sneered, but my words lodged in the back of my throat as my skin prickled again. *Last warning. I need to get out of here before the prince recognizes me.*

"My apologies, Your Royal Highness." I curtsied and then turned on my heel, fleeing before the prince could rebut.

I spilled out into the alleyway. The air, while warm, was a welcome relief against my aching skin as I pressed myself against the wall and sighed.

That was too close. I would time things better next time.

Still, the thrill of it all sang through me, and breathless laughter escaped my lips as I pressed a hand to my face. I clutched the bag of sandyms in my other hand as I hurried from the alley, eager to be home. The fighting pits were located in the lower districts of Kraeva, but I had learned which alleys and side roads to take to reach the royal districts more quickly as I tucked my sandyms inside my shirt, hiding the bag from wandering eyes. I knew better than to flash currency in the struggling parts of the city.

Wind trailed through the deserted streets as I stayed

within shadows, hidden from anyone who might be out. Knights patrolled the city in their light leather armor and khopeshes, but I managed to stay out of their observant gaze as I hurried up the cliffs towards the Royal Keep.

A low whimper echoed to my right as I passed by an alley. It was so soft it could have been the wind, but as my eyes adjusted to the dark, I flinched and ducked away as a fist swung past my left shoulder.

"Beat it, little rat," a man hissed, his eyes glowing in the darkness. Fae, perhaps? I couldn't tell as I scrambled away, my heart a wild, untamed thing in my chest. I couldn't see well enough in the dark, but it looked like there were two of them, and one had someone pinned up against the wall further in the alley, their shirt wrapped around his fingers. "Before you end up in'a sit'a'tion you don' wanna be in."

"What did he do?" I asked, gesturing to the man pinned to the wall. "Because if there's something I hate, it's pricks that think they can beat on someone half their size."

The man who had nearly punched me growled and lunged, his bald head gleaming in the moon's light. I swung out of the way just in time and then let go. Headache be damned.

The ache in my chest rekindled as it sang in excitement. I swept to the side and turned, instantly swinging out to grab the man's wrist as he lashed out at me with a curled fist.

Dodging the man's attack, I sank low. I needed to take him out quickly. I was already exhausted from my last fight.

He was quicker than I thought, though, and he laughed. "Tired, street rat?" His words were meant to poke at me, tug at my resolve, and make me reckless, but I had learned long ago that anger only led to mistakes and loss.

Somehow, I managed to get behind him as he darted past me.

Gotcha. Like the man from the pits, I latched myself onto the man's back, wrapped my legs around his waist, and slipped my arm across his windpipe. Tugging, I did not hold back as I had in the fighting pits. Here, there was no one telling me to show mercy.

The man struggled for several moments before he eventually gave up, his body slumping. I released him and managed to stay on my feet, my attention turning towards the others in the alley.

The other man cursed in a language I did not recognize and spit on the ground. "Not worth the trouble," he said in a heavily accented tone, pushing the man towards me and bolting.

Chest heaving, my legs gave out. I had borrowed too much time tonight and fought the odds stacked against me. The man they'd been bullying rushed over and knelt, his face swimming in my blurry vision. Oh gods, I was going to pass out. I couldn't pass out, not here. Not now. Someone would find me. Someone would...

"Breathe." The man's voice washed over me, and I inhaled sharply, forcing the darkness encroaching at my vision's edge to retreat. It was as if by magic, and I blinked rapidly as my eyes fell upon the stranger.

"Thank you for saving me," the stranger said, his eyes burning with the flourish of magic. It was otherworldly, and I immediately flushed as he smiled at me. The alley was too dark to reveal his features, but I knew he wasn't human. No human looked as he did now, with the soft glow of magic brushed against his skin.

"You shouldn't be out at night unless you know how to handle yourself. Or at least keep away from dark alleys. There's a fucking war going on," I scolded, but my voice was weak, wavering from exhaustion.

"Yes, well..." the stranger's thumb brushed against the sharp line of my jaw, and the tingle of magic returned. Suddenly, I didn't feel quite so weak, as if I could stand if I tried. Pain pulsed through my face, a reminder that I had taken quite the beating *before* I had fought the men in the alley. "They caught me off guard as I was leaving."

"What were they bothering you for anyway?" I trailed off, distracted by the man's thumb against my cheek.

He pulled away, adjusting his jacket as he rose and offered me a hand. "Wrong place, wrong time, I gather," he muttered as I allowed him to pull me to my feet. Yes, I could make it home now, and a startling clarity overcame me.

Not many knew how to wield magic, which meant this man was either a fae or a mage.

Both prospects made me uneasy, and I watched the man limp over and pick something up off the ground. A cane, one he leaned heavily against as he turned to meet my nervous gaze.

I shouldn't have been so frightened; I had seen him incapable of defending himself, but the idea of what he was capable of magically didn't sit right in my stomach, and I sidled towards the lip of the alley and cleared my throat.

"I'm glad I could help, but I should get home."

"Let me accompany you. As you said, it's dangerous at night."

I sneered, trying to tame the flurry of my racing heart in my chest. "And as you saw, I know how to care for myself. Good night..."

A low, breathy laughter escaped the man's lips. "Alistair."

I turned and fled the alley, sticking to the main roads towards my flower shop. The magic had worn from my face, freeing it from its disguise, and while I was usually one to stick to the shadows to avoid recognition, the whole night had left me rattled.

No one was out anyway. The warring kingdoms had left the streets of Kraeva silent; everyone was too fearful of Bracaea flying their dragons to lay waste to the cities and villages to dare brave the nightlife. No one knew of the sickness that festered in the belly of their city. Not yet. I knew it was only a matter of time, though. The Crown couldn't silence it forever.

Chilly sea air brushed my face as I rounded the corner, and my flower shop appeared. It was near the keep, which loomed high up on a cliffside edging the ocean, and relief overcame me. Everything that had transpired tonight left me rattled. It was becoming increasingly dangerous to travel the city at night.

A shadow blotted out the moon, and my blood ran cold as I looked up and met the sight of a dragon soaring overhead. It wasn't close enough to discern its size or what it looked like, but there was no mistaking it as it sailed over the city and bells began to sound, an alarm signaling that the city was under attack.

I quickened my pace and did not look up again as I found myself safely inside my shop, my heart thundering in my ears.

What the fuck was a dragon doing in Kraeva?

Continue reading now on Kindle Unlimited: https://mybook.to/6lFQ1

ROMANCING THE REALMS
MICHELLE MORAS
COURTING
THE
SWAN
PRINCE

COURTING THE SWAN PRINCE

The air is heavy with the Autumn Realm's constant amber haze, sunlight filtering through the oak trees' branches. I close my eyes, relishing in the warmth as it seeps into my skin. It's a perfect day for archery practice with my best friends. Best friends who are the princes of the kingdom.

"Ready to lose, Odette?" Odin asks, taunting me with his playful voice. He knows just how to provoke me. Ever since our earlier years in primary school, he was always teasing and toying with me, relentless in his pursuit to make me laugh or get a rise out of me. Ever the troublemaker, but I love him for it.

I open my eyes and shoot him a glance. "You only wish," I say, pressing my shoulders back and adjusting my bow. The target stands across the clearing, bark chipped where we've already missed a few times. "Besides, we all know Siegfried is the best shot," I say, looking over my shoulder at Odin's twin. Siegfried's cheeks flush after I wink at him.

If Odin is the jester, Siegfried is like the royal librarian, wise and quiet.

Odin's smirk deepens, his gaze flicking between Siegfried and me. "Well, then let's make it interesting," he says. "Whoever lands a bullseye first gets to marry Odette someday."

Freezing in my spot with heat rising in my cheeks, I glance toward Siegfried. His face is turning red too, but he tries to laugh it off, rubbing the back of his neck. I know it's just a silly game, but I'm baffled he'd wager such a bet. We're just friends, and to suggest we'd be more someday makes my stomach flutter with a thousand butterflies. Neither prince has ever dared to even hold my hand, let alone kiss me. Although, I've daydreamed of Seigfried doing those very things.

"Odin, that's..." Siegfried says, rubbing his temples. "Odette's too good for either of us."

"That may be true, but one of us will be king someday, so maybe she'll want to be queen. Besides, it's just a bit of fun, right?" Odin asks, flashing that charming, dangerous, gorgeous smile of his.

The twins couldn't be more different in personality or looks. Odin, with his dark, curly locks, wide jaw, and dimples, and Siegfried with blonde hair, a long nose, and high cheekbones. Their only similarity is in their stunning blue eyes that are now staring each other down. "Or are you too afraid to compete?"

Siegfried stiffens, the flicker of rivalry between them sparking as it always does when we do anything competitive. Neither wanting ever to appear weak, especially not in front of me. I'm not sure when things became this tense between them, this shift in their relationship to prove themselves. It's hard sometimes, balancing between them. Odin and Siegfried—they're like fire and water, and I'm caught right in the middle, tugged between their differences. But I don't want to choose. I prefer things to remain unchanged.

It infuriates me, especially when they should know they have nothing to prove. I'll always be their friend and refuse to be something that comes between them.

Siegfried squares his shoulders, staring at me for a moment before nodding. "Fine," he says, tightening his grip on his bow.

My heart stutters at that, and my face burns at the idea that they would bet on me. This is silly, and we all know it's not serious. They could never marry me anyway. I'm just a simple elven villager and not future queen material, I remind myself. It's expected that their future partners will hail from the royal families from the other kingdoms.

"Hey!" I say, my voice rising to match their intensity. "And if I win? What then?"

Odin cocks his head, a glint in his eye. "If you win, Odette, both of us will give you a kiss."

"A kiss?"

My voice comes out in a squeak, and Odin grins wider, pleased with himself. Siegfried's face goes pale. We've always been close friends, but never outright flirted. My stomach twists and the sun feels too hot. If I'm being honest, I've daydreamed of what it would be like to mean more to Sig, but Odin? We might kill each other with how we argue about the silliest things. Besides, it's inevitable we won't see one another once they turn eighteen and go off to the royal college. I want to enjoy their friendship while I can and not complicate things.

"Well?" Odin asks, gesturing to the target. "Ladies first."

I shake off the nerves, focus my eyes, and raise my bow. It's just a game, I tell myself again as I steady my breathing and let the arrow fly. It sails through the air, swift and true, and lands…just outside the bullseye.

"Close, but not close enough!" Odin taunts, chuckling to himself, before setting up his own shot.

I roll my eyes and step back, pretending I don't care, but I feel my pulse quicken. Odin pulls the string back, his eyes narrowing as he lines up his shot. There's a confidence in his stance that makes me flustered, as if he already knows he'll win.

He lets the arrow fly, and with a dull thud, it sinks into the bullseye, dead center.

"Woo!" Odin shouts, throwing his hands up in victory. "Looks like I've won myself a bride."

"Just a lucky shot," Siegfried says, muttering under his breath.

"Luck?" Odin asks with a scoff. "Maybe you're just jealous because you're not as good as I am."

Siegfried's jaw clenches as he stares at the target. I see the way his hands grip his bow, his knuckles turning white as he lets go and his arrow soars towards the target. It misses its mark, just outside the center circle. He glares at Odin, and for a moment, it's as if there's nothing playful left in their rivalry. His eyes flick toward me, but he doesn't meet my gaze.

Siegfried's face darkens, and before I can say anything,

he breaks his bow in half, turning and walking away, his steps quick and tense.

"Siegfried!" I yell, calling after him, but he doesn't slow down.

I round on Odin, fists clenched. "Why did you have to say that?"

Odin shrugs, unfazed. "It's just a bit of fun, Odette."

"Fun?" I glare at him, heart pounding with frustration. "You're being a jerk."

Odin raises an eyebrow, crossing his arms. "He'll get over it."

"You'd better hope so," I say, shaking my head. "I'm going to go find him." Without waiting for his response, I turn and hurry off in the direction Siegfried went, leaving Odin alone in the clearing. The sun dips lower, casting long shadows as I follow the path toward Siegfried's favorite spot—a tranquil lake where he goes whenever he wants to be alone.

I find him there, tossing stones into the water, each one making a ripple that spreads out across the glassy surface. His back is to me, shoulders hunched, his posture radiating frustration.

"Hey," I say as I approach him. He doesn't look at me, but I can tell he knows I'm here. "You shouldn't let him get to you."

He's silent for a moment, watching the ripples fade, and then he sighs, picking up another stone and hurling it into the pond. "Odin always wins, Odette. Always."

I step closer, reaching out but stopping just short of touching his shoulder. "It doesn't matter. It was just a joke.

Besides, I'm not some prize to be won. And we both know I'm no one's future queen."

Siegfried's jaw tightens, and he stares down at his hands, as if the stone he holds contains all the words he can't seem to say out loud.

After chucking it into the lake, he meets my eyes. "You don't realize how special you are, do you?" he asks, shaking his head. "Odin always gets what he wants, Odette, especially if he thinks it's something I want."

I'm surprised by his omission. Does that mean Seigfried likes me more than a friend? I feel warm all over and bite my lip, searching for the right words. "Odin wasn't being serious. We all know neither of you can marry me," I say firmly. "We will be lucky to be able to stay friends. You both will move on to bigger and better things without me."

Siegfried glances at me, his eyes dark and full of something I can't quite place. "It won't be long before everything changes, and I dread it."

I shake my head, trying to brush off his words, but a small part of me feels unsettled knowing that they'll leave for the Royal College when they turn eighteen in a couple of years. "I don't want things to be different, but I know you're right."

He almost smiles at that, but it fades. "I wish... I wish I weren't a prince."

"How can you say that?"

Siegfried glances back at the pond, silent again. He tosses the last stone into the water, and I watch it skip once, twice, before sinking beneath the surface. "Compared to Odin, I just don't feel cut out for royal life.

I'd much rather live in the village, like you. Enjoy a simple existence."

"That's why you'd make a great king. You understand your people and our way of life, and I know you'd fight to protect it."

He looks me in the eye as he takes my hand in his. "Thank you, Odette. You always know the words to say to make me feel better." He squeezes my hand before releasing it.

"Come on," I say, tugging his sleeve. "Let's go back. We can make Odin charm Madame Fallow for cookies as punishment for being an arse."

That earns me a genuine smile, and he follows me away from the lake, leaving the ripples to settle in our wake.

Two Years Later

"I wish you were coming with me," Siegfried says as he packs the last of his favorite books into his trunk. "You could fit in here and I'll sneak you into the college."

I let out a sad laugh at the visual of that. "Tempting, but what would I do once we've arrived? Hide in your room all day while you're attending your courses?"

Sig lets out a frustrated grunt, grumbling under his breath about stupid royal rules. "I should have pushed my mother harder about convincing your uncle to let you enroll."

"It would have been no use. My uncle tested my abilities, and I'm not powerful enough to study further.

Besides, I'm content with making teas and elixirs with my flora magic. You are meant for more. You'll have an amazing time, even if I'm not there."

"Doubtful," he says as he latches the trunk closed and turns to face me. His eyes are full of sorrow, and it breaks the false bravado I've been mustering up today. Despite trying to be happy for him, I'm hating this. I don't want him to leave; I want us to stay in our happy little bubble that we've been in the past year. Somewhere along the way, our friendship evolved into something more. Something deeper. Something I think might be love. But alas, all royals and nobles' elflings must go away to the Royal College at eighteen.

"You know this is hard for me too. I'm going to miss you so much, but it would be selfish of me not to want you to learn to harness your moon magic." Siegfried's powers emerged a couple of years ago, but it's been difficult for him to learn to wield them due to how strong they are. The moon's energy can flow into him, which he says will allow him to use it as a weapon and a shield. So far, he's only been able to use it to create light orbs and small beams. He needs to go to college.

"It's going to be the worst four years of my life. Every moment away from you will be absolute torture," he says as he steps closer, reaching a hand out to cup my face. I lean into the warmth, savoring his touch while I can. "But, I vow I will write to you every day, so expect a hawk delivery daily."

I smile up at him, bringing my hand up and resting it on his chest. "And I'll write back just as often, but I don't want you to feel pressure to keep in touch. You need to focus on your studies and advance your magic. Don't worry about me." We've known this day was always coming, and sometimes I wish I hadn't let myself fall for him. Everyone knows there's an expectation that the royals find a suitable match while at the college. As deeply as I care for Sig, I know it's futile to hope he'd wait for me.

He drops his hand and frowns down at me. I'm much shorter than him, my head coming up to his chest. He's gotten so tall over the past couple of years, and so handsome, even when he looks at me in dismay.

"You really think I could forget you?"

"I'm just trying to be realistic, Sig. Our paths are going in different directions, and I don't want to hold you back. Our kingdom needs you — you could be the future king someday, and I'll just be making tea."

"But, I need *you*," he says with a hint of desperation in his voice. "Odette, maybe I haven't made this clear, but I... I love you. I always have. Going away to college will not change my feelings. You're what I want. All I want."

I gasp at the words I've been longing to hear, but a little voice deep inside me reminds me he's leaving and we're too young to be making such claims.

I reach out and clasp his hands in my own. "Sig, you know I love you too, but it may not be enough. You must make the kingdom a priority, and I won't ever blame you for that. Promise me you'll focus on yourself while you're there."

He looks away from me, his jaw ticking. "I don't agree, but I will promise you that, if you promise me one thing before I leave?"

"Okay... what?"

"Just tonight, let us be enough. Stay with me. Let me love you fully, wholly."

"Okay."

"Are you sure? You want me as much as I want you, right?" he asks, and I can't help but blush. We've come close so many times to letting ourselves go all the way, but something has always made it nearly impossible to get enough alone time. If this is our chance, I'm taking it.

"Of course I do, Sig, you know that. I'd regret it if we didn't, but I'm also scared it'll make telling you goodbye that much harder," I admit, looking down, trying to hold back the tears that threaten to spill out.

He lifts my chin with his fingers, forcing me to meet his beautiful icy blue eyes. I think they might be what I'll miss the most.

"I know, and you may be right, but I can't leave without showing you just how much you mean to me. My heart, my body, my soul — they all burn for you," he says before crashing his lips to mine. I let him pour all his love and angst into me as I kiss him back with everything I have. He may not be mine forever, but he's mine in this perfect moment, and I'm going to savor it.

We kiss. And kiss. And kiss some more, before he lifts me into his arms, my legs wrapping around his waist as he carries me over to his bed. He lays me down so gently that my chest aches. I try to steady my breath so that I can commit every touch, every kiss to memory.

"You are the loveliest elf in all the realm, Odette," Siegfried says, standing over me. "I'm the luckiest elf in all the realm to be loved by you. I'll never take your love for granted." A tear falls from the corner of my eye and slides down into my hair. He wipes it away with his thumb and then takes his time undressing me. First, taking off my leather slippers, then rolling down my stockings and tossing them on the floor. He kisses his way up my legs, teasing me with one quick press of his lips to that magic spot above my entrance before pulling my pantaloons off. I can't help but groan in both frustration and need. My middle feels like it's burning up in anticipation, and I'm sure he can see the evidence of my desire.

Just when I'm about to demand he hurry, he leans over me, our bodies perfectly aligned. I moan at the delicious feel of the weight of him against me. He hikes up my chemise and dress, teasing my core with his fingers. We've done this part so many times that he knows how to make me explode, playing me like an instrument.

"That's my girl, soak my hand so that you're ready for me," he croons over me, making my toes curl.

"Oh stars, Sig. I'm so close, don't stop," I say, my breathing turning ragged as I lose myself to his touch. It doesn't take long before I'm shaking and coming undone beneath him. He bends lower, kissing me hard to cover my cries as waves of pleasure flow through me, eventually ebbing away into mere ripples. And yet, I'm ready for more. Craving it. Craving him.

Siegfried rolls onto his back, pulling me with him. Sitting, straddling his hips, I lean down to kiss him while holding his face in my hands before trailing kisses down his neck. I push myself up, sitting atop him, so I can unbutton his trousers and slide them off. He sits up to take off his shirt, and I help pull it off. Then he does the same to my dress, loosening the tie in the back and lifting it over my head. There's nothing left, just our burning bodies, begging for each other.

"Are you sure you're ready?" he asks as he brushes my wild red curls back behind my shoulders.

"I've been ready. Make me yours," I tell him.

"You've always been mine, and you always will be," he says right before he lines himself up and nudges my entrance. I'm still so wet and warm that he slides in easily. There's a pinch of pain as he stretches me wider than I've ever felt before, but it dissipates into pleasure as Sigfried moves slowly in and out of me.

"You feel better than I could have ever imagined," he groans above me, as he pinches his eyes closed and bites his bottom lip.

It feels so good that I can't form words, so all I do is nod in agreement. Chasing the friction I'm craving, I lose all sense of time getting lost in the electric feel of him. Our bodies collide over and over as I ride him. When Sigfried brings his lips to my breasts, zings of lightning zap through my body. His teeth pull at my hard peak, and I come undone once again. "Yes, yes, yes," is all I can say as I get lost in the pleasure flowing through me.

Next thing I know, Siegfried flips us over and pulls my hips up, pressing into me from behind. "You have the most perfect body," he says as he caresses my backside before holding onto my waist. He feels so deep at this angle that I think for a moment maybe I can't take it. I grip the sheets beneath me and hold on for dear life as Siegfried enters me faster and harder.

Nothing has ever felt this good and this right. I squeeze around him, eliciting moans from his mouth before his movements get erratic. "Odette," he whispers like a prayer over and over, except it's me he's worshipping instead of the woodland spirits. Turning my head to look over my shoulder, I watch in fascination as he stills inside of me, only feeling a slight twitching before he wraps an arm around my middle and collapses against me.

We both roll onto our sides, facing each other with heaving chests, trying to catch our breath. Siegfried interlaces my fingers with his and kisses the back of my hand.

"Thank you," he says and kisses me. He stares into my eyes so reverently, like I'm the most precious thing in the world. I've never felt so cherished, so adored, so worshipped. "Do you feel okay? I didn't hurt you, did I?"

"I'm perfect. I'm sure I'll be sore, but that's to be expected, I think. Don't worry," I tell him and I mean it wholeheartedly.

"I hate that I'm leaving in the morning. I want to stay here with you and love you over and over and over again."

"I hate it too," I whisper, my voice beginning to shake with all the emotions I've been holding in. I've never felt so happy and sorrowful at once. Burying my head in the crook of his neck, I try to breathe him in and fight back the tears. But as he pulls me into his embrace and runs his hand down my locks, I can't hold them back.

"I know, I know," he says into my ear, consoling me. "It will be pure torture being apart from you. I swear to you that when I return, we will be together again."

"I hate their stupid rules. How can they keep you

secluded for four years and not let anyone visit? It seems cruel to keep everyone away from their family and friends."

"I'll see if I can get my mother to get them to allow me visits, but it may not happen. That has been the rule for centuries upon centuries, unfortunately. Are you sure you don't want to hide in my trunk?"

"Wishful thinking won't get us anywhere. I'm just not ready to say goodbye," I tell him, wiping my eyes.

"Stay the night then. Let me show you the depth of my love until the sun rises."

"I'd like that," I say, as we crash our lips together once again. This time, our movements are not slow and sweet, but frantic and full of the desperation we feel to cling to each other.

We stay tangled up together, loving each other with everything we have until we are both too spent for more. When the first rays of sunlight stream through the cracks of the drapes, I can't bear the thought of saying goodbye. So, I kiss him one last time before slipping out of his arms. Out of the castle. Out of his life for the unforeseeable future.

Every step away from him feels like wading through mud. I know he'll be upset that I left, but I refuse to say goodbye. My heart already feels like it's shattering, and I don't want him to feel any worse about leaving than he already does. He needs to focus on honing his power and not have me as a distraction.

So, I'll do the same. I'll build my life here, contributing what I can to our kingdom. And I'll hope that the next four years go by like a flash of lightning and pray he'll come back to me.

Continue reading now on Kindle Unlimited: https://mybook.to/NKPMHD

ROMANCING THE REALMS
CHLOE HODGE
COURTING THE FAE CAPTAIN

COURTING THE FAE CAPTAIN

'The Mithrian Fae are among the most ruthless species recorded. Unlike their elemental brethren across the seas, theirs is a race that reveres bloodshed and darker power. If you cross them on a bad day, don't expect to see another.'
-*The Trials and Traditions of a Mithrian Fae*

I had always known I'd never outrun fate … that didn't mean I couldn't try.

Lightning forked through the sky as I made my way inch by careful inch down the rain-slick slate beneath my bedroom balcony. Thunder roiled; a large crack making me flinch so violently I nearly lost my grip and tumbled to the precarious drop below.

My heart bashed against my ribs. I'd done the climb many times before and was no stranger to the risk, but my fingers were so cold, it was an effort to curl them into the narrow ridges of stone. One wrong move and this foolhardy endeavour would all be for nothing.

But I had to go. My father would ship me off to Domeratt tomorrow to join a host of other would-be-wives hellbent on marrying the city lord's son—a captain of the Shadow Court's vast naval army, or so I had heard.

Frankly, I couldn't care less what the male's titles and achievements were. I had no desire to vie for his attention. Stories of how highborn fae treated their wives in the Shadow Court had often floated past my ears. The servants in my home liked to gossip over juicy scandals or female misfortune. And, seemingly, there was a lot of that in my homeland. When one was born into a world of immortal necromancers and dark magic wielders, one was bound to get a little more comfortable with death or other ill-fated fortunes.

There were four courts in the fae land of Mithria, each with their own class of magic wielders–Spell Weavers, Soul Speakers, Bone Cleavers or Blood Mages. I belonged to the Shadow Court, though my magic had yet to reveal itself.

I frowned, pressing myself flat against the stone as one of the castle servants reached out to tackle the banging shutters of a bedroom window beside me.

Halfway there. Just a few more balconies to navigate and castle guards to avoid. I'd prepared for this, though. This was a climb I'd timed more than once, considering patrols, guard rotations, and any other disturbances one might find when scaling a damn building as tall as this one.

Ironic, that I was the damsel locked atop my father's tallest tower. Only, he had no idea of the kind of extracurricular activities I got up to when he wasn't looking. Take rock climbing, for example. Not very demure. Not very ladylike.

A slow smile spread across my face. The conditions were less than favourable, but I'd trained enough times in hazardous weather to know the grooves and footholds as well as the back of my hand. Besides, this was just the kind of challenge that made me feel *alive*. The only other time I felt like this was when tinkering with potions and brews.

Alchemy. *That* was my true passion. Something I had done under my father's nose since I was a little girl, and something I had no plans of stopping. Which was exactly why marrying some pompous noble who thought of females only as breeding vessels was not on my list of things to do.

I was nearing the lower levels now. My fingers were turning blue with the cold, but I'd have time to lament the stiffness later. Just a little further and—I froze. Because just below me, bundled up in furs and staring out from the balcony edge, was one of the ladies of court. Melania, judging by the ginger hair wisping out of her braid. And that female? The only thing she loved more than herself was money and power. Or any means in which to get it. If she spotted me …

I sucked down a breath and forced my teeth to stop chattering as I waited. All she had to do was look up. Why in hells was she outside anyway? The winds were bitter and howling, the cold sinking deep beneath my bones. No one in their right mind would be out here unless … oh.

A male strode onto the balcony, gathering Melania in his arms as he turned her and claimed her lips. My body went taut. It wouldn't be any real scandal or surprise to see a noble getting cosy with another member of the court, but this was not a male any female had a right to covet.

That was Declan James, Blood Sword of my father's and, more importantly, a married male. Scandal, indeed. If word got out about this affair Melania would be finished. Declan would receive no real punishment, but that's the way it always went with the male fae in Mithria. Bastards.

My muscles were screaming as I held onto the wall for dear life. Sweat bubbled over my back, forming little rivulets that dribbled down my spine. *Please, please just go inside and go back to bed.*

He whispered something in her ear that made her laugh and blush prettily, then he was pulling her back towards his chambers. She protested coyishly, and it took everything in me not to roll my eyes. I'd bet my left tit she was already naked beneath those furs.

Five steps.

Four.

hree.

Two.

I almost heaved a sigh of relief when they took one last step, their heads nearly disappearing beneath the threshold.

Maybe I'd done something to piss off the gods. Maybe it was the boot that slipped ever so slightly out of the groove it was jammed in, but right before that last step, Melania fucking Harron raised those pretty blue eyes and gasped as she found me staring right back at her.

She took in my clothes, the braid, the gaiter pulled up over my face before her eyes slowly moved to my own. Recognition set in before the bitch smiled like it was the best day in her miserable little life.

Melania whispered to Declan, who looked up with

piercing blue eyes of his own. He'd always given me the creeps. That male was colder than the deepest frost or the most bitter of winds. And I knew when he looked at me that I was as good as dead.

He swore and stepped indoors briskly, though his face remained a mask of calm. I fucking moved, hightailing it across the wall as fast as I could go. My shot at escaping this hellhole just dropped by half, and the odds were never great to begin with. Declan was not a forgiving male, nor would he forget. Even if I made it safely back to my rooms, I knew he'd eventually come for me and make it look like an accident. Maybe even pay some lowlifes to do the job for him.

My heart thumped; my palms slick and clammy. I could either continue down the wall and run, or find a public place to lay low in. There was no way he could harm me in plain sight of the castle patrons.

I looked longingly at the ground. My future was at stake. My freedom. But what chance did I have of making it out now? My father would be furious with me if I returned and Declan informed him what had happened, but he wouldn't do much more. Not when the Rite was coming up tomorrow. Everything would be swept under a rug and kept hushed. I'd have my life, yes, but what was that really worth if I was never free?

Fuck it. I bypassed the closest balcony and kept descending. The heavens opened, and rain poured down in a sudden torrent of rage. My hair was sodden within seconds, my visibility drastically decreased.

I blinked back the water in my eyes just as Declan reappeared and nocked an arrow to a bow. My heart dropped into my stomach. He wouldn't take me out on the wall, surely? His arrow could be traced back to him, and then where would he be? That evil male looked down at me, took aim, and *smiled.* Terrible and cold, and joyful with the hunt. Oh yes, he fucking would. Perhaps he was a greater asset to my father than I'd realised. Perhaps my father would turn a blind eye for his precious Bloodhound. Declan had never liked me. Maybe covering the affair was just an excuse to shoot me down.

The arrow flew, speeding through the air towards me. And as a scream tore from my lungs, thunder cracked in answer, swallowing any sound. I took one look at that arrow, prayed to any god who might be listening ... then jumped.

Continue reading now on Kindle Unlimited: https:// mybook.to/EunI

MIRANDA JOY

COURTING THE MOON PRIEST

COURTING THE MOON PRIEST

SORAYA

Everyone on the island holds their breath, eyes locked on the night sky. We wait patiently for the twin moons to overlap, forming a single supermoon as they do one night every thirty days.

"Almost," Mariel whispers, gripping my hand tightly in both of hers.

The moons overlap, almost entirely consumed by one another. The moment the second moon is gone from sight —fully nestled into the other—a roar of appreciation rises from the beach. The conjoined moons' glow intensifies, sending radiant waves of iridescent light streaking through the dark sky.

In response, the jungle brightens, glimmering with the gifted power of our goddesses.

"Praise the moons," I whisper, excitement bubbling up in my chest.

The bright silver light casts an ethereal glow across the island. The rivers shimmer, running down the single verdant mountain and through the jungle like narrow arteries. They all feed into the ocean around us. The currents pulse softly, as if alive. Along the banks, all through the island, the plants harbor the same magical light. Their usually vibrant green coloring mirrors the ribbons of blue-green streaking through the sky beside the newly formed supermoon.

A smile overtakes my face, and my shoulders soften. Mariel drops my hands, throwing her arms around me.

"Blessed Union, Soraya," she squeals in my ear. I squeeze her back, and she pulls free. Music starts playing, and the gratitude of the villagers is palpable. "I'm going to snag us some nectar. I'll be right back."

She bounds off toward the hut at the edge of the sand, waving animatedly at everyone she passes. Most of us were born and raised on the Isle de Lunith, and we're a fairly tight-knit community.

Strong arms snake around my waist, startling me. The scent of salt and earth, mixed with a familiar musk, invades my nose, and I chuckle.

"This dress does things to me," Joss murmurs into my neck, invading my personal space.

Swatting his arms away, I turn to face him. Moonlight dances on the droplets lining his deeply tanned chest. He runs a hand through his short brown hair, slicking it back. It glistens from his dip in the ocean. His lips raise into a teasing grin, and my expression softens, mirroring his.

I playfully roll my eyes. "We're all wearing the same thing."

Gesturing around the beach, I take in the various celestial servants scattered on the beach, mingling with the rest of the island's population. Everyone drinks, dances, and feasts tonight, celebrating the moons' union.

The priests and priestesses are easy to pick out, all dressed in similar wispy, lightweight garments in the color of the moons—pale silvers and off-whites. Some don cascading gossamer gowns with thin straps, others have flowy pants with billowing arms, but they're all variations of the same look with cascading layers.

"No," he says, arching a light-brown brow. "You certainly are not." His fingers trail up my covered collarbone until his hand lands on my exposed shoulder. "I like *yours* best."

Planting my hands on his bare chest, I gently push him back. "We talked about this!"

"I thought we were friends." He fake pouts, running his fingers through his wet hair.

"Exactly—*friends*."

He gives me a broad, charming grin. "And I'm honoring your wishes… by being very friendly."

I can't help but laugh and roll my eyes, amused by his quick quip. "You know damn well what I mean, Joss Thalor!"

"It's impossible to keep my hands off you." He groans. "I miss you already."

It's my own fault for blurring the boundaries between us. I might've ended our official relationship, but I haven't kept him out of my bed.

I shake my head, scanning the beach for Mariel. She's out of sight, likely having made her way into the hut for our drinks. As much fun as Joss is, I ended things for a reason. No matter how handsome, kind, and funny he is, I just don't want *more*.

Not the same way he does.

My eyes flit to the moons. I want a love like *theirs*. Lore says the two moons were previously goddesses who sacrificed their mortal forms and cursed themselves, all to spend eternity together, hung in the skies side-by-side, only kissing once per month.

They're forever suspended overhead, only shifting to touch on Union Night and separating by morning.

I don't necessarily want their fate, but the thought of a passionate, all-consuming, eternal love lingers in the back of my mind. With Joss, things are comfortable, but the thought of being without him doesn't steal my breath.

When I glance over at him, he's staring out at the dark ocean, all the previous humor gone. My heart spasms violently. We've been there for each other our whole lives, including when he lost his mother to the very sea he loves.

The guilt gnaws at me, and I step beside him. I nudge him with my elbow. "Wanna go find some silverdew?"

The flower, indigenous to the Isle de Lunith, only opens at night. Though it sprouts in abundance, it's a cherished flower, mainly because it's our primary export and the source of our island's income.

It can be tapped for nectar—the delightful, fruity brew we enjoy for a buzz. It also provides a more intense, euphoric high when the petals unfurl and the pollen is snorted.

Joss shoots me a crooked smile. "Later? I'm going to

catch another quick dip with the other tideborn—before they get too nectared."

Squeezing his hand in understanding, I nod. When he leaves, I dig my feet into the cool, packed sand, watching the water gently lick the shore. With my back to the revelry, I take this moment to myself to just *be*.

My lungs fill with fresh, salty air with a fruity tinge. It smells like home—like *everything*.

I love Union Night. Not only for the obvious—the energetically charged revelry, the merriment, the magic— but because I feel as if I'm truly one with the island. Fingering a strand of teal hair, I smile down at the color, feeling less like an outcast because of its unnatural hue and more like I'm an integral part of the ecosystem.

Shoving my hair over my shoulder, I squint, catching the faint ring of the smaller moon as it nestles in front of its larger counterpart. One night a month, when the moons align, the Isle de Lunith comes alive with magic. Even though I've experienced it twelve times a year for twenty-six years, it never ceases to fill me with awe.

Amazement tickles my insides, and my heart pulses in time with the flickering fireflies lighting up the beach.

Familiar faces play the shell horns, blowing merrily into the seashells as they sway to the music. Drums and stringed instruments accompany them, blending into a tune that instills a need to move. It's melodic and hypnotic. A group of celestial servants throw their limbs around as they release pent-up energy in dance. Others chant in groups, leaning into gratitude mantras to thank the goddess moons for their protection.

Every soul dances barefoot on the sand, connecting

intimately with the land, and celebrating another night—another month—of life-sustaining magic.

Every soul except for one.

I gaze toward the temple atop the tallest hill, which settles into the trees far beyond the village. It's where the celestial servants live and work—the point of the island closest to the moons. Even from this distance, I glimpse a hint of light sparkling from the top where the moonstone lives, absorbing the energy on this powerful night as it does during every Union.

Sparkling waters crest over the stony side, feeding into our rivers.

"You'd think out of everyone, *he* would be down here celebrating," Mariel yells, thrusting a drink at me.

"Where have you been?" I graciously accept the beverage, wrapping my lips around the bamboo straw peeking out of the coconut shell. The fruity, slightly sour tang of nectar washes over my tongue, and I close my eyes to revel in it for a moment.

"Maybe one day he'll stop thinking he's too good for us," she says bitterly.

A soft sigh escapes my lips as I open my eyes and face my best friend. "You know how he is, Mariel."

"*Reclusive,*" she says sarcastically.

My lips press into a thin line as my head swivels toward her. "Hush." I glance around to ensure no one's eavesdropping on her talking poorly about High Priest Raziel Kasper. Granted, I've heard enough whispers to know many of the villagers think the same way. "He's our Moon Priest."

"Exactly." She lowers her voice, but the way she slurs

tells me she's already had a little too much fun during tonight's celebration. "With how up the moons' butts he is, you'd expect him to show face during the most sacred night of the month."

"I'm sure he celebrates in his own way." I squint at the temple, unable to understand why he'd choose to skip the Union. The High Priests before him were known for flashing their magic on this sacred night. He's an enigma for hiding his powers from the islanders.

She snorts. "I'm not the only one who notices his attitude."

Mariel isn't wrong about him being a bit of a recluse, but he's our island's Highest Keeper. *The* Moon Priest. The Goddesses' Anointed. The moons chose him to oversee the magic and, thus, the life of our island.

Yet, he snubs every ceremony.

Mariel raises her drink to the moon, and her bracelets clink together noisily overhead. She throws her head back, closes her eyes, and lets out a *whoop*.

"To the moons!" she yells.

"Praise the moons," I say with a soft laugh.

"Hey, there's your man." Mariel nudges me with her elbow.

I turn to catch Joss heading toward us. He charges the last few steps toward me, and despite his bare feet sinking into the soft sand, it barely slows him down. His muscular arms wrap around me, squeezing me as he playfully nibbles on my neck.

"Joss," I chastise, swatting at him. "You're getting me wet!"

"I wish," he murmurs.

He spins me around, and some of my nectar splashes over the side. The sheer, wispy bottom half of my gown floats around me, the slits parting to reveal my bronzed legs, toned from my daily treks up and down the temple's archive stairwells. The delicate silver chains crisscrossing my midsection hold the dress in place with effortless grace. The tiny star and moon charms tinkle with the movement.

I laugh. "Put me down!"

He obliges, placing me back on my feet. I stumble, quickly reorienting myself and adjusting my neckline to ensure my chest is fully covered.

"What are you two talking about?" Joss's green eyes twinkle with jest.

I'm glad to see he's swum his previous sorrows away. The grief hits him from time to time, and though I can't relate in the same way, I know what it's like to miss a mother. Unlike him, I never knew mine, though. Where he misses a person, I miss the idea of one.

Mariel, having refocused her attention on us, smirks with amusement. Her dress matches mine, but where mine is high in the front and plunging in the back, hers is the opposite, showcasing her glorious cleavage. The pale coloring contrasts beautifully with her brown skin and dark curls.

The outfits are symbolic, marking us as priestesses of the moon—a reminder of who we are and who we serve.

The Moon Priest.

My eyes flick back in the temple's direction. I find it rather blasphemous to talk poorly of him or the moons he protects. That *we* protect. Mariel, on the other hand, loves instigating and stirring up the 'monotony of our island'—her words, not mine.

"We're not talking about anything," I tell a waiting Joss. "Hey, would you mind grabbing me another nectar? Please?"

Joss gives me a broad smile and then glances at Mariel.

"Make that two?" Mariel says, twisting a curl of dark hair around her finger.

Joss thumbs us up, then jogs off toward the Nectar Hut —our beach tavern.

His muscles flex with power, only the tiny fabric of his hemp water shorts covering his ass.

"Your boyfriend is a delight," Mariel says. She grabs my hand, tugging me through the sand, closer to where the band plays their live instruments.

"You know we broke up." I raise my voice so she can hear me over the melody.

She whirls toward me, rolling her hips to the tempo as she raises a brow. "I saw him sneaking out of your bed this morning."

"Yeah, but we're not—"

"You *always* find your way back to each other." She spins, arms overhead, and her face tilted to the sky with glee.

"This is different, Mar." Shaking my head, I give up and let the music sink into my bones. I move naturally, matching Mariel's steps.

"He would've bonded with you in a heartbeat."

I flush at the thought of completing the Union ceremony with Joss—on a night like tonight, when such bonding events occur. I'd be lying if I said I hadn't imagined it a thousand times over.

I shake my head, and a few tendrils of hair fall into my face. "I don't want that—we're better as friends."

"No," she says sternly, gesturing from me to her as she dances. "*We* are better as just friends. That man is better as a husband, and you know it, Soraya."

"It was never serious." I stop moving to the music and dig my toes into the sand instead.

She snorts. "He loves you something fierce."

I kick a hearty amount of sand at her legs. She squeals, kicking sand back at me.

Joss appears with our drinks, cutting the conversation short. Mariel teases him about something, but his eyes stay locked on me. I flush under his attention, hating that I'm letting both of my best friends down with my decision.

Not wanting to think about it, I fiddle mindlessly with my straw and return my attention to the temple, catching the light refracting from the moonstone atop.

Everyone around me is focused on the music, the moon, or the drinks, socializing and dancing in spades. Though the source of the magic comes from the sky, the moonstone nestled in the temple's summit is the heart of our island. It absorbs the pulsating magic sent down from the goddess moons, after all. Without it, there would be no magic. No island.

Suddenly, the gleaming light flickers out, and the top of the temple goes dark. My heart trips over itself, and I nearly drop my nectar.

"Joss," I yell, grasping his arm tightly with my free hand.

He stops mid-conversation, turning to me with concern etched into his features. "What is it?"

"The moonstone." I turn back to the temple, raising my hand to point, but the soft glow has returned, wavering hazily above the temple.

"What about it?" The worry leaves his voice, and he gives me a curious look.

"She's obsessed with that thing," Mariel says, giggling. "Overcome by its sheer beauty from time to time."

"I can understand what that's like," he says wistfully, his gaze boring into me.

Mariel giggles.

Sighing, I glance down at my drink, shaking my head. I take a long pull, finishing it off in one go while my friends cheer.

"Nevermind," I whisper, blinking stupidly in the direction it sits. It flickered for a moment—I swear it. Or maybe I had too much nectar, and my eyes are playing tricks. My lips stay sealed, not wanting to rouse unnecessary fear on a sacred night, but sweat beads on my spine.

My hand rises to the center of my chest, mindlessly hovering there.

Joss and Mariel laugh at something, talking animatedly. None of their words stick in my brain. Instead, my eyes stay glued to the temple as if I might catch the moonstone winking again.

"I should check on the High Priest," I say in a rush, interrupting their conversation.

Mariel looks at me as if I've lost my mind.

"Is he sick?" Joss asks with a frown. "We have our island assembly tomorrow."

I shake my head. "Something just feels *off*." The words are weak—strange—even to my own ears.

"Ooookay." Mariel takes the coconut out of my hand, tossing it onto the beach. "No more nectar for you. Let's dance it off." She grips my hand and tugs me closer toward the shore, where waves gently caress the packed sand. "Come on, Joss!"

We navigate the merriment, smiling and nodding at everyone we pass.

A pit of dread builds in my stomach, but I don't fight my friends. I can't make sense of my feelings on my own, let alone verbalize them. Instead, I allow Mariel and Joss to sandwich me as we sway our hips in rhythm to the drumbeat.

We drink more nectar, and later, when Joss's hands snake around my waist, threatening to steal me away to the bushes, I let him.

My eyes continue to flick toward the temple, and the unsettled feeling lingers, even though I try my best to let Joss *distract* me.

Continue reading now on Kindle Unlimited: https://mybook.to/lmxJAj

www.ingramcontent.com/pod-product-compliance
Lightning Source LLC
Chambersburg PA
CBHW031737180726
48283CB00005B/1549

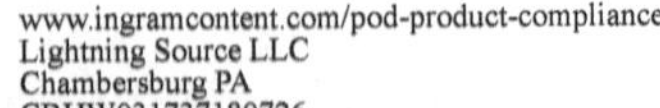